THE SHADOW OF MY LIFE

THE SHADOW OF MY LIFE

Where Cruelty Meets Love

Anastasia Mechan

authorHOUSE®

AuthorHouse™
1663 Liberty Drive
Bloomington, IN 47403
www.authorhouse.com
Phone: 833-262-8899

Published by AuthorHouse 07/13/2022

ISBN: 978-1-4567-6711-2 (sc)
ISBN: 978-1-4567-6710-5 (hc)
ISBN: 978-1-4567-6709-9 (e)

Library of Congress Control Number: 2011906198

Print information available on the last page.

Any people depicted in stock imagery provided by Thinkstock are models, and such images are being used for illustrative purposes only.
Certain stock imagery © Thinkstock.

This book is printed on acid-free paper.

INDEX OF CHAPTERS

ACKNOWLEDGEMENTS

Mom, there are not enough words for me to explain the immense love I have for you, and how grateful I am for everything you have done and sacrificed for me. I want to thank my grandma, "Panchi"; thanks for always being there for me, and for being my biggest fan! Dad, I will always love you. My sisters, Pamela and Fiorella, who are the strongest women on earth, you have shown me with tears and hard work that everything you want to reach in life you can achieve if you really go for it. Thank you girls for the support! My grandpa, "Viejo", who always felt proud of me, and told the whole world I was going to go far. Michael, thanks for being there since the beginning of this manuscript. But the person I want to dedicate this book to and thank for everything is my baby nephew, Joshua. Baby, I do not know how to express the love that I feel for you. You have shown me with your innocence and smiles that I can do anything in life, love freely, and not worry about tomorrow. I hope one day, when you read this, you will be proud of me.

Thank you guys, and I hope you all are proud of me.

I.

A CRUEL AND UNUSUAL BEGINNING

In a therapy meeting, people were sharing their testimonies and the following words were spoken:

"I still remember every little thing — every detail. I can even remember the program that was on TV that cruel afternoon. It was somehow windy, what can I call it — a melancholy day. I was coming back from the supermarket where I used to work. I opened the door and saw my brother and sister on the floor, in the same position Arabians pray in. They were naked. My sister was crying loudly and my brother had his face flat on the red carpet. And there he was, my stepfather, with no shirt on, pants falling, and holding a belt in his right hand looking at me, " Caleb recited with deep emotion.

The therapist looked at him and said "It's ok if you don't want to keep on with your story. We will all understand."

"No! I need to say it. I've been keeping it in for years, and today I need it out."

Caleb was a man who had it all: money, looks, great personality, education, and intellect; everything that would make any woman go crazy. However, it seemed that even with all those admirable qualities, he hadn't had any luck. But in his mind, he knew that one day he was going to find the love that he was looking for, and perhaps be reunited with his brother and sister.

Caleb looked at the people around him, looked up at the roof, the floor . . . and began his story once again.

"My stepfather looked at me and laughed hard. He saw the tears coming out of my eyes. He told me to get on my knees, but I refused. I didn't want anything to happen to me. Then he said, 'Oh yeah? Okay, watch!' He grabbed my sister and dragged her to the middle of the living room. He was screaming on top of his lungs. "Did you hear me or what!" he kept on screaming. My sister's eyes were as red as fire from crying much. I was shocked.

My sister screamed hard, her pain was hurting me too," Caleb sighs. "God! I didn't know what to do! That son of a bitch didn't care, he was looking at her facial expression, and — and I know he was looking at the blood dripping out from her tiny body. He was so sick that he started licking it. He was laughing, opening his mouth on purpose so I could see all the blood through his teeth.

I couldn't stand it anymore. I knew I had to do something. So I tried to grab anything I could use to hit him with but everything was so far away from me.

Then, as soon as I looked back, I saw my little brother, on his knees sucking my stepfather's, you know. I couldn't believe it. I wanted to throw up! My innocent brother and sister were abused and I wasn't doing anything to help them. So with all the hate and anger that was in my heart, I threw myself on top of him; pushing him against the TV, making him fall, breaking all the things around. We were fighting each other, and even if I wasn't as strong as him, I tried my best. My brother and sister were watching everything. They did nothing but cry, and those tears motivated me to try to kill him. But he got up and beat me. I fell and I couldn't get up. I was hurt. He kept on beating me, meanwhile. He kicked me in the face and stomach until my body was sore.

I was on the floor helpless. He was coming towards me, and I screamed, I felt something bad was coming… and suddenly I noticed a knife nearby. I stretched every nerve I had in my weak body, and when I got it, he screamed. He was bleeding off his right eye.

I summoned strength from my weak body and as I got up I told my sister and brother to hurry and run out of the house. I was going crazy." He sighs deeply. "My desperation was increasing faster than my heartbeat. Then my brother said, 'I can't leave mom alone! That's why I'm not going to run away with you.' Of course, I told him, 'Mom is here because she wants to be here. If she wants, she'll leave!' Neither of them listened to me; neither wanted to come with me. Then, I felt a bat hit me in the face. The hit was so hard I felt like I flew. I woke up after a very long time, probably hours later since there was no light hitting the kitchen's window, but only a deep shine in the middle of the dark sky. I was on the floor, numb. The only thing I could do was watch my stepfather's actions. He grabbed my sister and threw liquor all over her body, started licking it, touching her parts, forcing my little brother to watch everything. It was enough for me. I couldn't hold it any longer so I started crying. Yes! I cried like a girl, or maybe worse, I won't deny it. I tried to get up, holding on to the walls for balance. However, that disturbing day wasn't over. He wanted me to suffer since he couldn't hurt me, so he grabbed my little sister and, the worst happened... not only that, but forced my brother to watch what his psychotic mind wanted... I screamed and dragged myself across the floor. I was throwing up the little bit of food I had eaten during the day. I tried to get up, and even though I was falling all over the place, I made it to the door and I ran.

I ran as fast as I could. I left my house like a coward, leaving behind two innocent kids. I felt guilty, but I just couldn't stay there anymore.

That night, I went to my friend's house, and I told his parents what had happened. They fed me and gave me clothes. Later on, I was getting out of the shower when I heard his mom calling my house, and a man from the Department of Children and Families saying in the speaker, 'Yes, we just arrested Scott Stuart and we are taking both children to the hospital. Yes, Loren Smith is under arrest too. Are you with Caleb?'

Two hours later they came and picked me up. They sent me to a foster home, sent my sister and brother to two different places. I never heard from them again. I tried to look for them, but I only heard rumors; rumors such as my little brother had joined the Army and my little sister had changed her name, so now it would be even harder to find her. I used to go to jail to visit my mom and ask her about them, but she never wanted to talk to me. She got out of jail a few years ago. She lives in an apartment with her sisters, and I go and visit her even though she denies herself from seeing me. Oh, and my stepfather, he's still in jail. I heard he got raped and now is dying of AIDS," said Caleb, breathing deeply as he finished his testimony.

Everyone at the meeting clapped hard for him. Some were crying, others were hugging him, talking to him, giving him props for the courage he had for sharing such a strong and awful story. The therapist switched seats with another member of the meeting and, holding Caleb's left hand, said, "You are a very strong man. It takes a lot of courage and strength to talk about situations such as this. I'm so proud of you, and I really hope that this shadow won't follow you anymore."

After the meeting was over, Caleb, while on his way back home, felt an enormous relief, as if he had gotten a lot off his chest. Suddenly, intense clouds covered the dark sky, and the thunder started. He kept on driving until a red light, when he noticed, in the middle of the dramatic rain, a stunning being. She was sitting at the bus stop, covering herself from the rain. As soon as the light hit green, he drove forward, but her face was stuck in his mind. He couldn't help it and drove back to the bus stop. There she was, still in the same spot; shivering in the middle of the rain, wet, looking like an exotic animal about to go extinct. Caleb put his emergency lights on and ran out of his car to the bus stop. He couldn't leave her there or he'd feel like the world was coming to an end. But why, he wondered.

Caleb gently asked, "Excuse me, ma'am, do you need a ride home?"

"Fuck off!" she answered harshly.

Caleb, amazed by her words said, "Okay. I'm sorry. I just wanted to give you a ride home. I can't leave you here. It's dark and it could get dangerous."

The young lady, maintaining the same attitude, responded, "Fine then! If something happens to me, don't let it be your fault, let someone else take it."

"Miss, I'm not trying to seem like a creep but if you refuse to get out of here I will have to stay with you until you grab your phone and call someone."

"Why would you do that? You don't even know me."

"Let's just say we each have a chance to change the world just by doing one small thing. In this case, maybe not leaving you here will save you from something bad, and that will be the change."

The young lady stared at the rain. Convinced by his candid words, she said "Okay, but don't lock the doors when I get in."

"Don't worry. I promise, I won't."

The young lady got in the car and a conversation began.

"Are you always this nice and compassionate?" she asked sarcastically.

"I feel that every decision and every little good thing an individual does can make a whole big difference in the world," Caleb responded as he drove carefully in the rain.

"What are you, an environmentalist or the president of a foster organization for the homeless and family?"

"No, I'm just an ordinary man who hopes to achieve happiness one day."

The young lady stayed quiet for a moment.

He stopped at a red light and looked at her. Seeing her discomfort, he asked, "Are you okay?"

"I just got in a stranger's car. Why wouldn't I be?"

Caleb didn't have anything else to say. He knew she was right. Letting a few minutes pass by, he asked where she lived. "Pardon me. I'm so rude I didn't even ask your name. What is it?"

"Juliana and yours?"

"Caleb."

"That's a nice name," she responded as she kept staring at the wet streets through the window.

"Do you like Bob Marley?" Caleb asked.

"Of course, especially when I'm high," she smiled.

"High?"

"Yes, high. What? Are you going to tell me that you don't smoke?"

"I don't."

"Well, you are missing out then. You should do it once in a while. It will relax you, and perhaps even help you come up with more ideas for your civil rights movement."

Caleb laughed hard. "Who said I work for the civil rights, or environment, or so?"

"Well, I thought you were involved in those organizations. Sorry. I don't know. You are too much of a nice guy, so far."

"Look, I don't want you to think I was trying to harm you when I offered you a ride. I was just concerned. Why would a young lady, such as yourself, be outside, sitting on the street at this time, in this weather?"

"I got into a fight with my mom. Make a right here so you can get to my house faster," she said as she dialed 911 on her phone. His face was beautiful, but her nerves were forcing her to be careful.

Caleb, following her directions, said, "You shouldn't be mean to your mom. She probably was screaming at you because she is trying to protect you from something. She surely loves you a lot and doesn't want anything bad to happen to you."

Juliana, irritated, screamed, "She is stupid! I can't stand her anymore! She's always talking the same crap! 'Juliana does this, Juliana does that! Juliana, I grew up in a sad home. Juliana, I never had a good childhood like you did.' God! She makes me go crazy! Just because she wasn't normal doesn't mean she has to try to mess up my life."

Caleb wanted to smile at the childish behavior and conversation they were having, but he kept on driving, listening to her dramatic story.

Finally, after 15 minutes, they got to her house.

"Do you want me to talk to your parents?" he asked.

"For what?"

"To let them know that I found you on the streets and I offered you a ride."

"Are you crazy? Look! If you love your life just keep on driving, because my parents would throw you in jail for life," Juliana said as she took her wallet out of her pocket, grabbed some money, and handled it to him.

Surprised, Caleb looked at her and asked, "What are you doing?"

"I'm going to pay you."

"For what?"

"For the ride, what else?"

"No, thank you."

Juliana looked at him, surprised by his words, and said, "Oh, sorry, I forgot that you have such a great heart," very sarcastically.

"Have a good night."

Juliana just looked at him, stayed quiet for the longest four seconds ever, and said, "Okay, thanks, you too." She got out of the car and headed to her house. "Wait!" she said turning around, going back to Caleb's car.

"Yes?" he said.

"What's your name?"

"Caleb. Caleb Smith."

"Good night and thank you, Caleb Smith" said and walked over to her house.

He was waiting for her to get to the door safely. Apparently, she was a rich girl. The place where she lived was an expensive residence. She was a very pretty girl who had beautiful skin, black hair, and honey eyes that caught his mind 100%. He wondered, then, why such a beautiful and spoiled female would be so rebellious and want things that she didn't need to have.

Once home, he sat in his white sofa, which was covered by a big blanket that had the face of a tiger printed on it. He opened the curtains of his balcony with the remote control and watched the city, beautiful and dark. He noticed something different that night. It had no stars, but the moon was still there, nice and shiny, but it was still missing what it needed to be complete. Maybe he and the night had something in common. They were incomplete, had it all but still were missing something. Caleb was a successful electric engineer/software developer/computer programmer, owned a millionaire-dollar apartment, and his financial situation was persistent. A project he had been working on for years was almost done. Most of the companies in the city, reading about his project and programs, urgently wanted to do business with him, and he was happy about it. He was extremely proud of himself. But deep inside, deep, where no one could see, it didn't really matter. His days and nights consumed him with misery and loneliness. The memory of his childhood was affecting him a lot. He believed, and it likely was the reason, it was why he was scared to engage in relationships. He was traumatized and didn't want to make mistake after mistake. His girlfriend, the loneliness, he said to himself, swallowing the alcohol angrily, was the only one that always waited for him to come back home; the only one that was jealous of any one-night stand; the only one that would remind him of his past, his trauma, and how scared he was of falling in love. Probably one of the few things that was making him happy was the thought of having his own electronics company. He laughed, remembering how even the same gender would try to approach him for a hook up at night, or how his own secretaries would offer him free sex just to find out about his mysterious life. He wished to scream at the world how weak he was, how much agony he had inside his heart; an anxiety that needed to stop but wasn't going to unless he reached his main priority, and that was to find his brother and sister. A brother and sister he hadn't see in more than a decade. Swallowing his whisky, he fell asleep and dreamed. He dreamed of rocks, sex, money, and love. He dreamt it all. He dreamt that he was running, running, falling, getting up and continuing running until his heart stopped, stopped and then, exploded. He woke up sweating his nightmare off, sweating the fear, but not because he was going to die, not because he was not going to breathe anymore, but because he wasn't going to be able to see his brother and sister one last time.

He got up from his bed, walked up to the bathroom, and drowned his nightmare with cold water. He stared at the mirror for a few seconds, looking at the water running down his face, reaching his neck, and falling off back to the sink. Suddenly, his cell phone started to ring.

"Hello?" Caleb's deep voice responded, but the person on the other line remained quiet.

"If this is a prank call then just go and . . ."

The person on the line interrupted, "Caleb? Caleb Smith?"

Caleb, worried, responded, "Yes, this is Caleb. Who's this?"

The person on the line said, "Oh god!" and started to cry.

Caleb said again, "Hello? Who's this? You are really getting me mad. Can you tell me who the hell are you?!" Caleb's angry side started to come out.

The person on the line answered, "Caleb. Caleb it's me, Joey, your brother."

Caleb couldn't believe what his ears were hearing. It was his brother Joey, the one that he hadn't seen in more than 14 years. It was a big blow for him to get this unexpected news. One of his biggest searches had finally appeared. It worked. So many prayers, so many religions, expensive lawyers, detectives, so much money, and everything just for one phone call.

Caleb, crying on the phone, tried to talked, "Are you — are you serious? Are you serious? Because if you are fucking lying then we are going to have big problems!" he yelled over the phone.

Joey, his brother, crying, responded, "I can't believe you're still the same. You haven't changed. Yes. Yes, it's me, Caleb. Joey. I just got out from the Army. I've been doing so much to find you and I'm here in New York City. I want to see you. May I?"

Caleb felt like he'd won the lottery and without a second thought said, "Of course! Of course you can. Yes, please, let's meet up now! I don't care. Tell me. Tell me where you are."

"I'm in this hotel, near Times Square. Here, this is the address."

Caleb wrote it down and as soon as he hung up the phone, got a jacket, and left his apartment. He ran to the elevator, to the parking lot, leaving the valet parking men astonished for being in such a hurry. He got in his car and sped off as fast as he could. He was shocked about the situation. He knew it could have been a joke but he was still going, taking a risk. He couldn't stop crying. The closer he got to the place the more nervous he was. He had been looking for his brother and sister since they were separated and tonight, if destiny wanted it, he was going to hug his brother and talk to him face to face after 14 years. His brother, on the other hand, was waiting, drinking, and drinking. He felt the same as Caleb. It seemed like the same computer was managing their minds. Every little thing one was doing the other one did as well. If Caleb was running with his car, Joey was swallowing the alcohol faster. He was stressed out too.

The minutes were running, and both brothers were nervous. At the hotel already, Caleb walked up to the bar where they were going to meet up. Then, he saw a man wearing an Army uniform. Caleb wasn't sure if it was his brother, but holding his strength and swallowing his pride walked up to the guy and tapped on his shoulder. The man turned and, with tears running down his eyes, hugged him. Caleb couldn't believe it either. He was crying too. That moment became one of the happiest moments of his life. Finally, he hugged his brother, the one he hadn't seen in years; centuries it felt like. They both shared love through the connection of their arms.

Caleb, crying, looked at him and said, "I — I don't know what to say."

Joey responded, "I'm still in shock. I — I have so many things to tell you."

"So do I. I don't even know where to start."

Joey, looking at him, smiled and said, "Well, something that I can tell you is that I was in the Army. And before that, the family that adopted me gave me lots of love. They don't know I'm here with you, but I want to introduce you to them. They are going to love you."

"Have you found out anything on Lily?" Caleb asked Joey while he was sitting down.

"No, but I talked to the family that raised her and they didn't want to give me any more information. They said it was 'confidential.'"

"I heard the same too," Caleb said, swallowing the whisky that they ordered. "Supposedly she got married, changed her name, and lives here in New York."

"Wow. Did you ever go back to jail and talk to mom about it?" Joey asked, holding his glass of whisky.

"Mom?" Caleb said, sighing hard. "She's been out of jail."

"You see how lost I've been? I don't even know anything about my own mother."

Caleb sighed, "There's not too much to know. She lives with Auntie Carol. And him — Manuel, he is still in jail. He got raped in there and now he is dying of AIDS."

"Did you go and see him?" Joey asked.

"Of course not. Mom told me about it," Caleb said making a disgusted facial expression. "You know she's still in love with him. She told me that he stole money from this gang member, and well, this gangster found out and sent his people to rape him."

"Finally he got some of his own medicine. Now he knows how I . . ." Joey paused his words and looked down to the floor.

"Try to forget. Everything is over now. We can't live in the past anymore."

"It's just that every time I hear his name so many memories come to my head. I feel like the memories are coming back to life. It kills me. And my pride as a man starts burning."

"Well, put it this way — IT'S OVER. It's never going to happen again and I promise you that." Caleb said holding on to his brother's arm, strongly.

"Yeah. Yeah, you are right. You are right. Sorry about all this."

"Sorry? Look at you. You are a grown man and are still saying sorry to your big brother."

Joey sighed and a big smile came out. "So, tell me. Where you staying at now? What do you do for living?"

"I'm an electrical engineer and I live in this apartment . . ."

That night, the conversation seemed like it wasn't going to end. Secrets were shared and facts of life were learned. Drinks came. Drinks went. Laughs were heard, and they enjoyed every single second of it. They felt so thankful for having each other face to face, and learned that one doesn't know what one has until it's gone.

In contrast, Juliana was in her room talking on the phone with her best friend, Monique.

"Yes, Monique, I told you. He is so hot!" Juliana said while she laid on her bed, playing with her hair, holding the phone in her right hand.

"Well, girl, then tell me what he looks like," Monique asked.

"He is tall with blue eyes; very handsome. Perfect!"

"Is he white?" Monique asked.

"Yes. Why?" Juliana responded.

"White? Well, he must be hot enough for you to like him."

"Hey man, you're being a little racist there. You know I date all kinds."

"Girl, I barely see you with white dudes and you are white yourself. You always dating the dark skin or the caramel skin men," Monique said while she started laughing.

"Well, let me tell you, he is hotter than all the brothers I've dated before."

"I want to see him," Monique responded sounding anxious.

"Monique, don't even tell me about it. I didn't exchange numbers."

"Are you serious?"

"Yeah! I should have, but fuck it."

"How are you going to talk about this dude, saying that you like him, and you don't even have his number!"

"Don't worry, Monique. I know I'm going to see him again."

"Oh yea? How?"

"I don't know. I just know that I'm going to see him again. He is an electrical engineer, so if I want, I can search on my dad's computer all the engineers in the city."

Monique, raising her voice, said "Oh shit! That's my girl."

"I had to use my dad's services one day."

"Anyway, you want to come tomorrow to Danny's party?"

"I don't know. You know me and my mom have been arguing lately, so I doubt it," Juliana responded.

"Are you serious?"

"I may sneak out. I'm not sure."

Monique, laughing, responded. "Yes, you should. He told me he wants you there."

"What did he say?"

"Well, you know him, always being fresh. He is like my brother, and since the trust is so intense he told me that he wanted you to go to the party because he wants to remember old times; like that day you gave him a blow job in the detention office."

"I cannot believe he said that! I'm going to kill him!", Juliana said and laughed harder.

"Well, then, he was telling me how bad he wanted to eat you out and stuff. You know him, girl. He likes you a lot."

"Well, too bad. I don't like him anymore. I'm so over him."

"How do you know that?" Monique asked. "You guys dated for the longest. How long was it? Two years and nine months?"

"Well, Monique, let me tell you how I know, and learn from the master. I know it because his dad gave me better things than his son did. You get it now?"

"Unbelievable! I can't believe it! You did it with his dad! How did it happen? Well, his dad is hot, but, no, no, no! If Danny finds out, he'll kill you!"

"Kill me?" Juliana asked. "He wouldn't even look at me knowing that I cheated on him with his own father. He would probably pay a journalist to put a picture of me, front page, as an STD magnet or the new 'Superhead'. I don't know. I don't care. Anyway, I don't think he will mess with me knowing who my dad is."

"Girl, let your dad find out about it."

"He won't. Believe me. He won't."

"Okay, so then tell me, how'd it happen?" Monique asked impatiently.

"Gosh, Monique, you really are nosy aren't you? I'm going to tell you tomorrow at school."

"Are you serious? Why tomorrow?!"

"Because tomorrow is Friday and it would be better, more exciting, to start the weekend with surprises, you know."

"Okay, okay, then see you tomorrow," Monique said and hung up.

Juliana, for some reason, couldn't stop thinking about him, Caleb. What was so different about him from the rest? There was something so special that she wanted badly. She needed, not just wanted, but she had a necessity to see him again. She knew she had to. She wanted that man and she was setting her mind to get him. So not thinking twice, she ran to her father's office downstairs, locked the door slowly, opened the laptop, and quickly she searched for his name. She had found him, she thought, but unexpectedly her mother opened the door.

"You know your dad can kill us both right?" her mother said as she closed the door.

Juliana just stared at her and closed all the windows in the computer.

"Honey, I know today it wasn't a good day for us because . . ."

Juliana interrupted her mother and said, "Because? I'm going to tell you why mother. Because you are always up in my business! You are always trying to mess up my life! THAT IS WHY!" Juliana screamed.

"No my dear I don't . . ."

Juliana interrupted again. "Yes, you do mother! You want me to be as miserable as you were or probably still are, but let me tell you, mother, it won't happen! IT WON'T!"

Dara, feeling the disrespect too deep, yelled, "Look Juliana! I'm tired of you treating me like if I'm your enemy! YOU NEED TO STOP THAT!"

Juliana sat down and laughed sarcastically. "Wow! Finally, you are acting like a mom. Congratulations! Now you can leave me the fuck alone, please. I have to go to school tomorrow," said as she walked out of the room.

Dara watched her leave and, with tears running down her cheeks, walked out of the office right after Juliana. She asked herself what she had done for her daughter to hate her so much. She'd had a bad childhood. She'd suffered a lot and that was the reason why she lied so much about her past. She'd denied Caleb, her own brother, by saying that he was dead. She'd lied about Joey, her other brother, by saying the only reason he was missing was because he was a drug addict and her mother kicked him out of the house. However, something that she never denied was her daughter and the love she had for her.

She believed that lying and rejecting her roots, her past, and her own family was the only way to cover her tragic reality; the truth that would not only hurt her but also her daughter. She knew that at the end of the day, in her own beliefs, there was a God out there, and a *Karma* alive.

Meanwhile, Juliana, in her room, was tearing on her pillow. She felt something hurting her heart. She felt like she couldn't breathe. She was very sad. She knew she loved her mom. She knew her mom was always going to put her first under any situation, but for some reason she couldn't stop hating her. One side kept on saying she loved her mom and the other kept on saying she hated her, over and over. She didn't know why she enjoyed seeing her mom cry so much. She didn't know why she liked so much seeing her mom begging her for love. She wanted to stop, but she couldn't. And every time, after every argument, she would end up breaking into tears, like she had now.

"Hello? Hey, it's Juliana," she said cleaning her tears after she made a phone call.

"Hey, darling. How are you doing?"

"Better than you, so far."

"Wow, I see you are still a little aggressive with me," responded the man, with a deep voice, on the other line.

"I'm just saying what I feel. After a long day, you have to go back home and see your wife. Meanwhile, I'll be laying down or swimming in my pool, naked."

"I like your game. I've always loved it, ever since I made you mine for the first time. So tell me, what did you call me for? Do you want a designer bag; tickets for a cruise? What exactly does your sweet self want, because I know you didn't call me for no reason."

"Not really. You know, if I want an expensive bag I can ask my dad for it. I don't need to gold dig you like your secretary does. I called you because I can't sleep, so I want to play."

"You want to play, huh?" The man asked, excited.

"Yes, but I don't like phone sex. I want to see you tomorrow after school, if it's okay with you?" she asked.

"Perfect. Danny is not coming home tomorrow. He told me he has practice so I guess we could have time for us."

The man on the other line was Adam, her ex-boyfriend's father.

"Okay then, see you tomorrow. I'll catch a cab, don't worry, just pick up when I call you," she demanded.

"Okay, sweetheart. Oh, by the way, can you send me a kiss?" Adam asked, and Juliana hung up.

Early in the morning, Juliana, who was already late for school, turned on the radio and started getting ready. She got her backpack, said bye to Marilu, the maid that'd taken care of her since she was little, and left the house.

Her driver opened the door of the car for her and she said, "Don't worry, I'm catching a cab. Oh and shut your mouth if you don't want to get fired."

The driver just stared at her and closed the door, watching her leave.

Juliana got in the cab that was waiting outside for her and told him to drive around. She was calling Adam over and over but the phone just kept on ringing.

"Excuse me, Miss. Where do you really want me to take you? You have been making me go in circles," the cab driver asked.

"Look, don't be complaining okay? As long as I'm paying you, don't worry and keep driving."

The cab driver looked at her and kept on driving. He needed the money and since she was insisting he didn't say anything else. Then, her phone started ringing. She picked up and it was him, Adam.

"Where the fuck have you been?! I've called you like ten-thousand times. What the fuck?!"

"I was in a meeting! Maybe the day you get a job you will understand."

"Whatever. Do I still go to your house or not?"

"Yes, please do so. I'm on my way there. Are you in a cab?"

"Of course!" Juliana responded in a silly way. "What did you think? That my dad was going to take me to your house?"

"Okay just meet me there and . . ."

Juliana didn't want to hear anymore. She hung up, told the cab driver to change directions and take her to Adam's house.

In contrast, Caleb was running late to his job. He knew he shouldn't have gone clubbing when he had to work the next day. "At least it was worth it," he kept on repeating to himself to avoid feeling guilty for his tardiness. As soon as he walked into his office, everybody stared and whispered. The news at the office was always faster than the speed of light; and like the telephone game, every employee had a different story stuck in their head, but they all had the same assumption, SEX. How come the perfect man, who had no active social life, was late for work? Caleb, finally at his office, closed the door, sipped his coffee, and sat down. Then, a knock on the door stressed him, "Come in!" he said. It was Thomas, one of his closest and only friends from the company where he work at for years.

Thomas, smiling at him, said, "Wow! You have to give me the best explanation for why you weren't here for the meeting."

Caleb looked at him strangely and asked, "What meeting are you talking about?"

"You aren't serious, are you?" Thomas said looking at him surprised and confused. "We had a meeting today about your schedule and how the company was doing so well, and blah, blah, blah. But you weren't here."

"Oh gosh, I forgot! Sorry, I've been very busy lately. You know, I do this, I do that."

"It's okay, man. Don't worry. But honestly, what happened?"

"It's a long story," Caleb responded, leaning back in his chair, drinking his coffee.

"It looks like some curves didn't let you get up in the morning, huh?"

Caleb, smiling hard, said, "And why would you assume that?"

"Oh, c'mon man! You wouldn't be late to work unless you had a hot chick sleeping next to you."

"Well, it wasn't a girl," Caleb responded.

Thomas looked confused.

"No, no, I'm not gay. I love women, but it's something more important than that."

"Okay, may you tell me?"

Caleb whispered, "I found my brother."

"Are you serious?"

"Absolutely. Why would I lie about that?" he responded.

"Dude, that's awesome! How did it happen?"

"It's a long story, but look, let me get the papers I need to show Mr. Patrice and then I'll come back and talk to you," Caleb said getting up and walking out.

"Ok see you then."

Caleb tried to look as serious as possible, but with so much happiness in his heart he couldn't hide the smile on his face. However, he was nervous. He knew he had to give the boss a good explanation. He knocked on the door and heard his voice say, "Come in." He opened and walked up to his desk.

Politely, he said, "Mr. Patrice, I want to apologize for my tardiness. I know I should have called and explained before I arrived 30 minutes later than usual. However, I do . . ."

Mr. Patrice, who was sitting at his desk smoking a black cigarette, interrupted him. "Caleb I do not want your explanation. Save it for your appointments."

Caleb nervously answered, "Pardon, me?"

"Caleb, they loved your idea! They're going to design the electronics! The computers, the mp3s, the video games, everything is going to be as you wished. They already signed the contract. New York City now is going to know about your inventions! Imagine walking down the street of one of the most popular cities in the world and seeing through store windows your designs; seeing people buying them, using them, having them?!" Mr. Patrice said full of excitement.

Caleb, surprised and speechless, responded after a couple of shocking seconds, "Are you — Are you serious?!"

"Why would I lie to you about it?" Patrice said, smiling at him and getting up from his chair.

"Wow, I cannot believe it. This has been one of my biggest dreams. I can't believe they bought my idea. They bought my dream. People actually believe in me. I do not know what to say."

"Caleb, believe it or not, the world always believed in you. It just time for you to break that shell, come out, and show the universe how capable you are of throwing your dreams out there and seeing the best opportunities to catch them. I wish I was in your position so I could be screaming with happiness and excitement. Oh, and just to let you know, it only gets better," Mr. Patrice said as he walked up to him.

"I don't understand. What do you mean?" Caleb asked confused.

Patrice, holding his shoulders, said, "I'm going to let you manage all this, every detail, every contract, every little thing. You are going to work with attorneys, professional engineers, and perfectionists. I'm naming you the CEO of all the departments in this building, in this company, and in this project."

Caleb couldn't believe what he was hearing and living. He couldn't believe that all this was real. He had imagined and thought of this moment for so long, and now, today, out of nowhere, unexpectedly, it became real. Mr. Patrice's smile became bigger as he pulled out a contract, and grabbed his favorite pen, for Caleb Smith to sign.

However, not everyone was enjoying their day for their professional accomplishments, but for their sexual desires. Our dear Juliana, for example, was getting out of the cab and ran to Adam's arms.

"I was missing you last night!" she screamed.

Adam, hugging her back, said, "I guess so. Did you pay the taxi yet?"

"No, that's what you have to do. See you in the pool!" She kissed him on the forehead, ran to the pool and started taking off her clothes.

Adam laughed and looked at the cab driver. "I apologize, sir. Kids these days, no manners."

"Yes, I can see it," said the driver as he counted the cash.

Adam, walking back into the house, holding a newspaper in his right hand, looked for her. And there she was, his *Lolita*, acting as wild as an exotic animal in a new environment, taking off her skirt, just naturally driving him crazy with her beauty. She knew she had the power to manipulate him without saying a word.

"Are you going to miss all the fun?"

"You are such a little girl," Adam said as he sipped his coffee.

"I don't hear that when we are in your bed!"

"Listen, you better get out of the pool and take your clothes to the laundry. I don't want people to think I brought you over here on purpose."

Juliana looked at him and swam from the middle of the pool to where he was standing, and got out fully nude. "Didn't you?" She smiled as she wrapped her arms around his neck. "Tell me. Lie to my face and tell me you didn't want me to come, and I will leave."

Adam did nothing but stare at her.

"I want you bad," she whispered in his ear.

"So do I. You make me feel different. Your skin, your lips, your body, everything about you drives me crazy. Oh, my dear Juliana, you just have no idea. You just can't imagine how I feel right now," Adam said as he carried her to the white chair nearby. He passed his index and middle fingers together in between her legs, making her close her eyes and bite her lips. Not saying anything else, he carried her inside the house, not caring about the housecleaners that appeared on his way.

"Sandra, please go and pick up the clothes that are in the pool area," Adam said while he was carrying Juliana, who was making a big show with her laughs.

"Yes, sir," Sandra, the housecleaner responded trying not to look at the young, naked woman that her boss was holding in his arms.

Adam threw Juliana's body on his king bed, the same bed that he used to share with his wife, the same silk sheets that rapidly hugged her body as they started making out. It seemed like she wanted him more than he did. They were sweating within seconds and in a few, her moans invaded the room. Juliana demanded him not to stop. He couldn't catch his breath. He felt like his lungs and heart were going to explode. He paused for a bit and admired her young, smooth body laying on the bed alone as if it was desiring itself. He didn't, he couldn't hold it, and he exploded. Juliana turned around and begged him for more love, and he proceeded.

The room stayed closed for hours, nobody dared to knock on the door. The employees of the house knew what was going on. His son's ex girlfriend was sleeping with the dad now. As disgusting as it seemed to the majority, it was happening, but of course, no one would ever dare to talk about it. Some of them were from foreign countries and needed the job, and some of them were *'aliens'* according to the law. So the pressure to stay quiet revolved in their minds.

Adam looked at Juliana completely wrapped in his arms after his so-called victory of having sex with his son ex's girlfriend. "Wow, I think today was the best so far."

"You think so?" she responded.

"Yeah. You know how long it's been since my wife and I have any type of sexual contact?"

"How long?" she asked, getting on top of him.

Adam whispered in her ear.

Juliana loudly said, "Oh my god. Are you serious? That's long!"

"Yes, I don't even want to touch her when she begs me."

"I feel sorry for her."

"Me too. Look at us here, on her bed, just finishing making love."

"No, not because of this, but because you are nasty! You are just — a poor old man. Do you understand my double sense? You are the richest, poorest man in the word. You have it all, but still you don't."

"I don't understand," Adam said trying to laugh.

"I have to go. You think my clothes are ready?"

"Maybe. Would you like me to call Sandra and ask?"

"Yes, please."

Adam called his housekeeper, "Okay, Sandra, thank you so much," while Juliana started to smoke a cigarette.

"Hey, no! Don't smoke inside the room!" He said, getting up and taking the cigarette out of her mouth. "My wife is coming back from Paris today I don't want her to be asking me questions."

"You are so pathetic."

"Oh, c'mon princess, don't get mad at me," said and hugged her.

"I'm serious. You are an idiot."

The housekeeper knocked on the door and Juliana, pushing Adam, walked up to the door nude to get her clothes.

"Where do you want me to take you after here?" Adam asked. Juliana, getting dressed, responded, "I don't know. Take me to Times Square. I want to eat something."

Adam said, "Sure, let me get dressed."

Later on, somewhere in Times Square . . .

"Stop here!" She pointed out at a Starbucks that was around.

Adam looked at Juliana and asked, "Do you want me to go and eat with you?"

"No," Juliana said as she was fixing herself through the mirror.

Adam, surprised, repeated, "No?"

"No. Now get away from me. You make me sick." She opened the door and walked out. He looked at her amazed. He didn't know what was wrong with her, but also didn't want to tell her anything. He didn't want to end the day with an argument.

As Juliana walked away from the car, her body started to have chills. Her throat was giving her signs of a disgusting feeling from her stomach, coming up fast like an elevator that was ready to come out through her mouth. She felt disgusted, empty, and lonely. Maybe that was the reason why she kept on going back to him, she thought to herself. She didn't even have an explanation for it. She lived regret after regret, and little by little she started torturing herself with everything that she ever did in her life, and the memories were eating her mind inside. She wanted to change her life badly or she was going to end up worse than the criminals that her dad was always dealing with.

And as she kept on walking around through the shopping stores in the big apple, she suddenly stopped and saw him. Yes, it was that guy, Caleb, eating by himself in a local restaurant. *Hope* showed up in her life she told herself. Not thinking twice, she went in, walked up to his table, and stood right there next to him.

Caleb felt somebody standing next to him, looked up, and saw her.

"Hey!" Juliana smiled and her eyes were bright like a shining star in a dark room.

Caleb, standing up from the table as a gentleman, responded, "Well hello there! What a great surprise. How are you doing?" he said and pulled the chair for her to sit.

"Good. Are you alone?"

"Yes, and yourself? Aren't you supposed to be at school, by the way?" he asked.

"It has been a long time since I've been absent so I took a little vacation," Juliana said pulling her chair closer to his.

Caleb, smiling at her, started to admire her. He was enjoying her company and her beauty. As she started to talk and talk about her day and school, he imagined the dirtiest thoughts under her skirt. He was a man, after all. A man that didn't know what he was getting into; either his best dream or his worst nightmare was about to start.

The conversation seemed like it wasn't going to have an end. For the first time in so long, she was smiling because she wanted to and not because she had to. It was the first time she was being her own, outgoing self.

"Well, it was amazing talking to you, and I'm definitely calling you later on. It was nice seeing you again. I have to go now."

"Where?" she asked concerned.

"To work, my darling. I actually can't be absent like you."

"Oh. Okay, so I guess I'll be waiting for your call."

Caleb stood up, kissed her on the cheek, and walked out of the restaurant.

Juliana stayed at the table a couple of minutes after he was gone. She felt electricity going through her face down her neck, etc., etc. She walked out and called her driver to pick her up.

Minutes later, on her way home, she was having a conversation with her best friend.

"Monique, I need you to go to my house, now!" Juliana said excited.

"Girl, where have you been?" Monique asked.

"Monique, stop asking questions and go to my house. I need to tell you something extremely important."

"What is it? You know your mom came to the school today, right? I don't even know how you are graduating when you are never here."

"Monique, stop talking so much and get over here, please?"

"Okay, Miss. I just got out of school. I'll see you in a little."

"Thanks. I love you. You will always be my sister," said Juliana sending all her positive energy through the line.

In the mean time, Caleb was on the phone talking to his brother. "Yes, you are going to be surprised when you see your house," Joey said.

"Well, hopefully you didn't throw my papers away. As you can tell, I'm not quite organized," Caleb responded.

"Don't worry, you know me," Joey said while he was walking around the kitchen at Caleb's apartment. "At what time are you coming back, by the way? I'm bored."

"I get out at 4 pm today. Take a walk around if you want, but write a note before you leave. I don't want you to get lost again," Caleb said sarcastically.

Joey laughed and said, "C'mon, what do you think I am, 5? I don't be getting lost like that."

"I know you well, very well, and if it wasn't for your head being attached to your body you would have lost it too," Caleb responded.

"Whatever. I'll see you in a little bit, then. By the way, any plans for tonight? The weekend is here already."

"Yea, we can get with some of my friends from work and go to a bar or a nightclub. Let's see what happens."

"I want to see some *hoes* ASAP. I have necessities."

Caleb laughed.

"What?" said Joey.

"Calm down kid. I'm still at work. Why don't you walk around the condo and see if you can find some women by the pool or the tennis courtyard?

"Wow! God Damn, Caleb!" Joey exclaimed.

"What happened now?" Caleb asked while he held his cellphone on his shoulder, trying to multitask with the computer.

"Who is that blonde right there? Yummy!" exclaimed Joey.

"Oh, wait a minute. She has short hair, and a big . . ."

"Yea, that one," said Joey, cutting his brother's sentence.

"That's a man."

"What?! No way! You are probably hating that I'm going to go get her right now."

"Go head and find out for yourself. At the beginning I felt the same until I went up to her. Don't worry, *shit* happens."

"Yuck!"

"I'll talk to you later, *macho-man*. I have to work," said Caleb and hung up.

Juliana, at home already, found her mom sitting on the stairs as if she was waiting for her. She was nervous but knew Adam wasn't going to be foolish enough to talk about their **BIG** secret.

"Where have you been?" asked her mom.

"At school, where else?" responded, walking into the kitchen.

"Don't play games with me, Juliana. You know very well that you weren't there," said her mom as she chased after her.

Juliana, stopping in the middle of her way, responded, "Okay, then where was I, mother? Tell me, since apparently you know everything."

"Your homeroom teacher called the house today and for your bad luck I was here," her mom said getting closer to her daughter's face.

"And what did she say?" her daughter responded without any type of fear.

"She asked me where were you, and I had to lied. I said you were sick. Later on, I had to go to your school to talk to the principal so they wouldn't kick you out."

"Good, mommy. Now you are learning how to lie," she said as she took ice cream out of the freezer.

Dara, taking the ice cream away from her, said, "Now, tell me where the fuck were you?"

Juliana looked at her with hate. "Okay, mom. I'm going to tell you the truth. Why lie to you, right? Yes, I did skip school. I took a long walk to the city, looked at clothes, and ate outside."

"With who? Monique?"

"No."

"With who!" Dara raised her voice.

"With my iPod," Juliana said and smiled at her mom, wanting to laugh.

Dara was angry. She wanted to kill her daughter for a moment and then bring her back to life.

"Mom, I'm telling you the truth. It's up to you if you believe me or not, okay?" Juliana said and walked out of the kitchen.

Dara stayed in the kitchen, put the ice cream back in the freezer, and walked quickly after her daughter, trying to stop her, but the door bell rang. She let out a deep breath as she opened the door. It was Monique.

"Hey, Monique," she tried to say with so much irritation after confronting her daughter, as usual.

"Hey, Mrs. Russell. Is Juliana here?" Monique responded as both said hi to each other with a kiss on each cheek.

"Yes, Monique, she is here. Come in," Dara said moving to the side to let her in.

"How have you been?" Monique asked Dara.

"Good. How's your mom, by the way?"

"Perfect! She is going with my dad to Cannes for a week. Then they're going to Greece for another week."

"That's fantastic," Dara said faking a smile on her face. "I talked to her yesterday at the beauty salon. She told me you got 2nd place in the contest for best science experiments."

"Oh yea, my dad helped me a lot. I didn't win but at least I made it there," responded the young girl, smiling hard as her Asian-looking eyes shined.

"Congratulations! I wish I could see those types of prizes around here," Dara said looking to the side, trying to avoid more talk as soon as she saw her daughter coming downstairs.

"Okay, mom, thanks! Now you can let my friend go. We need to talk about little girl stuff. You know what, mother? You need to stay in your place."

Monique looked at Dara and said, "Well, I'll talk to you later, Mrs. Russell."

"Ok, love," Dara said and kissed her on the cheek, saying goodbye.

Juliana smiled at Monique and then gave a mean look to her mom as she grabbed her friend's hand and headed to her room. Juliana, closing the door, said, "Monique we have a lot to talk about."

Monique, sitting on the bed, responded, "Girl what happened? Where did you go? I was worried about you."

Juliana laid her body on her sofa and covered it with a fur coat she had around.

"Are you going to tell me what happened? By the expression of your face it seems like you had sex with your favorite rapper." Monique smiled. "What happened? Tell me."

Juliana laughed and responded, "Well, I didn't fuck him, but I fucked someone else."

"Who?!" Monique asked, her eyes opening wide.

"Danny's dad."

Monique laughed hard. "Oh my god! He's going to kill you! How did it happen?"

"Well, today I was getting ready for school, told my driver to shut his mouth, and caught a cab. So you know, I went to see him. We talked and swam in the pool. I danced in the most naughty way possible for him and he got hard. Ha-ha, it was funny, an old man getting hard so easy," Juliana said giving a smile of joy.

"Wait! What about the maids? Nobody was there?"

"Of course they were there. But you know the money shuts them all up. So then, we went to his room and the action started. I told him to take Viagra but he didn't want to, so fuck it."

"You are unbelievable! I can't believe you did that!"

"He was saying it was the greatest today, and I said yes, yes it was; but it was bullshit, he doesn't make me orgasm that much."

"Then? I don't get it. Why do you fuck him?"

"I'm not going to lie, he turns me on and he does well sometimes. But at the end he's not for me. I need energy; a free spirit, a young soul, a body that will make me go crazy."

"And that's all you did today?"

"No," Juliana said standing in front of her mirror. "I told him to drop me off in Times Square and guess who I saw there?"

"Danny?!"

"No! Wait, Danny didn't go to school today?"

"No, he didn't. I though you were with him."

"No, eww. What's wrong with you? Anyway, I saw him, the engineer I told you about, Caleb!"

"Oh my god?! What did you do?"

"I ran," Juliana said, lighting a cigarette.

"Are you serious?"

"No," Juliana said blowing the smoke out. "I walked inside the restaurant where he was eating alone like a nerd and stood right there, next to him."

"And what did he do?"

"He looked at me and we talked for about 30 minutes. Then he gave me his number and he left to work like a sucker."

"So you called him already?"

"No, he said he was going to call me."

Suddenly, her phone started ringing.

Juliana, grabbed it and looking at it, said out loud, "Shit Monique, it's him, Caleb!"

"Answer!" Monique responded excited.

"Hello?" Juliana answered the phone.

"Hey you! How are you doing?" Caleb asked.

"So far, so good. And you?"

"The same as well. I was actually wondering where you were going tonight?"

"Nowhere so far. Why?"

"Well, my brother came back from the Irak and we want to go out today. I don't know, perhaps you would like to join us?"

"Sure, why not. At what time?"

"What time do you think would be best for you? I don't want to get you in trouble."

Juliana laughed. "I'm 18 not 8. What do you think, at 11 pm?"

"Perfect! Do you want me to go and pick you up?"

"Yes. Do you remember how to get here?"

"Kind of," Caleb responded.

"Ok, then I'll text you my address. I'm going to be here waiting with my friend, Monique."

Monique looking at Juliana with a *'what!'* facial expression, kept on doing signs saying no, but Juliana still accepted the invitation including her.

Juliana hung up the phone, looked at her friend smiling, and full of energy screamed. "Monique get sexy tonight because we are going out with two real grown men!"

"I honestly cannot believe you," said Monique, feeling the pressure of not abandoning her friend to hang out with two complete strangers.

On the other hand, Caleb, who had just arrived at his house, found a big change inside.

"You really are a bad person to live with," said his brother Joey, welcoming him home.

"I told you I was disorganized," Caleb said, dropping his suitcase on the just-cleaned carpet.

"So what are we doing tonight?" Joey asked as he cooked dinner.

"Do you remember I talked to you about this girl, Juliana?" Caleb responded while he getting a bottle of water from the fridge.

"The rich girl that you picked up from the streets?"

"Yeah. I saw her today," Caleb said, walking up to the sofa.

"Where at?"

"Times Square. I was eating and then out of nowhere I felt somebody standing right there next to me. It was her."

"And what did you say?"

"We talked," Caleb said and sighed. "We actually had a long conversation. We exchanged numbers and all that."

"Nice. Did you tell her to bring a girl for me tonight?"

"She is."

"Nice."

"I called her a few ago. She told me she is going to wait for me to pick her up today at 11 pm."

"How old is this girl?"

"18," Caleb said as he drank water.

"Are you sure?"

"Well, she told me she just turned 18 a couple weeks ago. Her father sent her and her friends on a cruise and blah, blah, blah."

"Young sluts these days. She must be shitting money to do all that."

"Maybe, I don't know. Do you think I'm doing something bad, picking up this girl? I mean she is 18. She's still young."

"My dear brother, look at you! Look where you're living! Million-dollar apartment. Tell me, who is going to judge you? NOBODY! Money buys everything and controls everything."

"Not everything, Joey."

"With me it does."

Caleb smiled at him. "At 10:00, Joey. At 10:00, we out. I'm going to take a shower and then file some papers. Be ready."

"Like my Cuban homeboy from the war says, 'coño'! You work even when you are about to die," said his brother as he was opening a can of beer.

When the night approached, Juliana finished retouching her intense make-up and finished cutting the shirt she had on. She looked at Monique, full of excitement.

"I'm not trying to fuck anybody, just to let you know, Juliana," responded her friend, feeling disappointed with her tight, black dress.

"Those weren't my intentions. We are just going to have fun. And no! Don't give the pussy fast. You know, then, guys leave you after you give it."

The phone rang and it was Caleb asking Juliana to come out.

As Juliana and her friend walked out, Dara stood in the middle of their way. "Where are you going?" she asked.

"To the movies," her daughter responded without hesitation.

"Without my permission?"

"I called dad. I already told you not to worry about me," said Juliana, pushing her mother to the side while walking out.

Dara stared at her daughter in shock. She walked toward the clear, crystal window next to the door and saw them both getting in a car she had never seen before.

Dara rushed to get the house phone and called her daughter. "Where are you going?"

"To the movies, I already told you."

"With who?"

"With Monique and two other friends."

"Who are they?"

"New guys from the school, mom."

"Then I'm going to walk out and meet them! You better not be lying to me or . . ."

"Mom, mom. Listen, we have to go, okay? The movie starts at 11:15 pm and we are super late. Check it on the computer if you don't believe me."

Dara was about to speak but Juliana hung up. She was mad. Juliana was her only daughter and she loved her a lot. She feared that something so atrocious like what had happened to her could happen to her one and only baby someday.

She stood by the stairs, and called her husband. This one, who already knew the drama that was happening between the only two women of his life, hesitated in answering. But Dara wouldn't stop bombarding his phone and kept on ringing him.

"Isaiah, I don't know what to do anymore," she said as soon as he answered.

"I already told you, sweetheart, it's her age. Young people her age act like that. It's the hormones."

"No, no, that's not true. I wasn't like that when I was her age."

"Honey, do you remember that you were living in an adopted home?"

"Yes, but," Dara sighed, "Isaiah, you know I'm scared that something may happen to her."

"Nobody is going to touch her, especially if they know that she is the chief's daughter. Please stop worrying so much! Nothing is going to happen to our little angel."

"Maybe I am exaggerating."

"Yes, you are. I'll be at home in 10 minutes. I'm hungry. Are you going to eat with me?"

"Yes, I'll wait for you."

"See you then. I love you."

"I love you too."

At the movies, Juliana couldn't stop staring at the individual next to her, Caleb. She wanted him. She desired those lips. She couldn't wait for the right moment to make a move. But then, in her mind, she kept on repeating to herself that he wasn't going to be a mistake. She told herself that this time it was going to be different. After the movie was finally over and they were leaving, Caleb and Juliana started a conversation as Juliana re-touched her make-up.

"Why do you argue so much with your mom? I don't understand," Caleb asked.

"You don't know her. She is so fucking annoying."

"I wish I had a mom like that when I was younger. A mom that was always there, making me get away from the bad things I did."

"Yes! I get your point, but, she is just too much. She thinks that because we're rich we should always be thankful to God, be happy and never cry because we have everything. I mean, I'm grateful for it, but, gosh! I never asked to be rich. I really don't care!"

"When you get older, you will be able to understand all this. When you finish school, and I'm not talking about just high school or college, I'm talking about something as big as a university, grad school, you are going to see how real life is."

"School? Oh god, don't talk to me about school. I hate school! I told my mom I wanted to drop out and get my GED and, of course, she started crying, as usual." The young lady sighed as she chewed her gum harder.

Caleb laughed. Juliana smiled. He didn't want to admit it but he started to find something in her that was making him stay around. He had a list of the type of girl he wanted to date and she wasn't in it. But for some reason he just wanted to be around her. He felt that special chemistry. He felt like he had known her for so long; felt like he knew so much without knowing her. He felt like a strong magnet was pulling him to her.

"What are we going to do now?" Juliana asked him as she saw Joey and Monique approaching them after they finished playing some games.

"I don't know. Let's go play pool," Joey said.

"No, I'm tired of that. My dad got his own pool place," Juliana responded.

"Are you serious?"

"Yes. My dad is always there with him on the weekends," Monique responded, looking at him and Juliana.

"Little rich girls," Joey said staring at his phone.

"At least I get more money from my parents than you do from the Army," responded Juliana smiling.

Joey was surprised. He wasn't expecting that. "Wow, wow! Watch that mouth, girl."

"Why? You think because you are from the Army I'm going to shut up?" Juliana said getting an attitude out of her.

"Well, at least, show some respect."

"My dad is the chief of the police department in Manhattan. He works with the FBI, CIA, Secret Service, along with other shits and I barely respect his rules. What makes you think I'm going to respect you or the president?"

"What if we go to Danny's party?" Monique interrupted them trying to calm the aggravated environment.

"Who's there?" Juliana asked.

"He told me his parents are leaving today. I don't know where; well, Juliana, you should know more about that," Monique responded.

Juliana just smiled hard as had flashbacks of those times sexing Danny, as well as his dad.

"So what would you ladies like to do? We cannot get into a bar because you guys are underage. Is there any other activity you would like to do now?"

Juliana looked at him and smiled. The way Caleb was speaking, the elegant words he used to talk, the way he stood up, walked, and smiled was something different for her young soul. She was amazed, perhaps, or impressed at the fact that she never had contact with a respectful individual such as Caleb, who was young, and was so much different from the rest. It sounded funny. They were rich and always had important figures at their homes, and still they were ignorant of the education they had around.

"Well, we are going to Danny's party then," Juliana answered as they were in the parking lot looking for Caleb's car.

"Are you serious?" Monique responded.

"Yes, I'm inviting all of you, and after that we can go to the beach and get drunk."

"You are not drinking," Joey responded while he checked the time on his phone.

"Says who? You?"

"Yes, I say so. You are not of legal age to drink. You are in a car with us and if something happens to you we are going to get in trouble, and I'm not taking charges over you."

Caleb laughed and kept on driving while he was listening to the argument between his brother and the woman he liked. They had the music as loud as both young ladies wanted, and even if it was a cold night, the heat was standing out. The chemistry between Caleb and Juliana was obvious.

However, Juliana's mom wasn't as happy as her daughter was. She was in her room with her husband, talking about Juliana's future.

"Yes, I already told you, I don't understand what's wrong with that girl! Today. Today I saw her getting in a car with two guys that she said were new from school."

"Maybe they were honey . . . What if Juliana was actually telling you the truth?" Isaiah responded.

"I don't know Isaiah, maybe they are and I'm worrying too much."

"You are love. Juliana is a grown person now, why don't you think about us going to Egypt and having us a second honeymoon?" said Mr. Russell hugging his wife very passionate.

"Are you serious?"

"Yes, 100% C'mon, she's already grown."

"I don't know, I don't trust her that much with the house, what if something happens?"

"Dara, my love, don't worry . . . Look everything is going to be perfect, I promise." he said trying to get farther than kissing her on the lips.

Isaiah Russell was Juliana's father; or at least that was what she believed. He was truly in love with Dara, and even if he couldn't have kids, he took care of Juliana as if she was his. He also was a very possessive and jealous man. He didn't want anyone going around his daughter or wife. He hated the fact that Juliana had guy friends, but he believed that by allowing her to hang out with whomever she wanted, he was going to be closer with her, and it worked. He was a very mysterious, feared man. Many individuals, including prisoners from maximum secured prisons had respect for him, and had a type of fear towards him. He discovered many mysterious cases in the country, sent criminals to death row . . . He always had the last evidence in the most complicated cases in his city. "The devil of law" some called him, the "Own Satan" others said he was, and another percentage even mentioned that he had a path with the own devil for so much success. Nobody knew what he really thought, felt, or wanted, he was an individual with a different personality every day, and the only thing that calmed him, and made him smile was his daughter Juliana.

Now, the only thing that was left to do was tell the truth to Juliana. She didn't know her father wasn't Isaiah; she didn't know that she was the product of the sexual abuse that her mom went through when she was little by her stepfather.

At the party, Juliana walked out with Caleb, and started a conversation.

"I understand the fact that you don't want to go inside because you think you are too old for this young teenage party, but let me tell you something." Juliana said.

"What?" Caleb asked looking surprised.

"I rather be here outside with you than with them little kids." Juliana said smiling at him.

"Wow, that was really sweet."

"I'm just saying what I feel . . ."

"You want me to take you home now? I don't want your parents to get mad at you."

"Gosh! You really are a home person aren't you?"

"It's just that I don't want your parents to think that something happened to you. You told them you were going to the movies and look at the time."

Juliana laughing said "In what century were you born? People these days don't go home early anymore."

"Well, sorry, I though kids these days were . . . I don't know, a little bit innocent at least."

Juliana kept on staring at his blue eyes . . . "He looks like somebody I know, but who?" She kept on repeating the same phrase every time she look at him. She used to think about it so much but since she didn't find an answer she gave up.

"Tell me more about you. I know there's something you have hidden deep inside you." She asked as she got closer to his face.

Caleb sighted deeply.

"I'm saying, everybody has something that they have been hiding, you know secrets, and I want to know that about you, I want to know everything about you . . ."

"Wow." Caleb sighed. "Why now . . . so soon?"

"Caleb, I don't bite, I just think you are great and I would love to know more about you."

"Do you really think I'm good person?"

"Yes, and I know it's crazy because we just met, but I think you are just such an amazing, incredible, inexplicable human being." said Juliana sitting on top of the car.

"I had a bad past Juliana a long one too . . . if I start now I won't finish it because the tears would come down and I'm not ready for it . . ." he said walking a few steps away from his car.

"Oh now you walking away like a bitch. Why don't you want to tell me about your life? Why don't you just talk about it like a real, grown man will do?" said Juliana loudly, laughing. She was calling him all types of names, disrespecting him, perhaps she didn't think he was going to take it bad, since she was so spoiled, and everybody was always used to take her crap, and she kept on going with her rudeness.

Her words made Caleb went back in time like a flashback and remembered how his stepfather and him once were doing laundry and his stepfather made him carry all these heavy boxes, which were too heavy. He remembers clearly how he dropped them on the floor, and his stepfather started hitting him hard with an electric cable, yelling at him, calling him names, telling him *"A real man don't act like a fag!"*, and all types of phrases that a person don't tell to a child. Those same words were the ones that Juliana was similarly using.

Caleb had his heart speeding, got mad and screamed. "Stop it! Who do you think you are huh!? Do you think that because you have money you can step on everybody's back? Well let me tell you something Juliana . . . That doesn't work with me! I'm not going to let you disrespect me!"

Juliana shocked, tried to respond to such a horrible reaction. "What? What . . . What is wrong with you!? Are you ok? I mean, I was just saying, don't be giving me that type of attitude, I was just playing with you . . ."

"I'm a grown man! I don't need this crap!" Caleb moved Juliana off his car, got in it and drove away. At that moment, his brother was coming out with Monique. They both looked at Juliana standing in the middle of the street, speechless.

Monique ran up to Juliana worried, and asked her. "What happened?"

Juliana looked at Monique and didn't say a word.

Joey asked. "Are you ok?"

Juliana still didn't say a word. She didn't know, she couldn't believe how somebody could have taken her so cold little jokes to an extreme.

Juliana looking at Joey said. "I . . . I'm sorry. I think I confused him with a trashy person and he obviously didn't take it."

Monique hugged her. "Are you ok Juli? You are pale!"

In contrast, Caleb was crying, driving careless. He didn't even know what was going on with himself. He knew it was an exaggerated thing what he just did. What kind of person reacts like that by a girl's words? His trauma, as we can tell, hasn't left yet. One of his biggest secrets was standing up naked in front of the mirror for at least 20 minutes every night and staring back at his own reflection. He knew it was weird, but he was always doing it. Every Saturday night, he wanted to know what was so interesting about his body that could have made another man go crazy and try to rape him. He kept on thinking, having all these crazy thoughts while he was driving.

Later on, Juliana his brother, and her friend got to his apartment, but he didn't answer to the door, so they waited in the lobby. Finally, hours later, Caleb got to his place, and looked at all of them in the lobby sleeping of waiting so much.

Juliana opened her eyes, rubbed her right eye from the short nap and asked.

"Where have you been?"

"Driving around . . . I think you should go home." Caleb said, sitting on the table next to the chair where she was sitting at.

"I want to apologize for anything that I may have said wrong and maybe have offended you."

Caleb looked up and then looked at her face. "Look, it wasn't you, it was me." He sighed. "If I explain to you now and I sit here and try to give you the reasons, the why and because of my reaction, I wouldn't finish. The one the needs to give an explanation is me, I acted wrong."

"It's okay, really don't worry, no need to explain anything, no need. Just please, don't act like that again; you don't know how worried you had me."

"I promise . . ." he responded making Juliana feel more comfortable and relieved.

Juliana got close to his lips, and kissed him. She gave him one of those kisses that you only get when you say hi to your friends, one of those kisses that you give when you are either in a rush or busy. The kiss was short, but both individuals felt the fire in those limited seconds. They knew that kiss could have turned stronger if they were alone. That kiss, that kiss was the beginning of everything. They knew they wanted each other.

Caleb looked deep into her eyes and right when he was about to talk, his brother woke up and right after him, Monique. As the night was in the middle of its time, they said bye to each other, and each of them walked away.

In the cab, Juliana was daydreaming and Monique was staring at her, wondering what was going on.

"What is wrong with you?" asked Monique.

Juliana smiled, and stopping cause of the red light, said. "I kissed him."

Monique smiled a little, and putting the seatbelt on said "When?"

"We kissed and out of nowhere, then, Joey rudely interrupted us."

"It was time for us to leave."

"He is so different from everybody Monique, you just don't know. It's just probably because he is polite? I know my parents are going to love him. I want him so bad, and you know what? I think he wants me in the same way."

"Juliana . . . you just met the guy, you need to take it easy. Don't rush things, remember how bad your relationship was with Danny, and he was your longest boyfriend . . ."

"Fuck Danny! Who cares about him? He is stupid. He thinks because he has the money he can get what he wants, not anymore, not from me. I'm upgrading my game, you know? Now I have another perspective, I think, I think with Caleb, I'm going to see the world from a different view."

"I hope so Juliana, you hurt so many guys with your lies, and you must know that karma is going to hit you back one day."

"Fuck karma! I'm going to make it with Caleb, watch Monique, I will."

In contrast, Caleb, who was acting strange with his silence at his apartment, was standing on the balcony.

"What happened?" Joey asked laying his hand on his brother's shoulder standing next to him.

"She started calling me names, you know how I get when that happens." Caleb responded and took a sip of his brownish whisky.

"So? I have been in the army, and have been called a pussy, a homosexual; they even accused me of sucking on dick before. How do you think I felt when that happened? I remember things too Caleb. But

I'm not stupid enough to act so reckless especially to act like that with a girl. What if you would've hit her?"

"I would have gone to jail, perhaps I don't know . . ."

"And you think its all cool? Look, you are a successful businessman; you can't be damaging your image Caleb! Especially for a young, rich, slut who is not worth your time! Have you been going to therapy?" asked breathing hard in and out.

"Don't call her a slut, I hate those names for females, and yes I have been, I already talked about it, and its not easy Joey, ITS NOT EASY!" Caleb screamed walked to the living room, faced the plasma TV screen, reached for his pocket and pulled out a personal bag of coke.

"Don't do it." Said Joey.

"I need it, you don't know how bad this have helped me Joey, and it's the only way to forget all the hell I went through."

"It doesn't work all the time; it only works for a certain amount of time . . . I know it because I tasted her too."

"Her? Why you call it '*her*'?" responded Caleb holding a key with coke on it.

"Well, it helped me a lot after my fiancé abandoned me, and humiliated me in front of everybody . . ."

"Fiancé? You never told me about that." Caleb dropped the key on the floor, making the white powder spread all over the carpet.

"Two years ago, I met this beautiful Asian girl, god! She was so beautiful; she was a model. Well she still is . . ." Joey sighted. "We had the perfect relationship, there were no secrets between us, except for the existence of my cruel past, and since I thought she was the woman of my life, I decided to tell her the truth . . . But not too short after it, everything changed. We started arguing, she suddenly would stop coming to the apartment that I rented for us. She never had time for me because she was always traveling, shows here, and shows there, but I knew they all were excuses . . . and I began to figure out that she didn't want to be with me anymore. She didn't want to take me to her main events, she didn't want to kiss me, hold my hand, or even have sex. So the day of our engagement party she arrived late, and rejected me in front of everyone. She said, well she screamed at me, she hated me. She was yelling at me atrocious things such as she probably had aids because we didn't use protection and if she did it was because I was raped by a man, a crack head. She started calling me gay, accusing me of using her as '*cover*'. Of course she added that we couldn't be together anymore, because if the media finds out that her fiancé was raped when he was little, it will destroy her image, and reputation. She looked at me, apologized to everyone in the party and left. Eventually, I told everyone to leave, and two weeks later, I found out that she got married with her photographer." Joey was crying. "I did love her, so much Caleb! I still can't believe she left me! Why?! Do you think that was fair?! NO! IT WAS NOT! I'm not a bad person Caleb!" Joey's tears turned to a deep crying. He dropped his body on the floor and cried like a kid.

Caleb got on the floor next to his brother and hugged him. "She left because you were too much for her. She didn't deserve you Joey. Forget about her."

"It's been two years already and . . . and I still dream of her. I still wake up feeling her arms on my chest and smelling her perfume after the shower. I still feel her lips touching mines. Oh god Caleb, you don't know how much I need her with me . . . I wake up days going crazy knowing that she is not next to me. Knowing that someone else is with her, knowing that nothing will be ever back again and I just can't believe that the truth is that she left me because . . . I'm less of a human being. I'm a waste of space on earth, no woman will stay around because nobody wants a sick person like me to be the father of their child." Joey kept on crying.

Caleb was hurt. He didn't feel as much pain since the last time he saw his brother. That night felt like the first one. They talked about unbelievable things any of them thought of. Caleb was confessing his brother his mirror views in the middle of the night, while Joey was telling him how he threw up every night after dinner for scary scenes he used to see in the middle of the dessert. It seemed like the drama wasn't ever going to stop.

II.

SIMPLY BAD

Juliana's prom night arrived, and besides thinking of attending to it, she was imagining herself on top of him, Caleb. She was thinking how she was going to surprise him and let him know that he was the one for her. She was smiling just of thinking of having his mature arms all over her breasts and neck suffocating her with heat, and strong exhalation. She just couldn't stop laughing on her own as she imagined more perverted scenes at the mall while her inseparable best friend Monique was paying for lipsticks, and condoms. They knew they were going to make this prom night an unforgettable one. For some reason, even if Monique tried to talk to her friend about money, weed, or someone else Juliana was just not paying mind to any of her words, and responded with stupidity.

"We are going to see Caleb. I want to get him drunk."

"We?" Monique responded with a question.

"Yes Monique, us . . . you are not thinking about leaving me hanging by myself right?"

"Well Juli, I just thought you were going to spend the night with Danny . . . I mean, it's prom-night after all." Monique said while she was sitting down on the small chair that was inside the fitting room.

"Woah! No of course not Monique I thought you got the fact that it's over between Danny and I . . . Why do you feel sorry for him? You can go and fuck him if you want . . . I'm gifting him to you."

"You better not be serious Juliana, do not talk to me like that."

"Well Monique what do you expect me to say? All these past days you've been talking about Danny this, poor Danny that . . . gosh! I talk to you everyday about this guy I've met and you keep on bringing that fucker's name . . . For some reason I think you like Danny and that you are too scared to tell me."

"You know what? I don't have time for your bullshit!" Monique responded while she was grabbing the dresses she had on the garment bags.

"What are you doing?" Juliana asked while standing up.

"I'm leaving that's what that fuck I'm doing . . . I'm not going to let you disrespect me, just because the rest of the world is a sucker for you, and takes your crap doesn't mean I will."

"Monique calm down, it was a joke . . . I know you wouldn't do that to me, you are my best friend; Just sit down, it's over, I won't joke with you anymore. I'm sorry."

"At what time are we going to see Caleb?" Monique asked as she stopped.

"Like at 1 am, we are going to be at the prom party, you know having taking pics, and then we are going to his house. He is going to pick us up." Juliana said looking at her hair in the mirror.

"You mean he is going to pick us up from prom?"

"Yeah."

"What about the lambo we rented."

"I cancelled it."

"So how are we getting to the party?"

"My driver can take us in my dad's car."

"What did you tell your dad about the lambo?"

"I just told him I wanted to save him some money." Juliana laughed.

"Let's take my car."

"That's fine with me." Responded Juliana hugging her friend.

Monique smiled back. "I want to fuck Caleb's brother."

Juliana just looked at her friend in shock.

"He is hot! He is a soldier! You can't say he isn't. I imagined myself on top of him last night . . . you know wearing his uniform and me screaming like crazy, asking him to shoot in my mouth."

"Oh my god! Monique I never ever thought that you were going to be that dirty! Watch that mouth!"

Monique laughed. "What? Well, if anything that's your fault, I've been hanging out with you all my life, everyday of the week, what do you expect? Plus I'm just saying what's on my mind. I really want to fuck him, and I want him sucking on his . . ."

Juliana interrupting her said. "Shut up! Just shut up Monique you still a virgin, you can't be talking like that. Who has been teaching you this language by the way?!"

"I guess the pornography has been getting me on it." Monique said while her face was blushing.

The girls kept on shopping here and going there, hair done, nails done until the afternoon got darker and the night arrived. The time on dot was going against the clock they thought as they rushed to get ready. At Juliana's room, her big mirror with golden decorations standing in the middle was letting her know how perfectly God drew her. She was looking stunning; she had her hair up in a bun. Her make up was matching her white tight dress, which had a big opening in the back and on the side of each leg. It was going to be a great night; she kept on repeating in her head as her dad came in her room.

"Wow! My daughter should be on a magazine cover! You look beautiful!" Isaiah said extending his arms ready to hug her.

Juliana smiled and received the hug very happily.

"It's the truth baby; I know Danny is going to be one lucky man tonight with a princess by his side."

"I guess . . ."

Isaiah was staring at his daughter hard. He couldn't stop admiring her beauty.

"What is wrong?" Juliana asked.

"Nothing, it's just that a few years ago, you were graduating from kindergarten and you were just my little princess, and now you are a queen, and soon, you are going to leave and do your own life." Isaiah said looking sad.

"Dad, don't say that please." She responded passing her delicate fingers by his left cheek.

"Why? It's the truth! C'mon, let us go downstairs Danny is waiting for you." Isaiah said putting his arm up waiting for her to put hers under his.

"Oh really? That loser rushed." Juliana said and got out of her room with her dad.

As Juliana was walking downstairs in her father's arms, she looked at Danny, he was looking very handsome, but she didn't see him with that sexual anxiety she had anymore. She felt disgusted, she wanted to throw up, or run away from him. She didn't even want to kiss him in the cheek, she felt like ripping off her hair, dress, take off her heels, and go out to look for him, Caleb, the only man that she ever wanted.

"You look amazing my dear." said Danny, who started putting the Orquidea he got for her on her wrist.

"Take care of her tonight, and don't let anyone else, not even yourself touch her." Isaiah interrupted.

"No need to tell him dad, I can take care of myself."

"Stop being so rude tonight Juliana, please just for once." Danny responded.

The young couple said bye to Juliana's dad, and walked out of the house to get into the brand new Ferrari Danny rented for the night.

"That is nice."

"You like it my dear?"

"It's a sexy hot thing."

"Great, because I'm fucking you there tonight."

Juliana stared at Danny and smiled. "I doubt it"

"Why?"

"You don't turn me on anymore."

"A couple of drinks and you will be screaming my name."

"Not even the white girl would get me horny enough to suck your penis Danny, you are not hot in my eyes anymore."

"We'll see, if it's not you, it will be someone else . . . maybe Monique?" he said while he was getting ready to ride out.

Juliana laughed hard. "You can fuck all my friends, even my mother but NOTHING will get to me, I thought you knew me already love."

Danny smiled at Juliana, and started to drive to the party. Juliana and Danny were stunning that night. They looked great together, the elegance was dropping through the hallways of the ballroom as they were walking. Their classmates wanted to take pictures with them, the professors were congratulating them their young success together. They were like celebrities at their own school. It seemed like the night was going to be young for a very long time.

As the hours were passing, and the queen and king were crowned, the young night was getting closer to the end. The time started running. Young hearts, young souls, young and fresh looks were getting closer to each other more and more. It was the time for that last romantic dance, where all the curtains were closing, and lights were turning off. All the couples were holding each other tight and the moonlight was the only artist on the dance floor.

Danny was holding Juliana tight, whispering in her ear. "I didn't have time to say it again but . . . you look beautiful tonight."

Juliana sighed and smiled. "Thanks! You look pretty too."

"No, I don't, I can't look pretty because I'm a guy."

"Well, you get my point."

Danny stared at her hard, and getting closer to her, he kissed her on the lips. Juliana didn't expect it, but she didn't reject his kiss and proceeded with it.

Monique, who was next to them, smiled at her friend while she was dancing in the company of someone else. While Juliana kept on kissing Danny, Monique held her date tighter and kept on dancing.

"Wow, it's been a long time since I tasted your lips for a last time."

"I know, it shouldn't have happened." Juliana responded.

"Why?"

"Danny, you and I have been over a year ago. It was about to be almost a year that we didn't even speak to each other. I don't even know how we made it to prom together, but the thing is that . . ."

"Is what? Don't you feel something for me anymore?" Danny asked after interrupting her.

"We went out for a long time, but we can't be together Danny that's the thing."

"Why? I thought we were the perfect couple?"

"Because . . . I don't deserve you."

"Why do you say that?"

Juliana was thinking if she should tell him what was making her feel sick. She didn't want to be a hypocrite anymore, she couldn't, she shouldn't, she needed to tell him that she cheated on him with his own father, or she should just tell him that she simply cheated on him.

"What is it Juliana? Tell me" Danny kept on asking.

"I cheated on you." Juliana didn't know if what she just said was going to be the beginning of her tragic night or the argument that they were going to have in the following seconds. But she already said it, and he already heard it, and there was no going back.

"That was it? Is that why you don't want to be with me?"

Juliana looking down to his shoulder responded. "Yes, I'm sorry."

"Don't worry, it doesn't matter." Danny said sighing deeply. "I mean Juliana I have been with other girls too, I really don't care if you messed with other guys because the one that you are always going to be faithful to is going to be me. I mean, maybe you are crazy outside and perhaps you can't be faithful but I know your heart is devoted to me. You still a virgin right?"

Juliana looking at him quiet kept on saying in her mind "*Should I tell him I lost it to his dad?*"

"Danny, let's please drop the subject." Juliana said turning around dancing slowly.

Danny hugged her from the back and whispered in her ear. "It's ok, the past is the past. I played games too, but now is over. We should be together." Danny said kissing her right cheek. "You and I have everything. We can rule this world. I have enough money, and enough ambition to keep on succeeding. All I need is you by my side to be complete."

"Danny, please stop talking shit, not today, not here and not now. I really want to enjoy my night."

Danny swallowed his words and kept on dancing with his date. He then, slowly put his hands all over her lower back and slowly his fingers went up to her middle back. He stared at her so lovely, and kissed her lips. The night so far was going great he believed. He was going to make her his he was so sure about it.

Later on, as the party began to end Juliana walked as fast as she could to the bathroom. Monique seeing this ran behind her.

"Juliana! Where are you?" she asked looking for her friend in between the toilet rooms. Then, she heard somebody crying. She opened slowly one of the doors, and looked at her friend on the floor. Her make-up was a mess, her eyes turned red and her black mascara was dropping on her long white sheer gown.

"Oh god, what happened?" She asked hugging Juliana.

Juliana crying responded "I feel . . . I feel dirty Monique."

"Why? What had happened to you? You seemed so happy outside. The party is so pretty. What's the matter?" Monique said sitting on the floor next to her friend.

"I was talking to Danny . . . and we were talking about why we can't get back together, and he kept on asking me why and I was like because I cheated on you. I guess . . . he probably thought it was with some random guy. Then, of course he kept on insisting . . . Tell me Monique, tell me how am I suppose to be a lady for a guy like him? How am I supposed to have a serious relationship with just anyone, when I keep playing with all these guys' feelings, I just know when I have them on my hands, I just know how to manipulate them, and break their hearts . . . I can't . . . Oh God! I feel so dirty, how am I suppose to sleep with a clean conscious when I slept and I lost my virginity to my ex's dad? Tell me!" Juliana cried louder.

Monique hugged her strongly. "Don't worry baby, it's over already . . . don't think about it."

"Monique, I feel like . . . I don't even know what to think of. Sometimes I feel like I should start charging for every time I finish fucking anyone."

"Don't say that."

"I don't even know how the fuck I got to that point. How am I going to be fooling and cheating on people's trust?"

"Don't think about it anymore . . . if you don't tell anybody, nobody will find out . . . just leave it alone."

"Monique . . . I don't deserve good things, no good guys, nothing! I feel like the day I will get married is going to be the day all the guys I slept with will come out and confront me."

"Just let it go . . . nobody will come, I promise . . . don't ruin your make up, you paid too much for it, and we need to be out there stunning. Caleb is going to meet up with us later on, and you don't want him to see you sad do you?"

Juliana nodded her head.

"Then, let's get up, go outside and enjoyed the night."

Juliana cleaned her tears, tried to get up, and falling on top of her white dress laughed with her friend, and got up. When both young ladies got out of the bathroom, the professors, and classmates were clapping and congratulating the king and queen prom one more time. The party, the magic event finally ended according to the teachers, principal, and any adult present. Juliana and Monique were getting their stuffs, and gifts to leave. They said bye to half of her drunken classmates, and taking a huge risk Monique let Juliana drive her car to go to Caleb's apartment. Juliana didn't have a driver's license with her but that didn't stop her from going to meet with her love. By her side, Monique was preparing a blunt. She had a bag of weed on her right leg, and a lighter on her left leg. While in between her lips, she had the brown cigar ready to be light up. Monique turned on the radio and the music started playing. The smoke was invading the whole car until it started coming out of the windows and invaded the air of the city. Juliana looked at Monique got the blunt from her mouth, put it in between her lips, and started consuming her addiction.

"Are we going to his apartment or somewhere else? Monique asked.

"No, he rented a hotel room . . . he is waiting for us there."

"Is anybody else going to be there or is it only them two?"

"I'm not sure, I think it's only Caleb and Joey, but if there are more people, then we calling the rest of the girls . . ."

"They are all mad at us . . . they are mad at the fact that I left with you somewhere else."

"Fuck them . . . They are probably going to Danny's . . . well at least he is going to get some head tonight." Juliana said while she kept on driving and smoking.

When they got to the hotel, Caleb and Joey were waiting for them outside.

"Hi gorgeous." Caleb said extending his arms towards her.

Juliana ran to him, and hugged him feeling that magic electricity that connected them both.

"You have no idea how bad I wanted to see you."

"Come in with me" he said, grabbed her hand and walked her inside. The hotel itself was nice, but the room they rented was nicer. Caleb took her to the balcony where she admired the dark blue sky and the stars that looked like diamonds. That night wasn't real she said. Everything was so beautiful in her eyes it looked painted.

Caleb then popped out a small box in front of her eyes.

"What is this?" she asked.

"Open it . . . I hope you'll like it." Caleb said smiling, expecting her reaction.

She opened the little box and inside she found a gold chain with a little heart at the end. On the back it said *"ALWAYS YOURS, CALEB."* She did not know what to say. She was amazed. Deep inside she knew it was just an ordinary gold necklace, but just the fact that he thought of it, the fact that he picked it, chose it, bought it, and gave it to her made it the best gift she has ever received. She looked at it repeatedly, speechless and jumped into his arms.

"I love it! It is beautiful!" she exclaimed as happy as she could be.

"I know I shouldn't but, I really wanted to do it . . ."

"What?" Juliana asked feeling curious.

Right when Caleb was about to tell her what he wanted to express, his brother Joey came with two other friends.

"Hey Juliana! Where are the rest of your friends?" Joey said loudly. He was tipsy already.

"Tell Monique to call them, they'll be here soon." Juliana responded pushing him out of the balcony.

"Ok, ok, I'll leave . . . I'm sorry I don't want to be *cock-blocking*."

"So . . . what was that that you were saying?" Juliana asked Caleb with a big smile on her face as soon as Joey walked out.

"I like you Juliana, I like you a lot . . . every time I have you around . . . I feel like if I'm looking at your for the first time. Every time is new for me, I feel like I have to start over to try to get your attention." Caleb said as he held her hands.

"And?" she asked, staring at her lover's eyes.

Caleb got closer until his lips got closer to hers, and his hands were grabbing her waist tight to his body. A kiss, a powerful one, was happening while they were closing their eyes, feeling it deeply. Suddenly, the night was turned inexplicable. The peaceful lake, the isolated sky all dark and bright decorated by the stars made Juliana wrapped her arms around his neck and held him tighter. After the kiss was over, they looked at each other and the biggest silence ever was present. "Wow . . . if that's the beginning of us, then I never want to end it." She said smiling at him.

"I want you to be mine so bad, and I don't only mean that by your body but your whole self. I want to hold your hand around the public and walk down the streets of New York City and tell the whole world about us without speaking. But if you need time, I'll wait. I'm sorry." Caleb responded.

Juliana was feeling so great, so happy. She knew that question was going to come after that kiss, but she was so into her happiness that she didn't know what to say.

"Sh! Don't say anything else. I know you are the one I want. I know and I see you, and you are so different from everybody else I've met. I like you, just like this. Your clothes, the way you walk, your eyes, your lips now." She smiled. "You make me see the world and what is on it so differently. I really want to be with you, ever since the first day I met you and saw you, ever since that day that you dropped me off at home I can't stop thinking of you."

It was the first time she was expressing her feelings, the first time that she let her heart do the talking. She knew this was what she wanted.

"Are you sure? I want you to be sure of what you are saying; I don't want you to make any mistakes."

"Mistakes? Caleb, are you kidding me? You are the first guy I didn't have to show skin to, the first one I didn't meet in a party or acting crazy with my girlfriends to like me. You met me the worst day of my life, you took care of me, and you were making me smile when I didn't want to. Every time I hear your name, or your voice when you say my name my heart races like a horse in a marathon. I feel like if one day I wake up and I don't see a text from you or don't have you around I will probably be consumed by anxiety . . . I just have these strong feelings for you . . . It's hard to explain . . . but something I could explain is that every time I hug you, I could stay like that forever."

The exchanged of words made them kiss again and finishing the kiss with a powerful hug they went back inside the room. She was holding Caleb's hand ready to join her friends. What, and how she was feeling made the rest invisible, even ignoring her friends whom were acting pretty crazy. On the table there were lots of alcohol: Bacardi 151, beer, sex on the beach, tequila, vodka, patron, the famous *Henny* among other drinks, weed, cigarettes, the unforgettable pills, and white powder. Caleb wasn't expecting all this wildness. He completely ignored his brother's level of maturity and knew something was going to happen that wasn't going to be good. He thought if he let all this wildness stay it was going to be the worst example that he could give to his girlfriend and her friends. But the rest of his partners weren't thinking the same; they all followed these girls' games. He didn't know if stop it and get everyone one mad, or if let everything go along to adapt to her age.

Juliana walked out with Monique along with two other friends. One of them got a piece of paper from her bag, opened it, and the pills were shown. Juliana couldn't stop staring at the pills. Each girl got a pill, grabbed a glass mixed soda with liquor, and swallowed the pill. They smiled at each other, and went back to the party, a party that they didn't want to end. 45 minutes later, Juliana walked back outside to the grass, and laid down. Monique followed her friend, and sat down next to her. The rest of the girls were inside the room off in another world, and so were the lights. The only loud thing was the radio playing music that was turning their vulnerable minds up and down. The girls were feeling the pill's effects. They all were feeling hot and the sweat started showing off when it started coming down through their foreheads. Caleb looked at them strange he knew something was different. The young ladies started taking off their clothes and slowly started giving guys lap dances. Caleb's friends were happy and excited for the young bodies on their laps moving so sexually and desperate. It was the heat that the pill was producing in them. Caleb got up, walked out where his lovely sweetheart was laying down. Monique, who was laying next to her, lifted up her head to see who was stepping in front of her and said "Hey! Where is your brother?"

"Inside." Caleb responded upset.

"Ok, I'm going inside, I need something in my mouth." Monique said as she crawled a little to get balance to walk.

Caleb stared at Juliana. He knew something was not right. She looked poisoned, she was rolling on the floor, crawling around, trying to rip off her clothes, sweating, and wanting to touch Caleb, but this one rejected her.

"What is up with you?!" Caleb screamed.

"Nothing, what's up with you? Aren't you hot?" Juliana responded smiling, covering her head with her dirty sweaty hands.

"Why are you hot?"

"Well, I guess you should ask that to my parents . . ." She said ironically and an exaggerated laughed came out.

"You can't even be funny on drugs, how many you took?"

"How many what? Fuck off Caleb stop that bullshit please, it's my prom night."

"So? You think because it's your prom night I'm going to let you get fucked up like that?"

"You are acting like an old person, drop it! You are actually acting like my mom shut up already!"

"I didn't know little girls acted this way neither."

"Have fun Caleb, you work and stress too much!"

"So should I stop stressing you?" Caleb asked moving his hands away from her.

"What do you mean?" Juliana asked.

"Juliana get up. I'm taking you and Monique home, this party is over." Caleb said getting up ready to walk inside the hotel room.

"No! You can't do this to me Caleb! I'm having fun, this is my party!" Juliana yelled trying to get up from the grass.

"I'm going to take you home!"

"No! It's not necessary anyway . . . I'm going to drive or tell my friend to give me a ride to other party."

"You are not going to another party! You had enough fun with that pill!" Caleb said turning back facing her.

Juliana fell on the grass, and Caleb, angry, grabbed her, carried her and took her in.

"CALEB! CALEB PUT ME DOWN, WHAT IS WRONG WITH YOU!"

Caleb was taking her inside one of the rooms, while the party was becoming more in an orgy than the innocent prom after party that it was supposed to be. Juliana's friends were taking the effect to a sexual level. Some of them were on top of guys with no bra on, while others were fulfilling others with blowjobs. Caleb in the room already, dropped her on the bed, closed the windows, making sure everything was locked so she couldn't do any type of stupidity.

"What are you doing?!" Juliana screamed hysterically. "You really have to lock me in a room because you scared I may leave you?" She said and laughed hard as she laid back on the bed.

"You acting childish and you are not the only woman in the world just reminding you."

"Then go head Caleb! I don't care if you just asked me out and gave me a gift, I can get any guy I want! Don't you get it?" Juliana kept on screaming while he was walking out of the small room that was suffocating him.

"Yes, of course you can get them . . . throwing yourself really fast like that tell me what female wouldn't get them like that."

"FUCK YOU!" She screamed on top of her lungs.

"I don't need a girl like that, for that I just go to the streets and get one."

"Don't talk to me like that! You are nobody to be telling me or calling me like that. Well, what can I expect? You are a nobody! You don't even know who is your mother, oh no, my badness . . . let me say it again. You are so angry with your life because nobody ever loved you, and that's why your mom chose your stepfather over you and your brothers."

Caleb was covering his ears while she was throwing her poison in the room.

"And you want me to tell you something else Caleb? Your sister doesn't love you either, because if she ever had, she would have never ever changed her name. She doesn't want you to find her because she doesn't love you! You were born from the dust; you belong to the dust not to a woman, that's why nobody loves you!" Caleb hearing everything he once told her started to regret the day he picked her up and the day he opened her heart to her.

"STOP! SHUT THE FUCK UP!" He screamed back at her and opened the door, grabbing her by the arm throwing her out. Juliana was laughing as he was screaming. He didn't hold it and he got out of the room, looked for his brother, but he was too busy having sex with Juliana's friend, and so were the rest of the guys. They all were busy having sex in front of each other in the living room. Caleb walked out as fast as he could from the townhouse, got on his car, as Juliana in the background, ran behind him feeling a little guilty.

"Stop! Stop! Please stop I didn't mean it!" She screamed. "Caleb, I'm sorry, I didn't mean what I said I'm really sorry!"

"No Juliana, I really don't need you in my life; I regret everything I've said to you tonight and in general . . . I told you personal things, just a few personal things about my life . . . things that are hard to tell to anyone! And you throw them out like that?! Sorry but I don't need that."

"Please . . . Please I'm sorry . . . When . . . When I'm on drugs I don't know what I do, think, or say!"

"I don't think it's a good idea be together, you are the opposite of what I want. We can't work out together . . . I don't like girls that are drug addicts. I don't want that for me, I care about you . . . but I just can't deal with this." And as he said it he turned on his car and drove away.

"No, wait! Wait Caleb please . . ." Juliana watched him leave, and feeling an atrocious pain in her heart, the tears escaped from her eyes. She felt like the night was over, she felt like she lost the one of the most important things in her life, walked back to the hotel to get her bag and leave. On her way in, she saw Monique on the sofa, holding a pill in one of her hands. Juliana walked up to her and whispered in her ear. "Monique, I'll be back, I have to go somewhere don't leave ok?" She gave Monique a kiss on the lips, got up and left. She called and called Caleb, but he didn't answer, so she decided to leave him a message. "*Caleb . . . It's me . . . Juliana, I know I shouldn't have said those things but I really want to see you, I'm sorry, I was on it, I'm driving and I'm still a little bit on it, but I'm not going to stop driving until I find you . . . please call me back . . .*"

Juliana waited and waited for his phone call, sitting at some random cafeteria that she found on the highway, but still didn't get a call back. Later on, her body couldn't hold it anymore, and ready to leave the place she felt her phone vibrating and it was Danny.

"Danny? . . . Hey, what are you doin'?"

"I'm doing well, where are you? I though you were going to come to my party . . ."

"I had things to do first, is the party still on?" Juliana asked while she was looking at her coffee.

"Yes, I'm actually waiting for you."

"Ok, I'll be there in a few . . ." Juliana said drinking a sip of her coffee.

"Are you alone?" he asked.

"Yes why?"

"Because Monique got here a few ago . . ."

"She did?"

"Yeah, why?" he responded.

"No, nothing . . . Listen, I'll be at your house in a few." Juliana said, and ending her conversation with Danny, she dialed Monique's number but she didn't answer. There was something that Juliana didn't know, and never in her wild imagination and that was that her lovely ex boyfriend, Danny was with Monique, her best friend in his room, covered and wrapped in silk sheets. She was deeply sleeping, the pill and the weed made her do things she wanted but didn't want to admit. Things where she got lost in words and completely forgot the definition of respect, and loyalty.

Danny looking at Monique moved her and said. "Hey you, Monique your phone is ringing."

Monique moving slowly responded, "Oh my god, what have I done?"

"What? I'm about to do it again." Danny responded wrapping a condom on him.

"What?" she asked.

"You are right." He said stopping himself from touching her. "I think you should get dress and leave."

"God, I feel so bad, you are Juliana's . . ."

"No, no, no . . ." Danny interrupted her. "Don't even go to that Monique. Don't try to act innocent or like the one that was 'seduced' because it doesn't work like that. Now, don't worry, I won't tell her anything, you know me, I never talk, ever . . ."

"You have to promise it . . . she is my best friend and . . ."

"I swear . . . she won't find out that her best friend fucked with her ex most serious relationship, or should I say prom date?" Danny said smiling and kissing her on the cheek.

"Oh please, be quiet . . . I don't even want to think about it, I was too drugged up to know what I was doing because if I was sober, this would have never happened."

"Monique, Monique, even if you were normal, or just awake from your sleep, you know you would have fucked the shit out of me. You know you wanted me since long, but I made the mistake to asked Juliana out."

"So do you regret it?"

"She never gave me what I wanted." Danny responded.

"And . . . did I?" Monique asked.

"Yeah, that also means that I'm always going to look forward to you and be faithful if we ever date." Danny said showing a fake smile.

"You wouldn't ask me out?"

"I would have to think about it."

"You son of a bitch!" Monique said getting off the bed.

"Yes, I know . . . now please get out of my room before I scream that you came in and got naked so I could do you." Danny said while he was getting the glass of alcohol that was next to him.

"I hate you! You are nothing but a liar! You knew I always liked you, you knew I was waiting for you to leave that bitch and come to me . . . but you are nothing but a piece of shit that walks on this earth!" Monique said as she was getting her clothes from the floor.

"Are you done?" he asked while he was finishing his drink and Monique was staring at him deeply in the eyes.

Monique stared at him.

"I need you to get out of here; I need to take a shower . . . Juliana is coming and I don't want her to think that I was messing with other hoes that are trying to be like her."

Monique looking down at the floor, where the condoms that they used were at, looked up to him and said. "Is that how you think about each girl that ever thought you liked them at least for a little?"

"You know I have no feelings for anyone else but Juliana . . . yeah, she may be a slut . . . but something that Juliana won't ever do is betray me . . . or use me . . . she has the looks, she is smart, and I know she will go farther than all of you for me or to defend whatever she wants . . . so

Monique I'll give you five minutes to get out of here, if not I'm going to have to get you out of my room myself, and believe me it won't be nice," Danny said walking to the bathroom to take a shower, leaving Monique half undress, crying.

Meanwhile, Juliana was on her way to his house, she was sad about how the night turned out for her. She felt alone. She was telling herself and the voices or whatever that was making her act so reckless to stop. She was almost 100 % sure that she lost the love of her life, Caleb, and she needed to do something to get him back. She couldn't stop stressing over the situation. At Danny's house while the security opened the door for her, she was looking how everybody was getting drunk, dancing, sniffing, smoking, and having all types of sexual contact. For a moment, she wondered how could people damage themselves to certain degree, then she wondered why she was such a hypocrite, criticizing everyone that did drugs when she was so addicted to them. She looked for Monique, but couldn't find her; everybody was saying hi to her, well at least everybody who could since everybody was under all types of influences.

The party looked liked a nightclub in such a big house, the lights were sparkling, brighting, moving, and the ball that was all the way up in the middle of the roof made people get hypnotized every time it flashed. Suddenly, her phone started vibrating, she had a text message, and it was Danny.

Juliana read it, and went upstairs, walked to Danny's room. She opened the door and found Danny standing on his window, smoking weed.

"Where is Monique?" Juliana asked, and threw her bag on top of the bed.

"She must be downstairs . . . I'm not her pussy Juliana."

"Ha-ha, you are so funny." She said sarcastically.

"So, you like my party?"

"Yeah it's pretty cool . . . It looks like a nightclub . . ." She said walking to the balcony and stood next to him.

"My father told me, well he already showed it. As soon as I graduate I'm going to own a nightclub . . . in south beach."

"Oh yeah?"

"Yes, I'm going to Miami after graduation . . . I don't know if you would like to come with me . . ."

"For how long?" Juliana asked.

"2 weeks, 3 weeks I don't know."

"With you? No thanks I rather be at home masturbating."

Danny laughed hard and responded. "Wow, my dear Juliana what is up with you that you are so angry, what has turned you like that?"

"Society." she said getting the joint from his hand and smoked it.

"Really? When was the last time you got some? Because it seems like you didn't get it in years, Oh no . . . sorry you are a virgin right?"

"Don't worry Danny, don't even sweat it, somebody has been there already." Juliana said smiling at him.

"Oh yea? Who did you cheat on me with?"

"No, you don't need to know that . . . that would be too much for you to handle." Juliana responded while she was exhaling the smoke out from her nose.

"You think so?" Danny asked.

"I know so." Juliana said smiling, looking at him, touching his hair. While on her mind this phrase kept on repeating. *"Stupid, if you would know that your father was the one who took my virginity you wouldn't be here admiring me but dragging me all over."*

"Anyway, tell me Juliana are you going to enjoy the few hours of this night masturbating in the bathroom so I could die of blue balls from hearing you moaning?"

Juliana laughing, wrap her arms around his neck and said "No my dear, I'm going to let you eat me tonight for the first time."

"Wow, am I going to be that lucky?"

"Yes, tonight you are going to eat me and drink the milk that comes out from my bottom lips, if you know what I mean."

Danny asked exhaled the smoke. "I'm eating it huh?"

Juliana taking her arms off his neck responded. "Of course, what you thought? That I just want the normal, regular sex?"

"You want it all?" Danny asked hugging her from the back.

Juliana turning around responded to his provocative purpose. "All as I deserve."

Not too long after Juliana finishing saying her sentence, Danny started kissing her. He grabbed her hair, while his hands started going down through her back getting to her lower back. He was massaging her cheeks, then, slowly he started pushing her soft body towards to the wall. He lifted her up, walked towards his bed and threw her on it. He got on top of her, took off her dress, and licked her chest with an enormous passion. One of his hands was all over her right breast, while the other one was holding her neck. The more that he was kissing her, the hardest his reproductive member was getting. She started moaning from level 1 to level 4. Then, he took off his shirt and his pants like if he was in a rush. His body was throwing so much heat, that he couldn't hold it; he put on the latex and the penetration started. Danny looked at her face. She was in pain, but at the same time, she seemed to enjoy it, she seemed like she couldn't get anymore, her face was expressing an eruption coming. She didn't know how to express herself, her legs were shaking on top of his shoulders, rubbing her own breasts, and the more he was penetrating the more she was going crazy. It was something unexplainable, she was erupting, he was about come, and the act was incredible. After the explosion, both looked at each other, and rested their sweaty bodies. The night turned crazy, unexpected, and sweaty. She wouldn't expect it to happen like that, but it was happening. However, even if she was having sex with Danny and enjoying it, she was thinking of the real person that she loved, the one that to her mattered the most. After that quick rest, they kept on going for a long time, and as minutes were passing they finally gave up.

"I didn't know tonight was going to turn like this . . ." Danny said looking at her Juliana who was laying on top of him.

"I didn't know either . . . and I still wonder where Monique is at . . ."

"Forget about Monique . . . She is not your friend my dear, she is not . . ."

"Why do you say that?"

"I don't know I just have this feeling. I don't think she is your real friend . . . I think she envies you . . . just like the rest of the groupies from the school."

Juliana looked at him, and feeling her phone vibrating, looked at the caller ID, and it was Caleb. Juliana wrapped one of the white sheets around her body and walked out to the balcony.

"Hello?" she answered.

"Juliana?" Caleb said. "I think it was somehow my fault for locking you in the room . . . I don't think that the things you said to me were good either, and . . . I'm sorry but I just can't stop thinking about you . . . I care about you, a lot." Caleb sighted. "I think we should talk . . . in person, well at least I would like to."

"Yea . . . you are right . . . I have so much to apologize for . . . where do you want me to meet you up at?"

"I can pick you up, where are you?"

"No, meet me in Times Square in 30 minutes."

"Alright . . . May I ask where you at?"

"Unfortunately in a party."

"I'll see you then." Caleb said and hung up.

Juliana ran back inside the room, and looked desperately for her clothes to get dress, and leave.

"Where are you going?" Danny asked.

"I'm done with you."

"Really?" said Danny holding a drink.

"I'm going to meet up with some friends." said Juliana lifting up the zipper of her dress.

"Do I know them?"

"You don't have to know them . . ."

"Ok . . . Sorry for asking . . ." Danny said while he was watching Juliana get her bag and leave the room. He felt sad, kind of upset. He liked her, he liked her a lot he knew it, but he wasn't going to show her that anymore. He was just waiting for her to prove him that she was worth it and was good for him.

On her way downstairs, Juliana saw Monique sitting on the stairs, it was 5:30 am, and the party was still going on; some people were laying down, some people were dancing.

"Where have you been?" Monique looked at Juliana and asked.

"I should be mad at you . . ."

"Why?" Monique looked worried.

"Don't try Monique. If you are my best friend at least let me know where were you going."

"What you mean?" Monique said getting up from the stairs. "Are you mad because I came here without telling you?"

"It doesn't matter anymore."

"It does! What happened? Why are you mad at me?"

"I talked to Danny." Juliana said turning and giving her a really mean look.

"And . . . what did he tell you?" Monique nervously responded.

"Nothing. Next time, at least, let me know where are you going. I don't want to be worried, thinking where the fuck you could be at." Juliana said and walked out to the main door.

"I didn't do it on purpose . . ." said Monique by stopping her in the middle of her way.

"By the way, weren't you fucked up at the hotel?"

"Yes, but then . . ." Monique couldn't give her an explanation. She was scared that her friend might found out about her little adventure with Danny.

"Look Monique, don't explain me shit anymore because I really don't care, okay?" She said and looking at her in a mean way walked out of the house.

Monique following her asked. "Where are you going?"

Juliana who was walking to her car responded. "To meet up with somebody who is really my friend."

"I am your friend!" Monique said stopping.

"I hope so". Juliana said, got on her car, and drove away.

Monique was worried. She didn't know if Danny told Juliana about them two having sex. They have been friends since they were little, and Monique didn't want to lose her for a desperate night. However, Juliana wasn't going to let her last chance get ruined, even if prom wasn't what she expected it to be, her heart was feeling good, she was going to see her God. That's how she described him, he was like a worship image that she would pray for. Something she needed to take care of. She felt like her heart couldn't get more, she felt like he was too good to be true . . . she was in love.

Later on, when Juliana got to the humble restaurant-cafeteria where they agreed to meet through texts, she looked around looking for him through the windows, but she couldn't find him. She walked in and didn't see him. Thinking that she was at the wrong place, she turned around ready to leave and saw him coming out of the bathroom. Her heartbeat sped; she smiled and ran towards him throwing herself on his arms.

Caleb surprised for the hello, smiled at her back, and before he said anything, a big kiss came out from her lips.

"Wow!"

"What?" Juliana asked smiling while her arms were around his neck.

"I wasn't expecting that." he responded.

"I miss you and I'm sorry . . ."

"I'm sorry too . . . I think it was a little childish leaving you like that . . . Would you like to drink something?" He asked walking her to a table.

"Coffee." she responded and sat down.

"Ok . . . I'll get you a coffee." said Caleb and called the waitress.

Both lovers at the table just stared at each other and waited for the coffee to arrive. Her prom night wasn't as she expected it to be. She wasn't at a party getting wild as she planned since she was in freshman year. But she didn't mind because that night was the one that she was going to remember forever because for the first time ever, she knew she felt it, and it hurt her and gave her a tremendous joy in her heart. She was in love.

III.

IM NOT A BABY ANYMORE

The next day, Dara, was cooking breakfast and saw her daughter coming into the kitchen, and smiling at her said. "Hello honey, how was last night?"

"It was great mom . . . what did you and dad end up doing?"

"Nothing much, just went to dinner with some friends." Dara said while she was serving orange juice in a long crystal glass.

"Oh, that's good." Juliana responded and smiled.

"Are you going out right now?"

"Yes, I'm going to the mall with Monique . . ."

"The photographer called me, he told me to pick up the photos from your prom night."

"Oh yea? Where?" She asked while she was eating bread with butter.

"From the mall . . . maybe we can go together." Dara said while she was looking through the newspaper, hoping for a positive answer.

"I can't mom, I'm in a hurry, I really have to get there and meet up with Monique."

"And why is that?"

"Because I have things to do."

"Like?" Dara asked putting the newspaper down.

"Are you going to start interrogating me?"

"Juliana you are my daughter and I'm really worried about you, we don't talk as much as we used to."

"Because I'm not a little girl anymore . . ."

"So what Juliana?! I am your mother I have the right to know where you are going, what are you doing, who are you going out with, etc."

Juliana putting her bread down responded. "Did you forget that I'm already 18?"

"I don't care if you are 45, you will always be my baby."

Juliana getting off the chair responded. "That's the thing. I'm not a baby anymore."

"At least tell me who else you are going to be with." Dara asked, looking at her daughter leaving the kitchen.

"With Monique, Joey and somebody else."

"Joey? Who is Joey? And who's that somebody else?"

"Somebody else mom!" She said stopping in the middle of the kitchen.

"Can you tell me Juliana?"

"That's somebody else is my boyfriend, and Joey is my boyfriend's brother, you got it?

"I thought you were going out with Danny, who is this new guy you are going out with?"

"Danny, Danny . . . It's always Danny in this house . . . I don't like Danny mom you do! And this new guy . . . He is the most amazing, incredible guy I have ever met, that's my boyfriend."

"Well, I need to talk to his parents."

"No you don't have to talk to his parents mom, can you stop please?!" Juliana screamed.

Dara looked at Juliana impressed of her attitude. "What is your problem?!"

"Nothing is my problem, you are a problem mother!"

"Why don't you want me to see him? Are you going out with a boy from the projects? Or are you going out with a guy that lives in the garbage? With who?"

"Even if he was homeless, with no job, or just a drug-addicted, delinquent whatever you want to name him . . . you will have to accept it because I say so!"

"Juliana, what is your problem?"

"Bye mother. I can't stand you." She said looking at her deep into the eyes, and walked out.

Dara called her husband immediately.

"Isaiah, I don't know what is wrong with your daughter!"

"What happened now?" asked Isaiah who was at his office in the police department.

"She told me she has a boyfriend."

"And . . . you made a big deal about it?"

"I asked her who he was, and she started screaming at me."

"Maybe you asked her too much."

"Isaiah please, what is too much for a mother? I don't care if I was asking too much damn it! She is my daughter I have to know what is going on in her life! I think . . . I think she is going out with a guy from the projects . . ."

"What are you saying Dara! Oh c'mon! You know her! She is always doing stuff quietly." responded Isaiah who was getting stress out by his wife.

"She told me that even if she would be going out with a guy from the hood, we would have to accept him." She continued aggravating him.

"So she said she was going out with one?" asked Isaiah sighting hard.

"I think she is . . . I mean, think about it Isaiah. If she doesn't want to introduce us this guy is because she is hiding something."

"Where is she now?"

"She went to the mall with Monique, oh god; I don't like that girl Monique . . . I already told her."

"Listen Dara. I'm going to call her; you know she never denies anything to daddy. I'm going to call her and I'm going to tell her to meet up with me in the mall, she won't deny it."

Dara sighted. "Are you sure?"

"100% my love, don't worry." said Isaiah trying to keep his wife calmed.

"Ok, I love you, see you later."

"I love you too." Isaiah said and hung up.

Nothing was getting better than the moments that Juliana was spending with her lover, walking around the mall, looking around, going in and out from the stores, and playing with each other as if they were two little kids at a toy store. He was playing with her hair every time she was next to him. It was the perfect day, the perfect person, and the perfect picture. The future will be better she believed in it; she felt it. It was the best time of her life and nobody was going to ruin it she was affirming it. He was definitely the love of her life and she was loosing her reasonable side for him. She even got to the point of feeling in the necessity to kill for his love. But could that be possible? Kill for love? As I think and try to remember all the love stories I have ever seen, I could tell that once somebody has the perfect man or the perfect woman, they seemed like they will do anything that is possible to not let them go? But then again I ask myself, could it be possible that a human being would mix their own hands with blood, just to not end their happiness? Or what they believed it belongs to them?

"It's such an amazing day I swear, I've never been so happy!" Juliana said to Caleb as he was hugging her.

"I feel the same way . . . I also wonder, why haven't you talk to your parents about me."

"Because . . . I already told you Caleb. I'm going to introduce you to them . . . but . . . just not yet."

"Why?" Caleb asked getting close to her.

"Because my mom needs to know more about you, you know how that goes."

"What do you mean?"

"It's too soon for her to meet you . . . we just started dating a few ago, don't you think is too soon?"

"Well, yeah you right but I want to let them know who you are with I don't want them to think that you are with a bachelor, or dangerous guy out from your country club world.

"Don't say that *'the country club world'* please! And don't worry, I will introduce you my parents, specially my father, he is amazing!

"And your mom?"

Juliana's face turned disgusted and responded. "My mom . . . yeah, I guess she is good too . . ."

"Why do you talk about her like if you don't care? Or like if you hate her?"

"'Cause I don't know . . . I can't stand her . . . I think if she would let me live my life how I want it, everything would be perfect."

"She is your mother."

"I know! . . . too bad you can't choose who your parents could be."

"What are you saying? Why are you talking like that?"

Juliana smiled, hugged him and said. "My love, forget about it, and forget about everything else . . . I just want to enjoy the time that we have together."

Caleb looked at her and when he was bout to kiss her again, her phone started ringing, it was her dad.

"Shit, it's my dad . . . I wonder what that she said." She picked up the phone call and yes, she was talking about her mother when she said the word *"she"* with so much hate . . .

"Hey daddy!" Juliana responded.

"Hey sweetheart where are you?" Isaiah asked.

"At the mall and you?"

"At the mall as well, what a coincidence . . . where are you?"

Juliana laughed in a sarcastic way and said. "What do you mean where am I? I'm at the mall."

"My dear Juliana stop playing games, you know what daddy means."

"Ok daddy, where do you want to meet up at?"

"What about the food court?"

"Fine." Juliana sighted. "Who are you with?"

"By myself dear, I just got out of work."

"Oh ok . . . I thought you were with mom"

"Who's with you?"

"My boyfriend."

"Oh wow, I didn't know you have a boyfriend, well that's even better, it's a great time to meet him. I'm going to be waiting here, and don't even try to sell me out because I will cancel your credit cards . . ."

Juliana laughed sarcastically. "Oh, no daddy how could you think that . . . of course not, I won't sell you out, see you in a few!" She hung up the phone, and looking at her boyfriend, he asked. "So should we start walking to the food court?"

Juliana sighted, held his hand and they both started walking. Juliana was nervous feeling a little upset at her mom. She knew she sent her dad to the mall, to find out if she was lying or not.

Caleb opened the big, clear, wide entrance door of the food court, and there he was, her father, sitting by himself in a table reading a newspaper.

Juliana stopped slowly in front of Caleb and said. "Listen Caleb, anything that he may ask just please, please be honest with it."

Caleb smiling responded. "Ok . . . What's going on?"

"My dad would catch your lies believe me."

"Are you sure? There's no person in the world that would find out if the lies that I had said were true or not. Unless, the person works for the CIA or FBI, or is a psychic."

Juliana looked at him and laughed softly saying "Yeah . . . You are right."

"Are you serious?"

"I forgot to mention it. Sorry. I was so into you when I met you that I didn't want you to run away from me."

Caleb felt like two big walls were closing with him, and stayed quiet. There was nothing he could do, he was already in that situation, and he had to handle it as the grown man that he was.

"Yes, but you don't have to be scared of him, he is really cool, you just have to talk to him nice and be honest with him."

Caleb had no words in his mouth; positive and negative reunited in his head. Well, maybe her dad could help him with the search of his lost sister he thought. Or maybe her father was going to find out about all the girls that gave him blowjobs in unbelievable places such as libraries, courthouses, banks, he was probably going to find out about the strippers he took home once, the girlfriends he had, and even the wives that he turned into part-time lovers.

But no matter what was crashing in his head, they kept on going Juliana approximating to the table where her dad was sitting at.

"Hi daddy!" said Juliana giving her dad a kiss on the forehead.

"Hello sir, nice to meet you." said Caleb shaking hands with him.

"Hello." Said Isaiah looking at him from head to toes.

"Dad, this is my boyfriend."

"And . . . where is Monique? I thought she was going to be with you." Isaiah asked her daughter while he was putting the newspaper he inside his briefcase.

"How do you know she was supposed to be with me?"

"Well, I guessed she was going to be with you, I mean you two are always together."

"Did mom send you to stalk me and to make sure that my boyfriend was not a guy from the projects?"

"She just worries about you a lot sweetie." said Isaiah looking at Caleb serious.

"I can't stand her! I don't know how you let her manipulate you!"

Caleb looked at Juliana and said. "Juliana please, show some respect."

"Please don't get in the conversation, it's a family thing."

"Oh sorry, I didn't mean to." apologized Caleb.

"Juliana since when you two started going out?" asked Isaiah looking at Caleb. Deeply inside he wanted to kill him. He couldn't stand the fact that someone else was touching his girl, and on top it was a man much more older than her.

"A couple of weeks ago . . ."

"And how you two met?"

"At the library . . ."

Caleb looked at Juliana.

Juliana looked at Caleb, and smiling looked back at her dad and kept on saying. "He was in the library reading a book, and I was inside because I had to use the bathroom. So he liked me, I liked him, I sat down to read a book also, I can't forget that." she smiled. "And whatever, he asked me for my number so I gave it to him and we started talking, and now we are dating."

"Just like that? You gave your number to a stranger?"

"No, daddy, not like that . . . I've seen him around before . . . Hmmm . . . around the school I mean."

"So now, he is a pedophile? Driving around the school to see young girls?!"

"No! Of course not, he is friends with Monique's friend, friend. And one day, I was talking to them and he came around."

"And the day that you saw him at the library you didn't waste time and gave him your number right?"

"Ok dad, that's enough."

"Enough what? I'm trying to know who is my daughter going out with, you think I want you to go out with just anybody?"

"Dad, he is not random dude from the streets believe me . . ."

"Whether you tell me or not, I'm still going to find out who he is, what he does, who are his friends, etc. So if I was you Juliana, I would sit down in the table with daddy, and boyfriend, and talk."

Juliana and Caleb looked at each other, and sat down with Isaiah.

"What do you do for living?" Isaiah asked to Caleb.

"I am an electric engineer, and now I'm in charge of the whole department where I work at, I'm the CEO of all these upcoming projects . . . and well, I'm planning to put my own electronics company soon." Caleb responded.

"That's not bad . . . I was hoping that my daughter will end up going out with one of the president's nephews, but I guess an ordinary business man *'wana be'* is not bad. Do you work in Times Square? What's the name of your company?" Isaiah asked sitting up straight. Juliana stared at her dad in shock. Her hands were actually sweating, she felt as if she was a criminal, and the own police was interrogating him. She couldn't believe it.

"Solo Company Inc." Caleb responded.

"Yeah, I know who they are . . . so I guess many people in the whole New York want to do business with you . . . I mean you must be smart to design all those mp3s, and check the video games you know what I mean. I'm not an expert but I know the basics of everyone . . ."

"I never talk about my work, because I don't like to sound stuck up, but so far, my designs have been welcomed, and approved by many companies. Income won't be a problem in my life so far."

"Dad please, can you stop interrogating him? What do you think he is a terrorist?" Juliana whispered.

"So what about your family? How are them?"

"Well, my mother, she lives with her sisters and . . ."

"How come?" Isaiah interrupted him. "It seems like you have a lot of money and couldn't bought your own mother a good place to live?"

"Dad please . . ." Juliana interrupted wanting him to stop.

Caleb looked at Juliana, and looking back at her dad responded. "Oh no sir, I did buy it, but she didn't want to live there, she rather be with her sisters."

"What about your father?"

"My father died when I was 2." He responded looking straight at Isaiah's eyes.

"So you have a stepfather?"

"I had one."

'Oh he died too?"

"From what I know, he is in jail."

"Oh I see, I see . . . what did he do?"

Juliana was angry. She stood up and with a tough attitude she yelled. "Ok dad, that's enough! He doesn't have to talk about his life; I think you've been too much with us. Stop it now!"

Caleb looked at Juliana and said, "It's ok baby, I think I should tell your dad about my background, at the end, it's worst if he finds out by a computer." Caleb got back at Isaiah and kept on with his story. "I have 1 brother and I sister, which I haven't seen in almost 13 years, . . . I just got in contact with my brother a few ago . . . My mother was in love with my stepfather, she loved him a lot. So he moved into our house when we were still little. Everything was good, my mom had a good job, we used to go to school, and we were happy. But, one day they started arguing, and since that day everything went wrong. My stepfather started hitting my mom. Then, he started hitting my brother, my sister, and me. My mom lost her job because one day he hit her so hard that she couldn't even walk, that day I was out, looking for a job, but I didn't find anything. And when I got home, I saw my brother and sister naked . . . on the floor; he was raping them, hitting them. He was drunk. We fought, but nothing worked out, he kept on doing what he wanted . . . that day, I ran away like a coward, and that same day I was separated from my family."

Juliana hugging him.

"Sorry to hear that." said Isaiah. "I didn't know that you went through all this. I just asked because she is my daughter . . . and you need to understand how a father takes care, and looks out for his children. The day you have a kid, you will probably understand how her mother and I feel every time she tells us about a romance she's having."

"I completely understand sir."

"And that was the day, the police took your stepfather to jail right?" asked Isaiah.

"That's right. They found him raping my brother and sister. They also locked up my mother too, for child negligence."

"And . . . until today, you haven't seen your stepfather again?"

"No, but my mother does. She goes to jail every week to visit him."

"Sometimes love is like that, it makes you do things that you shouldn't . . ." Isaiah responded.

"I guess so . . ."

"What type of sentence he got?" Isaiah asked while he sipped a little of his iced coffee.

"I'm not really sure what is his sentence, but something that I know is that he is dying soon . . ."

"Why you say that?"

"He has AIDS."

"How you know it?"

"My mother told me he got raped in jail."

"Ok, dad, that's enough . . ." Said Juliana wanting to leave.

Isaiah interrupting her said. "I though you were a bad man, but you speak with the heart, I see it in your eyes."

"How can you tell that?"

"I've been working with criminals, cops, politicians . . . all type of people all my life . . . I know who speaks the truth and who doesn't. I see in your eyes nothing but sad memories that want to end up."

Juliana smiled and getting from the chair hugged her dad and said. "Okay dad, I don't want to argue with you . . . but we have to go."

"Take care you two, and bring him to the house whenever Juliana, I want to have a dinner with you, him, mom, all of us."

"Mom?"

"Yes, your mom why? You are going to prohibit your own mother from knowing who you date now?"

"No, of course not . . . I was just wondering why we couldn't have a dinner without her."

"I will see you later Juliana." said Isaiah and kissed her daughter's hands before she left with her lover.

Both lovers said bye to Juliana's dad, and walked out. Juliana never believed in love, happiness, or any type of joyful feeling that made people go crazy for each other. She believed that fairytales, and anything related to it were fake. But this time, she could felt the electricity running through her body giving her chills every time his hands were touching her skin. Electricity that made her stomach move of anxiety, and she wasn't cleared if she wanted to throw up because her nerves were pushing her to it. All these feelings at once were confusing her. Her heartbeat was always accelerating and sometimes she felt like she couldn't breathe making her have an anxiety of being with him. That was Juliana, and yes she was in love. In love for the first time in her life . . . Every time she stared at his lips moving was like if she was thirsting for the honey that was given after every kiss; that was the way she felt. Every kiss had a magic effect on her. Every time he looked at her, she felt like she could see a new world into his eyes, a world that she could be able to build and not want to destroy. The way she loved him was unbelievable, incomparable, it was a love that had no words in her dictionary, no meaning for this feeling, she wanted to be with him forever, and not want to miss a single second that she spent with him. She was amazed by the way she was feeling towards him, it was too soon. And of course, at time she remembered all the crazy things she have done before, there she was, falling for this thing that we call love. She knew it was rebellious the way she was waking up, sitting, walking, thinking, talking about him. Everything was different but was right in her heart. He had changed her, yes he did, but nor in purpose, nothing was planned everything was just happening. She started to believe that her life depended on him, he was a God to her. And few by few he was just becoming her life. He started taking over her mind, body and heart, everything was one now, everything was ready to be dedicated to only one person and that was him, her lovely Caleb.

As the hours passed, and the night became the guest of the day, the so in love couple drove to their "spot", Caleb's luxurious apartment that was exclusively designed by one of the best designers from the Big Apple.

"Do you want to drink something?" He asked.

"No."

Caleb walked up to his kitchen, and standing next to his bar looked at Juliana observing everything and feeling curious he asked. "Are you ok?"

"Yes . . . Why do you ask?" Juliana responded.

"You seemed like . . . if something is bothering you . . ."

"Your apartment." said Juliana making Caleb looked at her like impressed.

"You like it?" he asked.

"A lot, it's really nice." Said Juliana walking around the plasma TV

"I am glad you liked it."

"Really?" said Juliana smiling back at him sitting on his $2,450 leather sofa. "So . . . what's up?"

"Nothing, what do you want to do?"

"I don't know, you have any movies?" she asked.

"Oh yeah, a lot." responded Caleb looking for the remote control.

"Ok . . . what do you want to see?" she asked him.

"It's up to you, you are my guest." Caleb said getting the remote which was under the sofa.

Juliana smiled at him and said getting closer asked. "Do you have any *porno?*"

Caleb almost choking with his own drink responded. "Pardon me?"

"Pornography, you know triple X." said Juliana doing the X with her index finger.

"No . . . No I don't. Do you watch that?"

"No . . ."

"Then why are you asking me for movies?"

"Because I want to get you hard, and I don't know how to start . . ." said Juliana giving him a seductive look.

"Are you sexually active like that?"

"Is that how you call a girl who loves having sex?"

"I don't want you to feel any pressure in any way . . . I told you we could still wait longer . . . remember you don't plan these type of moments, they just happen."

"Yes I know you don't plan these moments, but I'm your girlfriend . . . is different now isn't it?"

"Are you sure you want to do this? I don't want you to regret it later."

"If I'm going to regret things then I should have started years ago."

"I don't want to disrespect you, I really mean it."

Juliana putting her glass of water on the crystal table which was in front of the sofa got on top of him and looked at him deeply. "I want to do it . . . I have been waiting for this moment . . ."

"Don't tell me that . . ."

"Yeah, I have been waiting for this moment since we first met and I got in your car."

Caleb quiet couldn't say anymore, he believed she wasn't a slut. She was his girlfriend, and no he did not want to think badly about her, but he wanted her, and wanted to take it slow. But her beauty, her body, her movements weren't helping. He was a man after all he thought.

Juliana started kissing him and suddenly she felt something wrong. "What's your problem?"

"I don't know if I can do it."

Juliana getting off his lap said. "Why not?"

"I want a serious relationship I want things to go well. Another guy would have been fucking you right now, but I'm not like that. When I asked you out, it was because I was really sure that you were going to work it out with me. I was aware that you were the crazy girl I wanted but not the crazy type that jumps on every guy's lap and start action in less than a month . . . I have asked you to be my girl, not just a simple hook up."

"So you think I'm easy . . . a whore?"

"I didn't say that. I want to make sure that you won't do this, what are you doing right now as soon as I turn around."

"You mean, cheat on you?"

"It's not about cheating, because if you are going to do it, go head, at the end no matter what, you will do it if you want it. But I want to make sure that I can trust you that if for any reason one day you get mad at me or we happen to be mad at each other, you won't throw yourself this easy to another guy."

"I won't, because I'm loyal to you." said Juliana, who was feeling embarrassed, and upset.

"Can I ask you something?"

"Yes go head" she said.

"How many guys did you do?

Juliana on her mind was saying: "*if I tell this fucker I fucked more than 10 guys, he may think I am a hoe, but if I tell him that I lost my virginity with my ex father, he is going to think worst. And if I tell him that I fucked my ex the same night we started dating out he is going to definitely think I give it up to easy and won't never, ever try to look for me again. I guess a little lie won't fuck anything up.*"

"I only slept with one guy in my whole life." said Juliana looking at his eyes.

"And who was this guy may I ask?"

"My ex, we went out through the whole high school years." Juliana said sighting. "And you?"

"I only had three real girlfriends in my life. The rest were nothing but meats on the tables."

"Oh, so you are like a player huh?"

"No, it's just that life hit me hard and I started looking at females like pieces of candy that you see in the store. You want them because they look good, but then when you start tasting them, and you find out that the flavor was fooling you, and you throw them away."

"Am I one of them?"

"Those candies were the ones I never took serious." responded Caleb. "Those were friends, roommates, girls I met in parties, streets, stores, libraries, church girls"

"Church?" Juliana said surprised opening her eyes widely.

"Yes church. I met this girl at this church and she gave me head as soon as we got out of it."

"How was the communication? I mean in a church you don't do anything but hear the priest talking?"

"She was looking at me with those looks that melts you, and so did I, her eyes told me everything, and we ended up sleeping together."

"You are such a bad boy!"

"I know, I didn't want to, I really regretted it."

"Well honey, we are not in the church. We are in your house . . . alone." said Juliana getting on his lap again, and slowly started licking his left ear while his hands were holding her waist. Both individual's lips were touching each other; both bodies started feeling the heat. Her hands were going down slowly until she got to his spot. She slowly pulled down his zipper and getting on her knees she started sucking on him. Moans with his deep voice were coming out from his mouth. Slowly, she started going up and taking off her shirt, she laid down on the sofa, making Caleb take off his clothes in a rush.

He got on top of her and kissed her slowly, moving his tongue everywhere inside her mouth as she was wrapping her legs on his back. She made him go down to her breasts taking off her bra. He stared at her nipples so hard which made him go down even more. Looking at her panties waiting to be off, he ripped them off and looked her delicate part where a lot was waiting for him. Softly he passed his fingers through her lips down there, and he started a penetration with them making her moan of pleasure.

She was massaging her breasts and biting her lips while his fingers were feeling her inside out. Not waiting any longer he put on his weapon and a lovely penetration started. Her moans were making him go from slow to fast, from soft to hard. Kisses here, kisses there, everything was going great. Juliana was moaning loudly every time the fight was harder, she was making him go crazy with her moans. It was an incredible darkness for his senses, looking at such a delicate and soft body laying down there, screaming of pleasure. In less than 4 seconds she was giving him the back and slowly he started as she kept on yelling for more. More moans coming, more claps sounds loudly, her breasts were bouncing as he kept on punishing her with a glorious pain she was enjoying. Caleb closed his eyes and kept on making his night a movie that wasn't going to be forgotten from his mind. The minutes that turned intense were passing by, and the victory was almost his. She couldn't stop screaming, he couldn't stop exhaling this heavy feeling he had in his chest, and the battle was over. He won. Sweaty both bodies laid on the floor stared at the roof, looked at the whole apartment which had all the curtains open letting the city watch them. They closed their eyes, and remembered what just had happened.

"How do you feel?" he asked.

"Great." she said sighting tired of pleasure.

"I enjoyed it . . . I did because I did it with you." he said staring at her naked breasts.

"I think I love you . . ." Responded Juliana as she was getting closer to his arms. "I think I feel it in my heart . . . I don't know how to explain it, I just feel like I've met you before, and I feel like I know you enough already. I feel like I know we are always going to be link up together somehow . . . I know it sounds crazy, but it is just a feeling I've been having since I first saw you . . ."

"I don't want you to go home."

"I don't have to go." she responded.

"Well I'm going to take you home whether you like it or not."

"Why? It's already late, I can tell my parents I'm at Monique's house she will cover me."

"I'm trying to be serious with you, no games, no lies; no covers . . . Let me know when you are ready." Said Caleb and hugged her.

IV.

TEMPTING DADDY TO KILL

The next morning at Juliana's living room . . .

How was the mall yesterday love? Did you have fun?" asked Isaiah waiting for his daughter to sit down and eat with him.

"Yes dad, it was very good."

"How is this new boyfriend of Juliana?" Dara asked her husband directly avoiding eye contact with her daughter.

"He's a nice guy so far . . ."

"Daddy approved him mom . . . he doesn't make a huge deal like you do."

Dara looked at Juliana upset and responded. "Your dad is not the only parent you have."

"Please you two are not going to start! Please Juliana show some respect to your mom!"

"Sorry. I apologize." She responded feeling angry.

"I haven't approved this guy yet, but so far I don't see anything wrong with him. I'm going to tell him to come one of these days to the house, so all of us can have dinner." said Isaiah drinking a sip of water.

"Are you serious?" asked Juliana.

"Yes I don't see why not."

"I though it was too soon to bring him to the house." Dara said feeling her stomach moving around.

"It is but, I already met him, and I can see how much Juliana likes him."

"Aw thanks dad! I love you!" Juliana got up and hugged her dad as she said.

"Are you going out today?" He asked.

"Hmmm yes, of course like every weekend why?"

"Because your mother and I are going out tonight . . . This General from the Army is having a party and we are attending . . ."

"And that means what?" asked Juliana interrupting her father.

"That means that you can come with us, or stay here at the house with Monique ONLY."

Juliana sighted. "Ok, I'll tell Monique to come and sleep over."

"Your mother and I would be back tomorrow morning, and I want to find you here at the house."

"Wow, I feel like if I'm still 15 again."

"Well, no matter what you still a baby." responded her father.

Dara looked at her daughter while she was swallowing her food; she really wanted to know who was this guy that Juliana liked so much. She wanted to know why her heart was beating so hard and feared the romance that her daughter was living.

"Excuse me, but I'm done."

"Where are you going?" asked Isaiah.

"To the beauty salon, I have to do something to my hair for tonight." responded Dara.

"Honey you look incredible the way you are."

"I don't think so." Said Dara getting up from the table, walking away.

"I don't know how you could do it dad." said Juliana after her mom was gone.

"Do what?" asked her father.

"Stand her." She responded as she ate her grapes. "If I was you I would look for somebody else already and divorce her."

"My daughter can I know why you hate so much the person that gave you life?"

"I don't hate her, I just don't like the way she acts sometimes, and she gets too annoying."

"Remember something Juliana, she is your mother, and nothing in the world can change that."

"No need to remind me."

Dara, on the other hand besides going to the mall to get ready for her event felt an enormous pain in her chest. She had something in her throat that was about to come out. She forced the driver to pull off in the emergency lane and opening the door she started to throw up. She threw up so hard she felt her ears closing and her eyes cloudy. She fell on the floor next to her recently disgusting garbage, and kept on crying, pulling her hair, kicking and trying to hit herself her driver stopped her from it.

She looked at him and said, "There is no other pain that can compare to what I feel. My daughter doesn't love me, treats me like crap, and I bet will wish me to vanish from this world."

Her driver didn't want to talk. He was her employee, he had no business in her personal life.

"Tell me how should I wake up everyday knowing that every fucking day I have to live like this! I don't know what I did to for her to hate me so much!"

Her driver kept staring at her, and helped her to get up. He walked her inside the car, and walked to the front getting ready to keep on driving.

"Hold on a sec please I need to make a phone call." She was calling her mother, the one that she only contacted in certain holidays to send her a miserable amount of money.

"Hello." said Maggie, her aunt, one of her mother's sister.

"Hey Maggie, it's me Dara."

"Dara?" said her aunt. "Wow, what a miracle, we haven't heard from you in years. You finally remember you have a mother."

"Oh auntie please, it's not even like that."

"Of course is like that, you don't call, you don't take your mother out, you don't even come anymore . . . no matter what happened she is still your mother."

"What mother are you talking about Aunt Maggie? Was she there when I got rape?"

"People make mistakes dear, you should know that better."

"Mistakes?" Dara said. "So letting your boyfriend rape your own children is a mistake?"

"I'm going to put your mom on the phone; I don't want to argue with you." said her aunt.

"Thanks aunt, that's the best you can do."

Loren, Dara's mom got on the phone line with a calmed voice. "Hello?"

Dara feeling awkward responded, "Mother?"

"I had waited 14 Christmas, birthdays, and mother's days waiting for at least one of my seeds to call me that again." responded Loren.

"I need to speak with you mother."

"Go head, here I am." said Loren feeling a little hope.

"In person."

"I don't have a car to drive to your mansion my sweetheart."

"Don't worry, I'll go, I really need to see you."

"Ok, then give me a call when you are here, and remember is apartment 5."

Mother and daughter hung up on each other as if they were expecting this meeting for so long. Dara told her driver directions and soon she was on her way to her mother's. Meanwhile, Loren, kept on sewing a red sweater that she started 10 years ago, which she still didn't finish. The streets where Dara was being driven by were different from the ones where she lived. Dara was a rich lady now, her friends, class, education, life view were extremely changed. Soon, getting closer to a green building with black tall gates, Dara parked, got out of the car, and walked inside. She waited for the elevator to come down, holding her $2,380 dollar leather bag, and fixing her huge black sunglasses, she walked in. She didn't belong to the places where she was raised at anymore. She belonged to the rich society that made her scared of everything that once she was friendly with. Walking through the hallway, where the greenish walls were almost yellow and creamy. Dara kept on looking strange at the place where her mother was living. She found apartment 5 and knocked on the old, brown door. Slowly that door opened, and a woman with white hair and light eyes came out. "Come in my daughter". It was her mom, she was old already, and in her eyes Dara could deeply see all the pain she had. Putting a man over her own children was her sin, and her punishment was the loneliness. Dara went in and Loren walking behind her, sat on the sofa next to her foreign daughter and said. "What could a princess like you, need from this old sinner?"

Dara gave her a deep sad look. "You are my mother, no matter what."

"Yes, I am. But you denied it, just like you have denied your own blood Caleb."

Dara turning to the other side quickly responded. "What are you talking about?"

"Oh my dear, you don't know your own mother? I guess you still haven't developed the 6th sense that every mother has . . . or maybe you just don't want to talk about my feelings from all these miserable years."

"Please stop it." Dara interrupted. "I didn't come here to talk about your feelings."

"Then what is it that you want from me?"

Dara looked at her mother seriously and said, "I need you to tell me the honest truth . . . Caleb, where is he?"

Loren looked down to her hands and remained quiet.

"Mom, please answer me."

"Why do you want to know about your brother? For what? Wouldn't that affect your marriage with that rich man?" said her mom standing up, walking towards the closest window.

"I need to know. I've been dreaming of him and Joey lately. I'm sure that if they still are alive, they have came to you right?"

"Oh Lily, or Dara? How should I call you? You changed everything from you; your past, your name, your blood. Even if you try to buy me with your money, I wouldn't tell you anything!"

"Why? Just tell me . . . I need to find Caleb." Dara begged.

"I won't tell you anything . . . even if you were on your knees. What do you want from him?! You denied him to your husband. You told him that you only have one brother, Joey! Then tell me why would you care about where is Caleb?"

"Because . . . I have been getting payback."

"How Dara? What is your husband doing?"

"Not my husband, he loves me very much . . . it's my daughter . . . she hates me."

Her mom looked at her and looking back at the window said. "Have you ever thought about the things you did? Denying your own brother, saying he is dead, saying that I was a prostitute just for you to look innocent and helpless, and saying that your daughter was the product of one of your boyfriends irresponsible sex when your own daughter is the product of the rapes that your stepfather did."

Dara covering her ears scremed. "Stop it please! Yes I really sorry and regret it, but I can't do anything about it but keep denying it. That's why I need to find Caleb and talk to him!"

"And what are you going to tell him? Sorry for the words that came out of your mouth to save your own skin?"

"No! I want to tell him to keep the secret. Isaiah won't ever forgive me if he finds out all these lies. He would probably divorce me and my life would end." Responded Dara sounding selfish, but feeling devastated.

"You are still greedy even with your own blood. Everything, every lie in this world is found out sooner or later my dear, no matter what. And at the end, the one that is going to get hurt is your own daughter."

"So . . . you are not going to tell me where he is at mom?"

"Never, even if I knew it. Caleb is a great, successful businessman, and he is doing so well, that now he doesn't need to type of stress in his life . . . And of course I won't tell him anything about you . . . he deserves only good not bad as you."

"Why do you hate me so much huh? You don't remember that the one that suffered the most was me? With a baby, always getting raped and beaten by him because of your ignorant love!" yelled Dara.

"While you were at home, your two brothers were helping me to get money so we could feed you. You never told me he was raping you . . . Never."

"And when you found out that he was hitting us? Why didn't you do something? Answer me!"

"He bought that house, he was giving us money, I was a single mom don't you remember? Where was I supposed to take all of you? What was I supposed to do? Sleep on the streets with you being so little, and probably letting my own two sons become delinquents because of poverty? No! I have never been a bad mother; I always tried to do my best for you all!"

"So what?! It didn't work! Because you still let us on his hands! You still knew he was hitting us and still let him do it! And when you found out he was cheating on you, that's when you got mad and started fighting back! You cared more that he was with another woman than hitting your own kids! Why!?" Dara screamed hysterically.

Loren looking at the window, tearing responded. "No, no, no! I was angry, frustrated yes! I was because I loved him and I still do! It hurt me the thought that he was touching somebody else but me . . . And then you saw what he did to me! Didn't you?"

Dara closed her eyes while her tears kept on running down her cheeks and responded to her mom in soft tone, "I remember". She closed again her eyes, and to her mind came the day that her father hit her mom so hard after an argument, and he left her numb on the floor. And opening her eyes again, she looked at her mother on the floor, on her knees, crying. "He raped me and Joey while you were in the room paralyzed."

"And I heard your cry and felt your pain, but I couldn't get up . . . you really think I let him raped you and your brother? I wanted to defend you and do anything for you two. But he had the money so he had the power." Said Loren, crying, throwing up. The pressure of the memories were too much for the hearts of both women.

"You still let him do what he wanted before that. What kind of mother let a stranger touch their kids, and hit them the way he did?"

"Get out Dara, please get the fuck out of here!" screamed her mom. "I don't want to see your face anymore!"

"Why?! Tell me why?! Tell me why do you hate me so much mother, please tell me why?!" Dara screamed following her all over the house.

"I never hated you, you are my daughter! I was . . . just jealous of your beauty, of your youth, but you still were my daughter!" screamed her mom falling.

"Jealous? Of what?"

"Jealous because I knew he wanted you, and I knew he was contemplating you. He wanted that young skin, young, fresh lips, touch that virgin hair and penetrate a young innocent girl!" responded her mom whos eyes were almost bloody red. One of the veins inside broke.

"Mother . . . please don't be sick like him! You weren't jealous, I was your daughter be fucking serious!"

"And you still are, and I'm still jealous! Jealous, because you got his seed, and even if you didn't want him as I did. You gave birth to something I was wishing for!"

Dara looked at her mom with so much hate and disappointment, ready to leave and said. "Oh mother, you make me not want to come back and see you again. You are making me not regret what I said about you. You are making me want to deny you and hate you forever."

"Then do it! Because I don't want to see your face again either! You are greedy! You are heartless, and that's why you are not going to find love from her. Your daughter is always going to hate you, until the day that the truth be out!"

Dara crying, walked towards the door as her mom was throwing as many poisonous words she could. Finally, she closed the door, sat slowly on the floor crying in the silent hallway. She couldn't believe what she just heard, she didn't want to hate what gave her life and what once she thought it was her life. She cried as if she was mute, she didn't make a noise, not a sound it was a quiet, long crying. But her oxygen didn't hold it any longer and cried loudly. She went crazy. She tried to get up holding on to the walls, scratching them with her short nails which bled right after. She tried to hold on for balance and walked towards the elevator with a hand in her stomach and the other in the walls. She walked towards the elevator crying, so hard, looking like an enormous pain was hurting her physically as well. Finally after waiting in and out of the elevator, she got out of the *guetto* building, and walked towards her car, crying, letting all the children from the *hood* watch her walk in such a tragically way.

Meanwhile, Monique was at Danny's house, arguing . . .

"Oh please, what makes you think that I'm scared of my own friend?"

"Then why are you so worried if she finds out?"

"Because I will lose her friendship forever."

"But didn't Juliana say that she didn't care about me?"

"Still . . . she is my best friend; she trusted me and look what I did!"

"You are too paranoid." said Danny walking towards the white chair that was next to white crystal table. They were by the pool. "Come . . . Come sit on my lap." he said extending his arms to her.

"No stop it! Oh god! I don't even know why I came here for." She said looking stressed out drying the sweat that was running through her forehead.

Danny looked at her and laughed.

"It's not funny!" she said as she got closer to him and slapped him on the arm.

"Yes it is . . . come on, sit on my lap." Danny said pretending to hypnotize Monique with his flirtatious eyes. Monique sat on his lap and wrapped her right arm around his neck.

"There you go. That's how I like you better."

Monique rubbing his chest said, "Can I ask you something?"

"Anything."

"If Juliana ever finds out about us, would you later on, ask me out?"

Danny stayed quiet. He breathed deeply and responded. "Yes, if you give me and do what I want."

"What do you mean?"

Danny looked at Monique direct into her eyes and an evil smile popped in his face. "When I tell you I want it, you give it, when I tell you bye you leave, please me as the king I am." he said passing his hand around her tights.

"What would you give me back?" she asked looking at his hand going under her skirt.

"The world and everything that would fill you."

"What do you mean?" asked Monique looking confused.

"Monique, Monique . . . every time you walk with Juliana they always see you second. Don't you want to be the first?"

Monique looked at him and then looked at the nowhere as if she was daydreaming.

"That's why you need to put Juliana on the spot with what hurts her the most."

"By doing what?"

"Talk about her, let me know her business . . . but tell me and show me her privacy . . ."

"That's too much . . ."

"Yeah, but who cares . . . she doesn't care about you."

"Yes she does." she said getting off his lap.

"Oh yeah? And where is she now? She forgets about you when she needs to do something 'important' doesn't she?" Danny instigated more.

"That's if what she is doing is important . . ."

"And what is so important than being with her best friend?"

"She is with her boyfriend."

Danny impressed felt as cold water fell on his head. "Boyfriend? Ha! Since when Juliana has a man that is not me?"

"Since a couple of weeks ago . . . you didn't know?"

"No, and I'm surprised . . . who is this guy that she goes out with?"

"A very handsome man. He is a good guy. He is established, smart, handsome, respectful, everything a girl can ask for . . ."

"I don't think he is better than me . . . I got it all."

"This guy has the business by his own self. That's why Juliana is impressed, he is independent and on top of the deal he is really humble."

"Whatever, I don't care."

"If you are wondering if they fucked, they haven't. Well, that's all I know." she said while she was kissing his neck.

"And where they at now?"

"I don't know . . . I don't care . . . I just want to be here, with you."

"Can I ask you something? But you have to tell me the truth . . ." he said moving her away from him.

"Ok . . ."

"Who did she lose it to? Is it this guy that she just started dating few ago? Or somebody from the school?"

"I can't tell you that . . ." said Monique looking and feeling nervous.

"Oh come on Monique, you won't deny me anything . . . I didn't tell your best friend that you fucked her ex so what makes you think I would tell her bout this."

"It's not about that . . . it's just that, I don't think you should know."

"Why? Is it my best friend who played the game as well?"

"No . . . something worst."

"Who? Tell me who Monique and I won't ask you anymore, I swear."

"I'm sorry I can't, I shouldn't . . ." said Monique getting off his lap trying to walk away.

"Monique . . . Monique!" he said running behind her grabbing her by the arm. "Would you be my girl?"

Monique was surprised.

"Come on Monique say yes, you know you love me more than anything so far . . . tell me if you want to be with me?"

"I don't know what to say." she said looking at him feeling bad. "I can't because what would happen, what would Juliana say, the school, my parents, her parents, your parents . . ."

"Fuck the school! Fuck Juliana! Fuck the whole world! If I want to be with you it's because I do!"

Monique scared responded. "I'm sorry, I didn't want to get you mad."

Danny breathing hard responded. "I apologize, but if you are going to be with me, I need you to always be honest with me."

"Yes . . . yes you are right . . ." she responded hugging him tight.

"Don't be like Juliana, she keeps everything from her man, and that's why she gets in trouble, bad reputation and bad friends." He said hugging her back. "Think that if you date me, you would be that girl who everybody envies because you got what nobody has as a boyfriend. If you be my girlfriend, I'll be your main, and so you will . . . Juliana would envy you . . . and she would want to be like you, just like the whole school."

"You are right. I'm tired of being the second option, and always behind her. Yes my dear Danny I want to be your girlfriend. Good and bad times together . . . everything together!"

"That's what I'm talking about . . . Now tell me, just answer me this curious question that I have . . . Who did she lose it to?"

Monique looked at him seriously and said. "She lost it to your . . ."

"To my what?"

"She lost it to your dad Danny."

Danny impressed sat down on the chair nearby, and stared at the nothing for the longest seconds.

"I'm sorry to tell you but it's the truth." she said trying to touch him.

"That fucking whore did that . . . she cheated on me with my dad? Wow!"

"I tried to stop her, but . . . you know how she is . . . at the end, she does what she wants."

"Yes, I know . . . don't worry Monique is all good . . . You don't need to tell me anymore."

"Are you mad at me?" she asked.

"Why should I be?"

"I don't know you look upset."

"I'm mad at myself. I stepped in the wrong place, and made a fool of myself by trying to make it work out with her. But what makes it worst is that I found out something that I should have known from my father's mouth."

"So . . . what are you going to do now?"

"I need you to go, please . . . I really want to be alone."

"You were going to find out sooner or later anyway, I just hope you won't say anything to her, you won't right? You promised." said Monique getting her bag getting ready to leave.

"I'll think about it." He said, got up from the chair and walked away.

"What do you mean by you will think about it?! Danny!! Danny!!" Monique screamed. But Danny wasn't having anything else revolving his head by an anxiety of wanting to kill her and his dad.

Monique stared at him getting in the house, turned and left.

Hours later, Danny's father got to the house and opening the door of his room saw his son smoking a fat tobacco on his bed.

Adam smiled and with sarcasm said. "Wow, look at my son trying to be like his dad."

"I don't think I would get to that level. I wouldn't fuck my son's girlfriend." Danny responded making his father's face turned to a different color.

"What are you saying?" his father asked.

Danny got off the bed, walked up to his dad, and slowly, and unexpectedly punched him in the face. His dad stepping backwards holding on to the table around him balanced back and looked at him amazed touching his colored cheek.

Adam with anger and attitude raised his voice. "What the hell is up with you son of a bitch?!"

"Son of a bitch? Maybe my mom was a bitch, but I'm happy she is not here to see the stupidities that her husband does!" screamed Danny furious.

Adam walking closer to his son slapped him hard and said. "Punk little boy, who the heck you think you are talking to like that! HUH?!"

"You! The one that took my girlfriend's virginity!"

"How did you find out?"

"It doesn't matter, I'm not going to fight, or argue with you for a slut . . . but get something in your head, I can't trust you anymore. You are not my father anymore!" And as he said, he walked out of the room.

His father furious and shocked about the situation chased after him saying "She was a slut anyway, why do you care so much!?"

Danny stopped in the middle of the hallway and responded. "She was my girl, that's what mattered."

"I am your father!" said Adam. "She tempted me, she came to the house and threw herself at me! I'm a man! What are you expecting!?"

"I wouldn't fuck the underage maid or your secretary. The point is that she was my girl, and you went far for that *pussy* and betrayed your own son's trust."

"Wait! Where are you going?!" Adam said chasing his son as he was going downstairs.

"I'm leaving the house, I can't be here!"

Adam running behind his son screamed. "Wait! You can't do this to me! You are my only son, my adoration, please Danny don't leave. We can talk about it!"

But Danny kept walking forward not looking back.

Adam screamed in the middle of the living room right when Danny was about to open the door. "ARE YOU GOING TO HATE YOUR OWN FATHER FOR A WOMAN?!"

Danny turned around, looked at his father for a few seconds, and left the house.

Adam was devastated, he felt like his heart was eating him alive. He couldn't believe that his only and adored son was going against him. That afternoon was the saddest afternoons ever. He quickly ran to his office and drank shots of whisky until the afternoon turned into nighttime. Two of his employees from the house tried to go inside his office to get him but nothing worked. Adam kept on calling Danny, but he wasn't picking up. He left approximately 20 voice messages, but still didn't get a call back. He was ready to kill someone. He stared at his gun, got his phone and called Juliana.

Juliana looking at the number on her phone's screen got nervous, wondering what he could want at this time. "Hello?"

"You fucking dirty hoe!"

"Excuse me? Who would you like to speak to?" said Juliana playing it off, so Caleb won't doubt anything.

"I want to talk with the hoe that put my son against me . . ."

"Hello?" kept on saying Juliana trying to avoid his words.

"Don't even play Juliana . . . you broke my relationship with the person I love the most . . . Danny is gone, and there is only one person who could put him against me . . ."

Juliana worried started whispering on the phone. "What are you talking about? Who's been telling you lies?"

"What lies?! Danny and I argued today, and now he's gone! But you are going to pay for this bitch, watch!"

"What the fuck are you going to do? Remember I was 17 when you started fucking me. So don't dare yourself to do something you will regret after."

"And you think I care? DO YOU FUCKING THINK THAT I GIVE A FUCK!?"

"Stop screaming at me you fucking idiot!" said Juliana as she walked out to the balcony.

"I don't care Juliana, I don't care who your father is, I don't! I have more power! I have more money! I can buy the police of the whole country if I want!"

"Oh yes, yes, yes . . . I don't fear you Adam. Even your name reminds me about how weak you are . . . you do can buy the police, the doctors, the sex . . . but you can't buy the trust and love that you lost!" she said and laughed.

"SHUT UP!"

"Why? Because is the truth?"

"Listen Juliana, you better go back and tell him that we didn't do ANYTHING!"

"Go and ask your own son who told him that . . . because it wasn't me." And as she finished the argument, she hung up on him.

Adam was so angry that he tried to invent something to make her pay what she caused, which was the rejection of his son. As he walked out of his office, he went to the security room where all the cameras where at. He rewind them all to see at what time this accident occurred, but for his surprised it wasn't Juliana who arrived to his house, it was her friend Monique.

Adam called Juliana back, but she wasn't picking up. Finally, after blowing up her phone for like the 10th time she answered.

"What do you want? Didn't I tell you not to bother me anymore?" whispered Juliana.

"Give me your friend's number . . . that girl Monique . . ."

"Why? You want to fuck her too?"

"You better give me her fucking number before I find you and strangle you with my own two hands . . ."

"No." said Juliana as she was walking to the bathroom so her boyfriend won't hear the conversation.

"Don't even try to play games with me . . . I can make your father lose his job."

"No you can't . . . and you better stopped calling me, before I report to the news and your JOB, and said that you are harassing me . . ."

"Give me her number Juliana . . ." Adam said hitting one of the cameras.

"Give me one reason why should I?" she said while she was fixing her hair in front of the mirror.

"Because I seen in the security videos and she was here 2 hours before I arrived home . . ."

"Monique . . . in your house? What . . . what was she doing there?"

"I guess fucking my son, I don't know, and I don't care. But something that I know is that she was the one that told him about us . . ."

"I don't think so. She wouldn't do that, she is my best friend!"

"Oh my dear Juliana, nobody cares about you as your parents do. Your friend did tell Danny about us because she likes him, and they've been having sex!"

"That's not true! She likes my boyfriend's brother!"

"Boyfriend? Since when you have a boyfriend?" said Adam walking around his office.

"Why do you care?"

"I don't. I just feel sorry for that bastard who doesn't know that his girl been getting fucked by the whole Manhattan."

"Enough ok! I'm not going to argue with you . . . I'm really thinking about what you are telling me, and I'm telling you I don't think that was Monique . . . she wouldn't do such a thing."

"Then come see it with your own eyes . . ." said Adam and hung up.

Juliana got out of the bathroom and told her boyfriend that she had to go over her friend's house for an emergency.

"Is everything ok?" asked Caleb.

"Yes baby, she is just going crazy over an argument with her mom, she needs me. I hope you don't mind."

"No, it's ok don't worry. Are you coming back right after?"

"I'll try. I love you." Said Juliana and left his apartment.

As soon as she got on her car, she speeded towards Adam's place, she didn't care about the lights, or people. She just kept on speeding. She was dying to know what was going on. She wanted the situation to be a big mistake, she was hoping that Monique wasn't the one in the cameras; she was hoping that her own best friend didn't betray her with something so serious.

Finally, at Adam's house, one of the housekeepers opened the door, and asked. "Are you looking for . . .

"Go back to the kitchen bitch; I don't need an invitation to come." Juliana said after interrupting her.

"Excuse me?" the housekeeper said.

"It's okay Carol, I invited her. Come Juliana, followed me." Responded Adam.

They walked towards the security room, and did not say a word to each other. Adam opened the door, let her in, locked it, and turned on one of the big monitors.

"Isn't that your friend?" said looking at Juliana who couldn't believe what she was seeing. Monique was sitting on Danny's lap, laughing, kissing, touching him.

"Yes, yes she is . . ." Juliana responded.

"She was the one who told him, listen . . .

Juliana looked at Adam and heard the conversation that Monique had with Danny and it said the following:

"I don't like her anymore, I can't stand her either. Yes, yes you are right I should tell the world her business, and I should be the one that the world looks at first. Yes Danny she lost her virginity to your dad."

Juliana's ears broke when she heard this. She never imagined that her so-called best friend would say something so private about her. She felt like the back of her neck was burning in heat. She felt empty, all her energy dropped to the floor, and her smile disappeared. Friends come and go, she heard it so many times but still didn't believe in that phrase until now. Monique was her only friend. The one that she trusted the most and now, everything was over.

"Where are you going?" asked Adam as he saw her walking out of the room.

But Juliana did not stop; she kept on walking, as tears were coming out her eyes. She walked up to her car, and started driving to Monique's house. She needed to hear it from her own mouth; she was not going to believe it until her own friend says it.

Once at her friend's house, Juliana rang on the bell three times.

Monique opened the door and her face expression changed as soon as she saw Juliana. "Hey, why didn't you call?"

Juliana crying said, "Tell me you didn't tell Danny, tell me you didn't tell anybody . . ."

Monique looked down on the floor, and looked at Juliana again. "I didn't . . ."

Juliana hysterically screamed. "What the fuck! Monique! What is up with you?! You think I'm going to believe that shit? You fucking told Danny that I fucked his dad, and his dad called me when I was with Caleb and told me he was going to tell Caleb, and my family about it!"

"Well how did you know it was me? You weren't there . . ."

Both young ladies stayed quiet for a few seconds.

"Monique, there is no more to say, I saw you in the security video . . . you were in Danny's lap, flirting, kissing . . . and talking shit about me . . . and now, you just confessed it." said Juliana looking at her disappointed.

Monique couldn't say anything. She couldn't even look at her. The silence spoke for itself.

"Thanks Monique, I hope Danny would pay the price that you put by selling your own friend." She finished, turned around and got back in her car.

Monique knew she was wrong and that nothing in the world was going to give her back the years of friendship that they had. Juliana on her way home, sad didn't know that splitting like that from a friend was going to hurt so much. Finally at home, as she was walking in the living room, she heard someone playing the piano, it was her mom. She was playing a song the started with a sad beginning and ended with a sad good bye. Juliana not making noise leaned on the wall and said "You play really good mom . . . you always did . . ." Dara turned and looked at her daughter and responded. "Thanks honey . . . you want to come and sit next to me?"

Juliana smiled sadly, walked up to the piano, and sat next to her mom.

Dara started playing the famous and beautiful melody "Swan Lake". And while this one was playing Juliana closed her eyes, and let the music elevated her depressed spirit.

Dara kept on playing, but then looked at her daughter and saw the tears coming from her eyes. As a mother she was worried and felt that crying. She stopped playing the song and asked. "What's wrong sweetheart?" said Dara cleaning her tears and putting her hands on her daughter's arms. "Don't tell me is nothing, because I see in your eyes pain and sadness . . . tell me, what happened?"

"Monique betrayed me mom, we are not friends anymore . . ."

Dara surprised about the situation, smiled at her daughter thinking it was maybe a small thing. "Don't worry. You two would be friends again."

"No, you don't understand, we are not mad at each other . . . she told Danny something that she shouldn't . . ."

"And what is it?" asked her mom.

Juliana got up from the chair and said. "I can't tell you mom."

"Why? How bad is it?"

"I just can't tell you . . ."

"Juliana, there's been days, weeks, months that we haven't talked. I remember we used to be great friends . . . You used to tell me your secrets and now . . . I feel like you hate me."

"I don't hate you, but . . . I just can't tell you everything like before."

"I can't see you suffering . . . tell me . . . what bad have you done that you don't even want to let your mother know . . ." said Dara getting close to her, touching her face.

"If I tell you, would you promise me, would you swear that you won't tell dad?" said Juliana looking scared.

"Of course my dear, I will die with it."

Juliana looking down, then, looked at her mom and responded. "I slept with Danny's dad . . . and Monique told Danny I did . . ."

Dara's eyes were wide open. Her ears were horrified after hearing such a terrible thing. She turned and sat down on the white sofa nearby the piano and stared at the floor.

"Mom. Mom tell me something please . . ." said Juliana walking upon her.

Dara lifted her head and looking at her daughter said "Something? Like what? You are 18 you do whatever you want and you should know how to react about the consequences."

"Whatever, I shouldn't ever told you shit . . . you are always with your drama!" Juliana said walking away.

"Juliana! Those are not the values I taught you. What would your father, friends, the whole world that knows us would say bout your behavior? Tell me!"

"TO THE HELL WITH THE FUCKING SOCIETY! FUCK ALL OF THEM! I'm tired of you living for the rich society . . . When are you going to be a mom? When are you going to live for your daughter and husband?" Juliana screamed.

"Juliana, Juliana stop it! I am not going to let you disrespect me like that!"

"Don't act like you are the good perfect mom . . . because you are not!"

"Juliana, Juliana come back! I didn't finish this conversation!" But it was too late; her daughter ignored her words, and ran to her room. Dara again, felt destroyed. She wanted to get closer to her daughter but Juliana was pushing it away. She walked back to the piano, lighted up a cigarette and smoked her stress out.

Caleb, on the contrary, was thinking about how his life was paying back all the suffering he had before. Everything was going so good to him, his job, friends, money, and the most important, love. Even if his family wasn't ever going to be what he most wanted, and that was being tight as a chain. He was getting everyday a little amount of love that was filling his heart and soul.

Weeks passed and Juliana's graduation day arrived, and today was going to be the day that Caleb was going to meet his girlfriend's family.

Today, destiny seemed like it was going to make him find out that he was dating his own niece.

While the seniors of the class 07' were in the main hall listening to the principal's words, Juliana was turning around every five minutes to see if her lover was around. But Caleb was trapped at a last minute conference. He was organizing the big project; he was talking to different executives about the new company he was going to put in the market.

As the ceremony was about to finish; and the students were receiving their diplomas. Juliana kept looking around, but he wasn't in the crowd.

Monique was next to receiving her diploma, when couple of boys from the crowd started to yell. "Suck me up!" They were laughing and making obscene signs. Juliana loved Monique very much, and even if they were mad at each other now, she wanted to talk to her. Then, her name was called. She got up and walked up there to receive her high school diploma. Her parents were in the front taking pictures, shouting her name. Her mom was crying, and her dad was holding her. They were so proud of the only daughter they had . . . She was finishing something good as high school. But Juliana wasn't as happy as she wanted to be, her love wasn't there, she felt like she didn't deserve to graduate when she didn't do much, and she had no friends. And as the graduation finished, she kept on calling Caleb, but he didn't pick up the phone, angry about the situation, she turned off her phone.

"Congratulations my dear Juliana! You made it! Who would have thought!" said Danny while Juliana looked at him with that look that makes you say what a hypocrite, and responded "Aw, thanks my dear Danny you made it too! I'm so proud of you! Well, anybody can buy the diploma and the school with the money that you have right?"

"Congratulations miss, now you are welcome to the real life." Said Danny's father walking closer to her.

Dara, who knew about the adventure of her daughter with that man, walked up to them and said "Yes, now my daughter is not a baby anymore. She is going to see the reality of life through the time, but if she gets hurt in any moment, here I am to defend her with my own life."

"Wow!" Adam said smiling "From mother to daughter you two look alike even in the attitude!"

"You are right father, to date Juliana you need to be a man that likes . . . beauty and . . ."

"And what?"

"Nothing beautiful, enjoy your day and I hope see you in the after party." Danny said as the conversation finished.

Dara and Juliana stared at them with a hateful look.

"Don't worry baby, I'm here to defend you against everything, even if I have to kill."

Juliana looked back at her mom and said "It's not necessary, I can handle it by my own mother . . . Where is dad by the way?"

"There he is." Dara said and pointed at him

"Daddy!" Juliana yelled running up to him. "C'mon lets go to the restaurant, I'm hungry"

"Where is your boyfriend? Did you call him yet?" her mother asked.

"Mom please stop!"

"I thought you invited him." Dara said trying to calm down her daughter.

"Mind your business please, you are always interrogating me, that's why I can't stand you!" said Juliana and walked as fast as she could to the car, but a hand stopped her. It was Monique.

Monique looked at Juliana with an *"ashamed look"* said, "Can I please talk to you?"

"About?" Juliana responded.

Monique stayed quiet, and threw herself on Juliana giving her the strongest hug she ever gave. Juliana hugged her back, but she was still wondering what was going on.

Monique crying said. "I miss you, I miss you a lot! I hope you could forgive me . . ."

Juliana smiled at Monique and sighting said. "I missed you too, but what you did was too low Monique."

"I know, I know . . . I'm sorry . . . I really do . . ."

Juliana smiled at Monique hold hands with her and said. "Promise me you won't do it again, swear it!"

"I do, I do. I promise." said Monique with a cheesy smile on her face.

And finishing the conversation, they hugged each other and the friendship was back again. From far, Juliana's parents were talking to Monique's parents, an African American couple that had the best 5th economic position in the whole Manhattan.

While they were holding a nice conversation with Monique parents, and Isaiah was showing the whole world his perfect known side. Dara was angry. She never liked Monique as a friend for her daughter. She was sending all the negative energy around, making her husband asked. "Honey? What's wrong?"

"Nothing my love . . . I just don't feel good . . ."

Isaiah looked at his wife and waited for his daughter and friend who were coming closer.

When our two favorite families were done talking, each family started walking in different directions. In this case, The Russell family was heading to a restaurant, where they were going to meet up with the rest of the other family.

Dara, who was sitting in the front seat turned and asked her daughter. "Why are you friends with that girl? I don't understand . . . you know I don't like her."

"Honey." said Isaiah interrupting.

"I'm serious, I don't like that girl . . . I think she is so fake."

"Ok mom, stop it! She is not your friend, and you are not the one who hangs out with her so don't stress it."

Dara looked at Juliana impressed by her words. "So, are you going to tell me not to think bad about that girl, after what she did to you?"

"What really happened Juliana?" asked her father feeling lost and looking confused.

Juliana looked at her mom with anger after her father's questioned her, but stayed quiet.

"I bet it was something little." Said her father while he was turning on the corner. "Probably an issue over a guy." He said entering to the parking lot of the restaurant.

"Yes daddy, you know us . . ."

Dara turned back facing the front window again, and stayed quiet until they got off the car.

When Caleb was done with the conference, he ran out of the building to his car. He knew somebody was going to be mad, and he called her. He called and called. He called so many times, he left her infinity of voice messages, and an unlimited amount of text messages and still she didn't reply. Juliana, on the contrary, was at the restaurant faking the smile, and faking that she was listening to her dad's and family's words. She wanted to see Caleb, she needed an explanation, so she excused herself, and headed to the bathroom. She turned on her phone and saw all the calls and messages that Caleb left her. She called back.

Caleb desperately picked up. "I'm sorry love!"

"What's your explanation?"

"The conference lasted longer love, I couldn't make it."

"Caleb at least you should have called me, I was so mad!"

"I know my love I'm sorry!"

"No, don't tell me you are sorry . . ."

"How can I make it up to you?" asked Caleb while he was sighting

Juliana smiled at her reflexion on the mirror and answered. "I'm in a dinner with my dad's family . . . maybe we can meet up later . . . If you want."

"Ok . . . that's good with me, but I really want to see you . . ."

"Ok you will, but I will call you . . ."

"No, I want to see you now . . ."

"What? Where is the educated, respectful man I've met?"

"He is here, where is my girl?"

"You want to see me because you want to give me my price right?"

"Yeah I bought you something . . ."

"I'm talking about my other price . . ." she said and laughed.

"It has been waiting for you . . ."

"Let me see what excuse I give to my dad so I can go see you . . ."

"No, no, you are eating with your family, I don't want you to leave them because of me."

"I don't care, I have to see you, I need you."

"I do too, but if it's a problem I don't want to cause it."

"My god, don't be silly! You don't want to admit that I got you sprung." Caleb laughed.

She blew a kiss over the phone and hung up.

Juliana changed in the bathroom really quick holding her cap and gown on both hands. Then, she walked up to a waiter and gave him a note and pointing at her mom and she told him the following "*Go and give this note to that woman over there please*". And as she finished smiling and flirting with him, she kissed him on the cheek and walked out of the restaurant through the back door, passing by the kitchen. She stopped a taxi and headed over her lover's apartment. When her mother read the note, she wasn't happy at about it. She excused herself, and faking that she had a headache, walked out of the restaurant, ran to the parking lot, and looked for her daughter. Dara was mad and worried, what kind of guy was this one? He doesn't go to his girlfriend's graduation but he makes her run to look for him?

The note said the following "*If you are wondering Mom, I'm going to meet up with my boyfriend somewhere around Time Square. Invent an excuse; I leave it up to you . . . Juliana.*"

Dara got her cell phone and called her husband, who was inside the restaurant with the rest of the family. She didn't want to go inside and apologize for her irresponsible and careless child.

"She did what?!" screamed Isaiah. He got up and apologizing to his family, he got out of the restaurant.

"Where is she?!" he screamed at his wife.

"I don't know! She said she was going somewhere around Time Square . . ."

"To see him right?" said Isaiah looking around as if he wanted to kill somebody.

Dara didn't want to tell him, she didn't want to give her the note that her daughter gave her, but she did it. Isaiah read it and said. "I'm going to kill that motherfucker!"

Dara scared of his words said. "Isaiah please! Don't talk like that!"

"She is going to extremes. I don't give a fuck if she is 18, I swear I'll put her on the lash I don't give a damn! It's enough with her!"

"What are you saying? What are you going to do?!"

"She is not going to stop until that guy be away from her . . ."

Dara worried responded scared "What are you going to do Isaiah? Don't go crazy please."

"If I don't invent something for him to leave her, she is going to keep seeing him . . . I'm a cop with businesses everywhere; I'm also in charge of the police department. Tell me what a simple engineer can do against me?" said Isaiah throwing hate through his words.

"You are not thinking about sending him to jail are you?" asked Dara.

"I'm going to talk to him . . . if he doesn't stop, then you will see what happens . . ."

"Are you going to get on that level?" asked Dara holding his shoulder strongly. "You can't go against the justice Isaiah."

"I create the law Dara . . . and no man is going to put my daughter against it."

"She didn't tell me how old is him, she just told me he is an electric engineer, that is going to have his own store of electronic devices."

"Yeah, he told me the same . . . but I don't know, there is something that I don't like . . . and if he doesn't back off, he is going to pay the consequences . . ."

"And Juliana? What about Juliana Isaiah?"

"If that girl doesn't listen to her daddy, then she is going to pay as well."

"Don't you dare to put your hands on my daughter Isaiah."

"She is our daughter, don't you forget that!" said Isaiah heated.

"She is mine more than yours. And you know that."

Isaiah looked at his wife with so much anger, walked up to her and slapped her hard. "Don't you forget that she is my daughter too Dara, I don't care if she is not my blood, I raised her, I gave her everything the world wouldn't have gave her with you by yourself . . . and don't forget you are my wife and you can't go against me . . ."

"Why? Because you are a cop? Because you bought this house and gave us all this luxury? I'm not scared of a corrupted cop like you, who makes profits from poverty . . . I don't fear you Isaiah."

"I have the education, the power, the strength . . . everything . . . don't you forget . . ."

Dara looked at her husband with anger. She couldn't believe what she was hearing, they were married for about 12 years and she never expected her husband to act this way.

However Juliana wasn't stressing what her parents were probably thinking, she was so into her love, nothing really mattered to her. As soon as she met up with Caleb, she just couldn't stop kissing him and rubbing his back while she was hugging him. She loved him more and more, each second, every minute that passed by; she just wanted to live to love him more. On the express way, she couldn't express how happy she was feeling, getting on top of her lover while he was driving, taking his shirt off, and making scandalous moves in front of whoever was on the other lanes. They were driving to Coney Island, where Caleb's friend Lucas was throwing a party. Caleb and Lucas met at Harvard School. Caleb was majoring in business, while his friend dropped out in the middle of his studies, because he found out that he wanted to be an actor. He came from a wealthy family, where his uncle later on, gave him a position in his company.

"My dear Caleb! Welcome to my house!" said Lucas coming out from the main door.

Caleb and Lucas gave each other a hug. Caleb then, introduced him Juliana, who's eyes started shinning when she met Lucas. Lucas was a good-looking man, he was about 6'2 tall, incredible body, amazing hazel eyes and perfect face features.

"Hey!" Juliana said smiling.

Lucas smiling back responded. "Nice meeting you . . . You are?"

"My girlfriend." Caleb responded.

"Wow! You always come up with surprises Caleb, I wouldn't expect it from you . . . it has been years that I haven't seen you so serious." Lucas said while he kept on staring at Juliana.

"Well, I guess people changed."

Juliana kept on smiling at Lucas, what was wrong with her? Wasn't she in love with Caleb? Didn't she say she would do anything for him? Why does she want to be with every attractive guy that she meets, and at the same time she wants to keep Caleb around?

Walking to the house, they walked through the big living room, which had crystal windows, and most of the furniture was white mixed with wood. The party seemed so perfect for such a lovely house. But that wasn't it. Juliana was amazed when she saw that half of the pool was the shape of the moon, and the other half the sun.

"I didn't know you had a party today." Caleb said.

"Well, I wasn't expecting that much people, but you know me, when I throw a party everybody is always welcome."

Juliana wasn't the only attractive girl there, there were women of different races, shapes, and all of them seemed to be between 23-34 years.

Her smile changed quickly when a beautiful blonde girl walked up to them and said hi to Caleb directly.

Juliana was sitting on a white chair, watching the scene. The blonde girl was hugging Caleb, it was so much their "friendship" that the blonde girl started kissing him consecutively on the cheek. Juliana got up from the chair and throwing the sun lotion on the floor, walked up to her boyfriend. She pushed the blonde woman and said. "And you are?" asked the blonde woman who looked at her from head to toes

"Juliana Russell, Caleb's girlfriend. Nice to meet you by the way, you are?"

The blonde's face turned full of surprised when she heard the words that were coming out of Juliana's mouth. "I am Amanda McMahan, Caleb's ex fiancé . . ."

Juliana's face turned red as a tomato, the heat that the sun was producing felt like it went straight to her feelings and head. "I'm guessing that was decades ago, because I'm his girlfriend now." She said smiled and kissed Caleb on the lips.

Caleb was mute.

"Well, yeah that was a few years ago, but that doesn't mean the feeling disappeared." Amanda responded.

"Really? Well, if the feeling didn't disappeared I don't think he'll be going out with other girls don't you think? I know I definitely erased you from his memory."

"Erase my memory from his mind? I don't think so, that's going to be impossible." said Amanda laughing sarcastically.

"Ok guys, that's enough." Caleb said by getting in between them. "I hate arguments and you two know it, so please drop the subject."

Juliana stared at Amanda hardly and she did as well.

"I'll see you around Caleb, next time just put your dog on a leash." Said Amanda and walked away.

Juliana furiously screamed. "Why you never told me about her, huh?"

"I didn't want to tell you, I mean, she is the past already. She doesn't mean anything to me."

"Yes, she does matter! She is your ex fiancé! What do you mean she doesn't matter! And you let her hugged you and kissed you on the cheek. Did you bring me here on purpose? Did you know she was coming?"

"Baby, I swear I didn't know she was coming, I didn't even expect her to say hi to me. I swear, I wouldn't even think about cheating on you. You know if I want to be with somebody else, I just break up with you . . . or matter fact I wouldn't even have a girlfriend. You think I'm going to make you waste your time or waste mine? Please, I'm a grown man I know what I want."

Juliana stayed quiet. She couldn't say anything, especially about cheating. She already lied, and destroyed the trust between them, and that was hurting her conscious.

The party started getting wilder, when a couple of girls started to kiss, and took off their bathing suits slowly.

Juliana and Caleb were eating in one of the tables with Lucas, when a girl walked up to their table. She was around 5'4, brown skin, brown eyes, curly hair, and the most outstanding part of her body was her butt.

"Who's she?" asked Juliana to Caleb.

"That's Lucas's girl" he responded looking at her from far. Lucas then, introduced her to Caleb and Juliana.

"Hey nice to meet you, what's your name?"

"Calypso and you?"

"Juliana, that's a beautiful name . . ."

"Thanks! Are you two going out?"

"Yes, oh sorry I forgot to tell you, she is my girlfriend." responded Caleb.

Juliana smiled at her, she never felt an attraction for women as much as she was feeling it when she saw Lucas girlfriend. The minutes started passing by, and the alcohol was taking over. Lucas's mansion turned to a movie event, where orgies, drugs and sex were controlling the party.

"Calypso come with me to the bathroom please?" asked Juliana to Calypso, who held her hand, and walked with her inside the house.

In the bathroom, Juliana felt her phone vibrating it was her mother.

"What you mean you showed him the note mom?!" screamed Juliana over the phone.

"Juliana I had to do it, he is your father!" said her mom who was on the other line.

"Oh my god, now he is going to dislike Caleb forever!"

"Juliana I did it because it was the best, I can't lie to your father!"

"Well mom, let me tell you something, this is it! I won't trust you anymore; the small friendship that we had it's over. I can't believe my own mother would betray me like that . . . and listen to one more thing. Not matter what you or dad want . . . I'm still going to be with Caleb, nothing will ever separate me from him, and if I have to kill, run away, disappear, or even get pregnant by him so you guys could leave me the fuck alone, I will."

"Juliana, don't make things worst, your father and I think that the best is for you not to be with him!"

"Mom, fuck what you and my dad want! I don't care! I'm 18 years old and I do what the fuck I want!"

"You have to come back to the house, Juliana at least tell me where you at?"

"I don't know if I would be able to go home after this."

"Juliana if you don't come home now then you aren't coming back!" Said Dara fearing the words that were coming out from her mouth.

"Ha! Okay, then I guess you just made that decision. I'm not going home anymore mom, bye." Juliana said and hung up.

"Is everything ok baby?" asked Calypso seeing Juliana hold on to the wall while she was getting out of the bathroom."

"Yes . . . I mean I just argued with my mother . . . we always argue, she makes my life so miserable."

"Don't say that . . . don't get angry over a little argument princess . . . you are too pretty to be feeling down . . . specially now, when we are all having fun . . . there is so much sex outside, so much to pop, so much to drink . . . don't be down."

Juliana stared at Calypso and Calypso getting closer to her grabbed her face and started kissing her. Juliana wasn't expecting it, she didn't know if she should push her off, or keep on going with the kiss.

"Sorry, I just find you very attractive" said Calypso after kissing her.

"I've never been with a girl before." Responded Juliana.

"You want me to show you?"

"Where are we going to do it?"

Calypso grabbed Juliana's hand and walked around the house getting to a small room that only had a sofa, a TV, and movies all over the floor.

"This is where I do it with Lucas."

"Are you sure no one will come?"

"I promise, just lay down."

Juliana laid down on the couch, and stared at Calypso's lips while they were exploring her body. She didn't want to believe what she was doing while her boyfriend was outside, waiting for her.

"You are so delicious baby, you are so yummy, tell me if you like it." kept on asking Calypso to Juliana who was moaning as if she was crying.

It was a different experience, something new to her, she was going crazier than when she was with Caleb, and she wanted Calypso down in between her legs. She didn't want her to stop, and she kept on going crazy. She couldn't stop the earthquake that her legs were producing from the volcano that she was feeling inside.

A couple of minutes later, Calypso and Juliana left the room and found Lucas and Caleb in the kitchen drinking.

"Where were the two of you?" asked Lucas.

"Playing around." responded Calypso.

"Do you guys have 3somes?" asked Juliana.

"Once in a while, it depends when are we on the mood." Responded Lucas.

"Why Juliana?" asked Caleb looking at Juliana

"I'm just wondering . . ." she responded.

"Well, we have to go, it was a fun day Lucas thanks for inviting me."

"No problem Caleb, just come back whenever. Sorry Juliana for the sexual scenes outside, but here everybody pops pills, and sniff coke, it's hard to avoid this when all that is around."

"No problem, I just can't do any of that."

"See you soon Lucas." said Caleb while he was walking away with Juliana.

"Where are you going?" Juliana asked.

"To your house?"

"No, I don't want to go home, let's go to your apartment."

"Are you sure?" Caleb asked.

"Yes I'm sure . . ." she responded rising her voice.

"Are you still mad about Amanda?" he asked.

"No, why should I be? I believe you."

"I don't know I was just wondering . . . you didn't seem too happy in the party when everybody was dancing, and singing."

Juliana sighted, and laid back on the car's sit.

When they got to Caleb's apartment, they didn't do anything but talk and talk. Juliana was telling him how she became Monique's friend again, and how Danny tried to make her feel down at graduation. Later on the night turned very hot. As soon as Caleb got out of the shower, he saw Juliana sitting on his bed completely nude.

"Come." she told him.

Caleb slowly contemplated her body and responded. "You are so beautiful."

Juliana slowly laid down on the bed and slowly started touching herself in front of her boyfriend. She closed her eyes and slowly her right fingers were going down through her own body. They started going from her lips to her neck, from her neck to her nipples, from the nipples to her belly, from the belly to her vagina, and from the vagina to her clit.

Caleb was sweating, he didn't want to miss the show, and he kept on contemplating.

Juliana then, started fingering herself, from slow to fast; her moans started speaking for themselves. While she was moaning she started calling him to eat her alive.

Caleb, who was completely anxious, threw the towel, took off his boxers and grabbed the condom that was in the left drawer near him. He was ready to give her a second eruption. He put it on, and he ran up to the bed. He got on top of his lover, and the penetration started slowly.

She was so wet that it made it faster for him to blow up. Her moans were consecutives; she didn't stop screaming his name while she was wrapping her arms on his neck.

Caleb, who had already come, was acting like a beast with her. He didn't have such an amazing sex like this as tonight, so wild, so passionate, and so erotic. He kept on going, as fast as she wanted, as hard as she wanted. From the back, front, side, legs up, legs wide open. But he kept on, when the eruption on her face was about to explode, and he suddenly stopped.

"What happened?" Juliana asked tired.

"The condom broke."

"Ok, but I don't think anything bad is going to happen, you held it when I moved right?"

"I had already came . . ." Caleb said trying to calm down.

"What? What do you mean?" she asked.

Caleb voice changed, and taking the condom off out of his penis said "I came in the condom when I was fucking you. When I felt that the condom broke, it was already inside you."

Juliana stayed quiet for impression; she didn't want to think that the worst was happening Caleb sat on the bed, and stared at the floor.

"You think . . . you think I may be pregnant?" she asked.

"I hope not." Caleb said trying to be calm.

"Oh my god, what . . . what are we going to do?" she asked starting to feel paranoiac.

"I guess wait . . . until your period comes . . . when is it supposed to come Juliana?"

"Today . . ." she said looking paled.

Caleb looked at her, sighted. "I guess we can wait for the next month to come?"

"I don't know . . . I guess . . ."

Caleb stared at her, put his arm around her, and said. "Don't worry, I'm with you no matter what . . ."

"Caleb, what are going to do if we find out that I'm pregnant?"

Caleb sighted. "I'm not going to lie, I'm not ready for a baby, and I know that nobody is born with the skills to be a father . . . but if I was man enough to put my pants down, I'm man enough to accept my responsibility."

"I hope when I take the test it will come out negative . . . I don't want to have a baby now . . ."

"Well, Juliana if God sends us that bless, we have to keep it . . . I don't believe in abortions . . ." responded Caleb and kissed her on the lips.

"I do!" said Juliana with an enormous furious. "I don't give a fuck what God is sending me, he better not send me a fucking baby because I don't want it. I want money, fame, everything but a baby no! Not for now! I rather abort it than destroy my amazing body with it."

"Juliana, are you hearing the things that you are saying?" said Caleb getting upset.

"I don't care Caleb, you know I can't keep the baby anyway . . . I won't be the model I want, I won't go to parties, no more weed, no more drinks, nothing! All that over a fucking baby!" she said getting up from the bed, and started getting dress.

"You are getting me upset."

"It's truth Caleb. You are not even ready for it. What are you going to tell my parents that hate you so much? Huh? Tell me? You haven't even met my mom yet . . . I don't know why, every time I try to introduce you something happens."

"I don't know either." Caleb said and started getting dress as well. "Come on, I'm going to take you home." Juliana, feeling bad about the argument they had said before she walked out of the room. "Hey, I'm sorry for the way I act sometimes ok? You know me, I just can't imagine a baby now."

"It's ok . . . God forgives everything, even the beasts like you."

On their way to Juliana's house, Caleb and her didn't talk at all. From just a moment of pleasure to a big problem of stress, they were feeling like if the sky was falling on top of them. For things that happen in life, the condom broke and it was for a purpose, he thought. But then again, what was the purpose? Why would be the purpose of them having a baby together? Why would God send them a blessing like this, when they are relatives? Even if they didn't know it yet, they were going to find out later or soon, but the damage was going to be worst for the baby that was possibly coming.

V.

I HATE YOU, MOTHER

As the days kept on going . . . As the society kept on growing, and as the people kept on living, reproducing and dying. The lovers were still together; they were still seeing each other, loving each day and night. The more arguments Juliana was having with her parents about seeing this guy, the more that she was falling in love with him. She told herself that she was going to do the impossible to keep the relationship alive, and unbreakable.

Until one day, she got home from Caleb's home, walked up to her room and ready to take off her clothes looked around and saw her mother sitting down in the sofa across her bed.

Her mom, who was mad at the whole situation, the fights, and her relationship with this man that neither of her parents accepted, got up, closed the door of her daughter's room and said. "We need to talk immediately."

"What do you want?" while she was holding her phone on her ear.

Dara stood up in front of her bed with serious face. "Hung up the phone . . ."

Juliana stood up and walking to her responded. "I can't . . . it's an important call, way more important than talking to you . . ."

Dara grabbed the phone from her ear and threw it on the floor, breaking it.

Juliana looked at her with hate.

"What the fuck! Who the fuck are you to be doing all this huh?!" Juliana cursed at her mom loudly.

Dara angry screamed until her face turned red. "I AM YOUR MOTHER!"

"I KNOW IT! AND I FUCKING HATE YOU! I WISH GOD HAD NEVER PUT ME ON YOUR FUCKING BELLY! YOU JUST DON'T KNOW HOW MUCH I HATE EVERYTHING ABOUT YOU! I HATE YOU! AND YOU EMBARRASS ME!" Juliana screamed back at her.

Dara's eyes got cloudy and softly she asked. "You hate me?"

"YES, I hate you mother, I don't consider you my mother either, I wish I could be adopted so like that I would say that you are not my mother!" Juliana said getting close to her.

"You can deny me, you can hit me, you can hate me Juliana . . . but NO MATTER WHAT IM STILL YOUR MOTHER! AND NOBODY CHANGES THAT! NOT EVEN THAT BOYFRIEND THAT YOU HAVE!"

"Well let me tell you something mom! He begs me everyday to introduce you to him, and you know what I said? I say no! Because it embarrassed me to tell the world that I came out of you! I hate you! I just fucking do! I can't stand you, I can't breathe the same air that you do, I can't fucking live! I want you to die!"

"I don't care . . . I do not care how much you hate me . . . I'm going to still love you . . . but I'm not going to let you disrespect me anymore . . ."

"Oh yea? What are you going to do?" Juliana asked laughing. "Prohibit me from going out? Tell me not to fuck my boyfriend? Oh, oh! In case you don't know it, I do fuck him, every night and let me tell you I ENJOY IT!"

"STOP IT!" Dara screamed crying.

But Juliana kept on going. "Stop what? That I enjoy his sex? Deny that I do suck his dick? Well mom let me tell you, I do enjoy being with him and I don't care if you or dad don't want me with him because I'm going to be with him all the time that I want!"

"STOP IT! I DON'T WANT TO HEAR THIS ANYMORE! PLEASE!" Dara kept on screaming while she was covering her ears and closing her eyes.

Juliana kept on talking following her around the room.

Dara crying said. "What have I done for you to hate me so much?"

"I just hate you mom, I hate the fact that I came out of you . . . I don't know why but I hate you . . . I can't stand you!"

"He made you like this right?"

"No . . . you should thank him for everything! Thanks to him at least I come home to sleep, and finished school . . ."

Dara cried, tried to hug her daughter, but this one rejected her and pushed her.

"Why did you do that to me? Why?" she asked her daughter.

"I don't want you hugs mom! You disgust me!"

Dara tried to hug her again, but Juliana was trying to get her off. Juliana threw her mom to the bed and lifted her hand up ready to slap her own mother, but another hand stopped her. It was her dad, who was tired of the arguments that were happening in the house every day.

"Dad" Juliana surprised said as she turned.

"Don't you dare to touch her because you are going to regret it" he said holding her arm up, ready to do something against her.

Juliana giving him attitude said "Why? What are you going to do to me?" She said and smiled.

"Juliana, Juliana don't you dare me because I'm not weak." he said throwing her arm down.

Juliana smiled on her dad's face. "I dare you."

Isaiah looked at her hard, trying to hold his hands. He was ready to hit her.

"I dare you to hit me and try to make injustice as you do it in the police department. Come on!" Juliana shouted. "Are you scared of your own daughter?! DO IT!" she screamed. "DO IT! HIT ME, AS YOU HIT THOSE CRIMINALS FROM JAIL! EVEN IF THEY ARE INNOCENT!"

Isaiah couldn't keep his hands down anymore and he hit her. He hit his "daughter" so hard that made her fall on the floor.

Isaiah closed and opened his eyes quickly and said. "I wish I could have a daughter"

Dara crying screamed. "NO! DON'T SAY IT!"

Juliana lifted her head up with tears running down her face, while her hand was touching her left cheek. "Say what?"

"Nothing baby, you know your dad." Said her mom trying to hug her but Juliana pushed her away from her.

"Don't touch me mom, please!" Then, she looked at her dad, and slowly walked up to him. "Say what dad?" she asked again.

Isaiah sighted, put his head down while he was sitting on the bed. and he responded. "I'm just asking you to leave him alone because he is damaging you . . . you never did such a thing . . . leave the family in the middle of the reunion the day of your graduation, come home drunk, smelling like cigarette, and now try to hit your mother . . . you never did such a things."

"Did you forget I'm 18?"

"It doesn't matter to me!"

"Yes it does. Now I choose what I want, I do what I want, and I be with who I want . . . what part don't you get?"

"I'm trying to protect you!"

"Hitting me is not going to stop me! I'm going to keep in seeing him, I love him."

"No you don't! What kind of man turns the one that he loves against her own family?!"

"He never turned me like this! You just weren't here to see me!"

"My daughter is not a rebel!"

"Well Mr. Chief, your daughter is a rebel, and if you don't like it then fuck you!"

"Don't talk to me like that! Isaiah said getting up from the bed.

"Fuck you!" Juliana screamed again.

Isaiah walked up to her ready to smack her, when his wife got on his knees. "Please, please don't hit my daughter, please Isaiah . . . don't do it." Dara begged him.

Isaiah stared at his wife on the floor, but he did not feel pity for her. He looked back at his daughter and said. "I'm not going to hit you like this . . . but if you can't stop being with him, then I'm going to take different measures . . ."

Juliana seemed scared of his dad's words and asked. "What . . . what are you going to do dad?"

"If you don't learn from the good way, then you will learn from the bad one . . ."

"Don't you dare to touch my boyfriend, I swear dad you will regret it!" she screamed.

"What are you going to do? Kill me?" Isaiah asked.

"He is my love, and I'll do anything for him . . ." Juliana responded tearing. "I will do anything even if I have to kill my own father . . ."

"Let's see who wins my daughter . . . let's see." said Isaiah turning back at her. "Just stay away from him and you won't see nobody hurt . . ."

"You can't do anything to him!"

"Give me a good reason why, why shouldn't I keep him away from you?"

"Because . . ." she cried.

Dara looked at her daughter, fearing. She had a bad feeling eating her heart.

"Because I'm pregnant!" she said letting her body dropped on the floor.

Isaiah eyes spoke for themselves, and so Dara's did. She was feeling like if the world was coming to an end. Juliana looked at her mom, then at her dad, and slowly walked up to the door and ran. Dara wanting to go behind her, tried but her husband stopped her.

"Let her go . . . today is going to be the last day that she will see him." Said Isaiah.

"What?" Dara asked.

"He's going to die. She is going too far with this."

"Isaiah, Isaiah . . . don't you dare to dirt your hands with blood!"

"I don't want her to ruin her life. She will not be a young mother . . . she is my daughter . . . and I'm going to do anything to keep her good." He said and walked out of the room.

That night was the saddest night that the Russell family had. Juliana spent that night on Caleb's apartment crying and crying like if it was the day of someone's funeral. She was feeling as if she didn't have any hope. She feared her dad's angriness, her mom words and her lover's love. She was scared to lose her family, but she was more scared to lose her love.

However, as Juliana was living a nightmare, her friend Monique was getting high, drunk, and having intercourse with Danny. Danny who turned completely to an "asshole", after finding out what happened between the only girl that he has only ever loved, and his dad.

Monique looking at Danny asked. "Whom are you calling?"

"My dad why?"

"For what? We are busy . . ."

"He wants to get busy too . . ." Danny said and smiled.

Monique gave him a strange look.

Danny was about to talk, when his dad opened his door and slowly closed it.

"Wow, do I interrupt?" asked Adam, his father.

Monique surprised by him coming in the room cover her chest with the sheets.

Danny looked at her and smiling said. "No, don't worry don't cover just show it, that's how you look sexier . . ."

Monique looked at him feeling awkward, and let him put the sheets down, so his dad could see her naked breasts.

"Wow Danny, you have a piece of art right there, chocolate skin, just how I like them. Well actually I like pink nipples but I don't mind, she looks delicious." Said Adam.

Monique felt upset.

"Wouldn't you dare yourself to get down with us two?" Danny asked her.

"What?" asked Monique looking confuse.

"My dad and I think that you are very attractive . . . and I was wondering if you would let us play with you . . ."

"What?! . . . Danny, but . . . No, no I can't sorry . . . No, I'm not like that . . ."

"Come on, I'm pretty sure Juliana would do it if I ask her . . . well, she already fucked my father, but you could be the first one to do it with us together."

Adam laying down next to them said. "The first one and the lucky one". He said wrapping his arms around her.

"That's truth. No girl ever had the pleasure to fuck us together . . . Come on, let us and you will be feeling better tomorrow, you will be more than Juliana . . ." said Danny smiling at her and looking at his dad. Monique quietly laid down back on the bed. Danny was on her right side and his father on her left side. They both started touching her, kissing her, and then played with her body.

"Danny, I don't think this is good." Monique said looking at him feeling strange.

"Monique please! You are messing up the whole scene, I love you, now you have showed me that you will do anything for me . . ."

"You really love me?" she asked.

Danny kissing her neck responded. "A lot! You just don't know . . . I love your body, your lips, the way you give me head . . . just everything."

Adam then started kissing her, and slowly prepared, expecting her to blow him.

Danny smiled at her and nodded his head saying yes.

Monique looked at his dad, who was on top of her while she was participating on the blowjob, and Danny started the penetration.

Monique was feeling sick. She felt like throwing up. She couldn't breathe.

"What's wrong?" Danny asked when Monique pushed him and his dad.

"I don't feel good . . ."

"What you mean you don't feel good? What's happening is completely normal . . . you know how many girls do it?"

"Yeah, but I don't know, I felt like I wanted to throw up . . ."

"Maybe I was fucking you too hard . . . well dad, let's change positions."

Danny smiled and gave her a kiss on the lips while they finished convincing the young girl to let them do what they wanted. Danny was kissing her, getting liquor and throwing it on her, while his dad was penetrating her. Monique face was covered in tears; she was feeling awful for what she was doing. She knew somebody couldn't love you if it makes you do all this kind of sick things. She closed her eyes, and her hands held tight the pillows. She couldn't hold it anymore, and started pushing Danny off, but this one didn't want to move. She was desperate, and started kicking his dad, and this one stopped.

"What's wrong!" Adam screamed getting off the bed.

"Sorry, but I can't do this anymore . . ." she said sitting up on the bed.

"Why?" Danny asked.

"Because I want to throw up . . . and I just feel like I don't have to do this to prove you that I love you!" she responded.

"So you are going to leave us like this?"

"Yes, I want to go home . . ."

Danny smiled at her and said, faking his smile. "Ok my love, don't worry . . . I still love you . . ."

Monique's eyes smiled and full of hope and said "Really?"

Could a girl be that stupid or it's just that she wanted to get his attention? How could it be that a girl would let a guy take advantage of her, fool her in that way, and promised her that she will receive love in return?

Danny got off the bed, and walked Monique outside the room. As they were going downstairs they started a conversation . . .

"Yes . . . I'll be back tomorrow . . ."

"Tomorrow I'm going to bring some of my closest friends, so all of us can have fun . . ."

"What do you mean by all of us?" she asked.

Danny smiled, and playing with her hair responded. "Monique, Monique . . . tomorrow you are going to be done with your proofs"

"What is happening tomorrow Danny?"

"Tomorrow I'm going to invite 3 of my closest friends, who I told them about you . . ."

Monique smiled. "You told them about us going out?"

"Mmm . . . yes . . . I did, but tomorrow they want to see if you are going to be the perfect girlfriend for me . . ."

"Oh, they know about you and Juliana?"

"Yes, they know . . ."

"And?"

"Tomorrow you are going to get naked in front of us, and dance, and please us . . . but don't worry you are not going to do anything of what happened today . . . because each one is going to have you individually . . ."

"So I have to sleep with them?" she asked looking confused.

"Pretty much, and after that, we are going to be officially going out . . ." he said.

"Why are you making do all this?"

"Because that's the only way that I'm going to see how far would go, just for me."

"Ok . . ." she said looking worried and sad. "So tomorrow, call me."

"I will me dear, I will." he said.

Monique tried to kissed him before she left, but he stopped her and smiling at her he said "No please, let's save them for tomorrow." Monique looked at him, and turning her face, walked away. She waited for her driver to pick her up. Suddenly, her phone started to ring. It was Juliana.

"Hello? Juliana, what happened?"

"Monique, I ran away from my house . . ."

"What? Why?"

"Because . . . oh my god, it's a long story . . . you think you can come see me right now?"

"Sure . . . where are you?!"

"At Caleb's"

"Ok I'm going to be there like in 10 minutes . . ."

"Thanks! I knew I could count on you . . . where are you coming from by the way?" Juliana asked throwing a big hope of happiness and hope.

Monique nervously responded. "Hmmm . . . I'll tell you when I get there; it's a long story . . ."

"Thanks."

Monique told her driver to take her to Caleb's house. Meanwhile, she was thinking how she was going to explain what she was doing with Danny, how she was going to tell her best friend that she betrayed her again.

"Wait for me right here, I'll be back in 20 minutes ok?"

Her driver smiled at her and nodded his head.

Monique smiled at him back, and walked in the building. On the elevator already, Monique stared at her reflection in the mirror. She looked dreadful; she didn't make anyone stare at her anymore. Her beautiful face and body were disappearing for the drugs that she continuously was taking every day. She was turning into a monster not only physically, but also emotionally. Her self-esteem was so low, that she believed that by doing exactly everything that Danny was asking her for, it will make her feel useful. As she got out of the elevator, she walked up to the PH 43, and rang on the bell.

Caleb opened the door and seeing her said. "Hey Monique, come on in!"

Monique didn't want to look at him; she felt like everybody knew what she did before she got there.

"Hey! I was waiting for you!" said Juliana who got up to hug her.

Monique smiled at her back and sat down on the couch.

"Thanks for coming Monique I really needed someone to talk to." Said Juliana.

"What happened? Why you ran out?"

Juliana looked at her, and then looking at Caleb looked back at her. "I'm pregnant."

Monique stayed shut for a moment and then said. "What?"

"I'm pregnant . . . and I was arguing with my parents . . . screaming, crying and bullshit . . . I told them I was."

"Did you just invent that or is it truth?" asked Monique who was in shock.

Juliana looked at Monique seriously and said. "I'm pregnant Monique, I don't play with shit like this, and you know it . . . the condom broke weeks ago, and I took the pregnancy test right now, and I guess I cursed my own self out . . . they all came out positive."

"Wow! Are, are you guys going to keep it?" Monique asked.

"I don't know . . . We don't know yet."

"I don't get it . . . I thought your dad liked him . . . Why would he tell you he doesn't want you with him?"

"He didn't like the way I was acting with everyone for him. He didn't like the way I love him, and now that I told them that I was pregnant, I guess he hates him even more."

"They both hate me, mom and dad." Said Caleb walking to the living room, and sat on the crystal table that was next to the sofa where Juliana was laying down. "And the funny thing is that I don't even know her mom . . ."

Monique stayed quiet for a few minutes, drank a little of water that Caleb served her. "I have something to tell you too."

"What is it?" Juliana asked.

Monique looked at Caleb and asked him nicely. "Would it bother you leaving us alone?"

Juliana looked at her, looked at Caleb again and asked. "Is it that personal?"

"Yeah" Monique said sighting

"Ok, don't worry. I'll go to my room." Caleb said getting up from the table, kissed Juliana in the lips and walked away. But then looked at her friend and asked. "What's going on?"

"Caleb!" screamed Juliana making him go away.

"I didn't want to tell you, but I need you to listen to me before you judge me."

"Ok . . . I won't judge you, but what's going on?"

"I'm . . . I'm going out with Danny Juliana . . . I'm dating him." Said Monique putting her head down

Juliana opened her eyes expressing surprise said "What?"

"Yes, but . . . but listen to me, I can explain and I need to ask you questions."

Juliana didn't want to say anything, and the silence took over.

Monique closed her eyes, and slowly opened them, and her story began. Juliana couldn't believe what her ears were hearing. Why would Monique, a good girl, who graduated with the best grades in the whole class, get on this level? Where her education was left? What happened to her dreams, goals, and self-respect went? Juliana was in completely shock about the atrocious words that her friend was saying.

And as Monique kept on telling her about all the things that she was doing for Danny just to make him happy, tears started coming out of her eyes while her lips kept on talking with fear. Her hands were touching each other like if they were scared of somebody else.

Juliana surprised, amazed, grabbed her friend's hands. "And today Monique . . . what happened today?"

Monique looked at her and said "He told me . . . he told me to do it with him and his dad . . . that like that he was going to actually figured out that I would do anything for him . . ."

"And . . . why did you do it!?" she screamed. "Don't you have a brain to think?! I mean, I thought you were stupid Monique, but not that stupid! You are abasing yourself for him!"

"I didn't know . . . I mean, Juliana I knew it was wrong, but I did it because . . . I really want to be with him, and I, I thought it was going to be fun, and just . . . I don't know, I thought that by doing it, I was going to forget it . . . you know they say what is done is forgotten . . ." said Monique crying.

Juliana gave her that illogical look; she was incongruous about her friend's answer. She was thinking, wondering what was worst? A woman raped or a young girl letting the whole family do whatever they wanted, and humiliated her.

"Listen, listen to me Monique. I want to know why you did it for?! What did he give you back?! Did he pay you for it?! Huh! Because if I was you, I wouldn't let no guy do such a thing to me, I would get off that bed and walked out!"

"He said that he didn't need to ask you for a 3som, because you already fucked his dad, so it didn't matter . . . and then, he told me that . . ."

Juliana, who was walking around the sofa, back in forth, turned and looked at her and responded. "Told you that what? What did he tell you Monique?!"

"That to officially go out with him, to publish it in the newspaper, tomorrow I had to fuck 3 of his close friends . . ."

"WHAT?!" Juliana screamed.

"He . . . he said that they needed to see if I was good enough for him, to please him, to be the girl that he wanted . . ." Monique said standing up.

"And what did you say?" asked Juliana who was going crazy in the room.

"I asked him . . . well, I told him, because I'm sure that you didn't do that . . ."

"Of course I didn't do that! I don't need to fuck guys to get to one!" screamed Juliana again.

"He said that you didn't do it, but also he said that's why you weren't the one for him . . . and that . . . he never enjoyed anything with you, not even what happened on prom night when you left him after Caleb called you."

"What? How . . . how did you find out? I never told you that."

"That day, at Danny's party, you did it with him . . . I was hiding in the closet, but you thought I was downstairs . . ."

"Monique, why were you in the closet?" Juliana asked hysterically.

"He told me to get in the closet to watch you and him doing it, so I could learn all the things that he liked . . ."

"He didn't know, I didn't even know if we were going to do it . . ." responded Juliana.

"He didn't know if he was going to fuck you, yeah I know . . . but if it wasn't you it was going to be another girl."

"Monique, ok, that's enough . . ." Juliana breathed. "You betrayed, you snitched on me, your parents, my parents, the whole world thinks I'm such a bad influence for you . . . but look at you . . . you are the biggest . . . ! Should I keep on trusting you Monique? Should I? Or if I let you hold my trust in your right hand, you are going to try to give it away with the left one? Answer me!!! Did I make a big mistake by telling you what's happening to me now? Are you going to betray me and Caleb?"

Monique didn't do anything but looked down . . .

They stared at each other for a few seconds and suddenly Juliana slapped Monique hard.

Juliana stared at her. "What are you going to do? Huh? You think that guy, what's his name? Oh yeah, DANNY! . . . Tell me Monique, you think that guy is going to take you serious? They treat you the way that you treat people . . . and if you are behaving like a loose woman, they are going to treat you as one!"

Monique screamed. "WHY ARE YOU TELLING ME THIS! WHY! YOU ALWAYS HAVE HAD EVERYTHING JULIANA! EVERYTHING! IM TIRED! I'm tired of the world treating me as second! I always wanted to be the pretty girl that has everything, the popular one; the main star of the galaxy . . . but you! You always had it all . . . and it's not fair! Because you don't even deserve it! You treat everybody like shit, even your own mother!"

"Shut up, SHUT UP!" Juliana screamed. "Don't talk about my mother Monique, don't you dare to get to that level . . ."

"Oh wow! Now you are defending the woman that you hate the most?! Don't you remember how in school, when they wanted to call your parents you always used to give your father's first than you mother's, because you didn't want them to see her?" said Monique getting closer to her face.

"Why do you care huh? Why?!"

"Because your mother is such an incredible woman, and I wish, I wish I could have a mother like that . . ."

"You are stupid Monique, you are stupid, a traitor and a little bitch . . . I don't know how the fuck I have been your friend for all these years . . ."

"You are not going to help me?"

"Help you?

"I want Danny, I want him bad . . . but I want to gain his heart in a different way . . . I don't want t fuck his friends . . ."

"Go to hell Monique." Said Juliana walking away from the living room, leaving Monique alone.

Confusion, fear, what was going on with Monique? What was making her think and act like this for a man, when there were thousand of them out there? Would anybody get to this point, get this far, just to keep that person that they want the most? Well, apparently yes, and Monique was a big example of it, and a big example of ignorance or love?

The next morning, Juliana woke up alone on Caleb's bed. He was at his job; it was 10: 34 am.

At 10:38 am, her father, Isaiah was making several phone calls. He was ready to make Caleb disappear from his daughter's life.

At 12:30 pm, 3 men stood outside of his job. Not trying to be obvious, they walked around and around, drinking coffee, eating hot dogs from the Hispanic woman in the corner who sells them every morning.

Caleb, who was in charged of his job, including everybody in it, forgot to eat breakfast, and forgot his lunch. His stomach was craving urgently for food.

"Lucy, I'll be back I'm going to grab some lunch, cause I'm not leaving the office until late . . . so if anyone looks for me tell them I'll be back in 15." Said Caleb to his secretary and walked away. He went to subway but it was busy, and the cafeteria across the street was closed. So having no other option, he walked up to one of the Hispanic woman that was always selling hot dogs in the corner.

"Buenos días señora." He said smiling trying to speak Spanish as much as he could making the lady laugh.

"1 hot dog?" the chubby, short, Hispanic woman asked.

"Yeah, how much is the big one?"

"$3.50" the woman said getting the hot dog, putting it on a paper dish.

"Ok, give me two please." And as he finished talking, he looked for his wallet in his right pocket, and taking money out, a tall man ran by him, pushed him and took his wallet with him.

Caleb confused, turned, and ran after the man that robbed him. Everybody was looking at them running. 3 cars stopped, 2 women fell on the street being pushed by the thieve and 2 policemen who knew what was going down just looked to the opposite side pretending like nothing was happening. Behind Caleb there were 2 men running too. One of them was on the left side of the block, and the other one a few feet away from him. The thief ran to an alley, where he threw himself on the floor, making Caleb think that he was tired. Caleb, mad about the situation, grabbed the man by the shirt and right when he was about to punch him, he felt a strong pain on the rib. He fell on his knees, and touching his rib, tried to turn to see who was behind him. There were 2 men, each one on both sides, and one standing right there in front of him pointing at him with a gun. Caleb closed his eyes, he couldn't even talk, and thinking that he was about to die, instead of shooting him one of the thieves stabbed him on the chest several times. Caleb's body dropped on the floor, looking at the blurry sky, he closed his eyes and the lights of his world turned off.

The thieves ran away, to the spot where their car was parked. They got in it, and one of them made a phone call.

"Good job. Now leave before I arrive to the scene." Said a man with a deep strange voice on the other line.

The ambulance and police arrived at the same time for his good luck. As soon as Caleb was taken into the ambulance, the police started investigating his case. The police officers that arrived to the crime scene didn't understand how such an act was able to be committed in the middle of the day, in front of thousands of watchers, and police all over.

Isaiah's plan worked out. Everything came out as planned it, Caleb was stabbed, and hopefully dead, and nobody was going to find out about it. He was also thanking to the policemen that were working around the area that knew about it and pretended well that nothing was happening.

At 1:30 pm Caleb's phone didn't stop ringing, Juliana was going crazy, she had been calling him for the longest and he still didn't call her back. She was alone at his apartment, cooking, washing dishes, cleaning the house, doing things that she's never done before.

At 2:05 pm, Caleb's house phone started ringing; it was one of the police officers who found his wallet on the floor.

Juliana hoping that it was Caleb, answered the phone.

"Is this the residence of Caleb Smith?" a cop asked.

"Yes, yes it is, who's this?" Juliana answered worried.

"This is Officer Gonzales, who am I speaking with?"

"With his girlfriend why? Where is Caleb?"

"Ma'am, Caleb is here in the hospital . . . he was stabbed today."

Juliana who was about to faint tried to respond to the officer. "What . . . ?"

"I'm sorry that you have to hear this, but he is in the emergency room here on Belview hospital on 28 street." Responded the officer.

Juliana, who was in shock, hung up the phone softly and sat down, on the cold marble floor. Her soul was scared, her heart was beating fast, She was afraid. She wanted him to go back; she wanted to hear words coming out of his mouth so she could make sure that everything was ok. Putting both of her legs close to her chest; she put her head on top of them and cried, cried like if she was about to throw up. She felt like her world was about to end, she felt like everything that was good in this world was against her. She started hating herself, hating her God for not letting her be happy with whom she wanted. She was wondering what she has done wrong, what was going on that it was making her not be with her love. She wanted to kill herself, she felt like if he wasn't alive for her, her own child didn't need to be born. She was just, in few words, heartbroken, devastated, almost in a comma. She opened a drawer, grabbed a knife and laid down, and her tears along with her hair, body, and saliva invaded the floor. She wanted to welcome her own death.

She knew that crying nothing was going to be solved. *"Come on Juliana get up!"* Was saying her head. *"Come on Juliana get the courage that you have out and go and see him, he needs you"*. Juliana got up from the floor, threw the knife around, and running downstairs with the same clothes that she on, jumped in her car. Tears and tears, and nothing but a sea of tears that were full of sad memories and unsecured prophecies were going down her face. As she was driving, her dad was as well. He was on his way to the hospital to talk to the detective that was there. Unfortunately, he got there before his daughter, and walked up to the emergency room, showing at everybody that was on his way, his high rank plaque.

Isaiah shook hands with the detective, who was taller and swollen than him. And as they said hi, Isaiah started asking questioning him.

"So . . . what have you found out about this case?"

"It's so unpredictable the way these gangsters have been killing people lately . . . specially for a couple of dollars. Apparently, they were 3, but after that they ran to a car, an expensive one. So we can definitely say that they were sent to kill this businessman by somebody."

Isaiah smiled at him and said. "Do you think someone would waste their time and money by hiring cheap hood boys to kill an ordinary man for a few dollars? I don't think so."

The detective looked at Isaiah serious and responded. "Excuse me Mr. Russell but we are living in one of the cities that have one of the highest averages of delinquency. Of course I can believe that anything can happen."

"I don't think somebody sent 3 individuals to stab somebody just for a simple wallet, unless this individual was a very powerful person in the country, which I doubt."

"So, what are you saying?" asked the detective.

"I'm saying that they were simple delinquents, and we just have to look for them by the cameras, arrest them and that will be it."

"So, you are telling me to drop the case here?" asked the detective surprised.

"Of course! What else can you do? I mean, nothing bad happened, they didn't kill him."

"Sir, the man is about to die, and you are telling me just to drop the case?"

Isaiah looked at him with a mean look and said. "How long have you been in the investigation department of Manhattan?"

"A couple of months." the detective responded.

"Do you know who I am right?" Isaiah asked him.

"Yes sir." the detective responded.

"Well, if you don't want to lose the opportunity of becoming the best detective around, then quit it."

The detective looked at him and stayed quiet for a few seconds, and then he spoke again, "Then, who is going to take charge of the case?"

"That's none of your business."

The detective looked at him amazed; he could not believe what was happening. He was starting to believe that Isaiah was probably one of the many men whom were part of the contribution to the pollution of the criminal investigations and crimes that never had solutions.

Juliana at that moment got inside the room, looked at her father and at the detective surprised.

Isaiah looked at her and asked. "What are you doing here?"

"What you mean what am I doing here? He is my boyfriend, you thought I was going to leave him alone?!" she responded with a huge attitude.

"Juliana don't start with the attitude please . . ."

"Attitude? What attitude dad? I didn't come here to see you, I came here because of him, the reason why I live for . . ."

The detective looked at Isaiah surprised about what was going on. Then, he wondered, why Mr. Russell wanted to make him drop the case for? The case where his own daughter's boyfriend was involved? Why would he let this case be forgotten as if Caleb was a random individual?

"If you are going to stay here dad, please I'm going to ask you . . . I'm going to beg you not to make your comments. I'm not in the mood to hear your ignorant phrases; I don't want to argue with you." Juliana said mean as ever.

The detective stayed quiet, he never though that someone in this world would talk to Mr. Russell in that way. But yes, someone did, and that person, the only person who had the balls or ovaries to talk to him like that was his own daughter.

Isaiah gave him that mean look, and walked out of the room, leaving the detective and Juliana alone. Juliana cried when she got closer to her love. She knew that if Caleb disappeared from her life, she wasn't going to be the same person. She knew she was going to change and ran away from the only society that knew her. The detective looked at her, and whispering said. "I'm sorry that you going through this pain Miss . . ."

Juliana was looking and touching Caleb's hand. "Miss Russell, yes, I am Mr. Russell's daughter."

"Oh, wow, I was just wondering why your father wouldn't want to investigate about this case." the detective asked.

Juliana wiped her tears and turned, and looked at him. "What?" she exclaimed.

"I was in charge of this case, but then your father told me not to get involved. He told me to drop the case. He told me that it wasn't that much of a big deal . . . a minor crime.

"Are you serious?" she responded.

"Yeah, and I had to say yes." The detective sighted. "I had to say that I wasn't going to be involved in this case, because if not he would make me lose my job."

Juliana, who wasn't impressed about her father's attitude, started walking up to the window that was across from Caleb's bed. "I'm not impressed about his words . . ."

"Why?" the detective asked.

"My parents don't like him, so I'm not surprised if my father won't even take importance to this case."

The detective looked at Caleb, and then looked at her. "Miss Russell, if you wish, I can take the case . . ."

Juliana turned and faced him and interrupting him said "Go head, do it . . . Because if you don't do it, believe my father won't do anything for him."

"But I need to ask you something before."

"What is it?"

"What is the reason why your father and your boyfriend hate each other?" he asked.

Juliana walked up to Caleb, and touching his hands said. "I don't know, I don't know how it started. My father said I changed too much since I met him. Then, my mother started telling him things about my relationship. Then, later on, I got into a big argument with both of my parents . . . and I ended up telling him about me being pregnant."

"And . . . are you pregnant?"

"Yes." She said tearing.

"Have you ever thought that your father, being a powerful man could maybe have managed all this?"

Juliana looked at him and with an attitude responded. "What the hell is your problem? What are you saying about him? Because if you are I think you should tell him on his face and see the results after it!"

"Ms. Russell I didn't mean it in a bad way." he said apologizing.

Juliana took a deep heart breath and said. "Ok, you know what? I'm going to try to relax, because I don't feel like arguing with anyone, especially with a cop."

"I am not a simple cop, I'm a detective, and I guarantee you one of the best."

"And . . . what's your name by the way?"

"Detective Robin."

"Ok, Mr. Detective, can you please leave the room? I do no want to see your face anymore." The detective looked at her as if he wanted to slap her. But in silence, he walked out of the room. And as he opened the door, Monique came in the room. Juliana seemed surprised and not that comfortable about her presence at that moment.

"What are you doing here Monique?" Juliana asked. "Didn't I tell you I don't have time to hear your stupidities?"

Monique threw a deep heart breath. "Juliana, I know I shouldn't have came, but . . . I really wanted to see you . . ."

Juliana got up from the chair and looked at her friend. "You are already here; I guess there should be a good reason why you came right?"

"I wanted to tell you that I love you and that I'm going to be here if you ever need me. I mean, I know right now you are going through a lot. I know your boyfriend got shot and everything and I know that you feel so disgusted about me because of my actions. But I still wanted and I came to tell you that I really care about you. I really want to be here for you . . . I love you, you are my best friend and . . ."

Juliana cut her words interrupting her. "You WERE my best friend, the only best friend I had and I know I'm going to have forever is Caleb."

"Juliana, please don't say that . . . I am your friend . . ." said Monique as her eyes got cloudy.

"Monique, you have betrayed me so much. First with my ex boyfriend then . . ."

Monique interrupted. "But you don't care about him!?!"

"Oh yea? Tell me how do you know that? Are you on my mind? Are you the thoughts that I have every morning when I wake up?"

"No. But I am your friend, and you always tell me everything."

"No Monique I did tell you my deepest secrets and you betrayed them too. I should have never trusted you."

"Juliana, please don't say that . . ." said Monique trying to hug her.

"I gave you my trust, I trusted you Monique, I told you everything, everything! And you told Danny all that! You told him and did things for him that I know you wouldn't ever have done for me. You ruined my reputation, you tried to destroy my image, and you did all this just to get what you wanted. You are greedy Monique, and I don't want somebody like that as a friend." Said Juliana as she walked to the door, and opened it waiting for her friend to leave the room.

"I'm sorry, I know I was wrong, but everybody deserves a second chance Juliana."

"I gave you too many chances, and everybody deserves it, yes. But that doesn't mean that you have one from me."

"Why?" Monique asked wiping her tears.

"Because Monique, if I give you a 2nd chance, who knows what would happen to me. Maybe I would end up killed like . . . like Selena too."

"Oh please Juliana, you are exaggerating."

"No I'm not! As she put her trust on her so-called "best friend" I did too. And as she gave her more opportunities, I gave them too, as she thought she was going to do well, she lost, and I did too. You told him things that were my personal secrets. Things that the world shouldn't know."

Monique stayed quiet, letting the tears roll down her face.

"So please, I'm going to ask you nicely to get the hell out of this room." Juliana said looking at her, expecting her to get out of the room already.

Monique, who had the face red and full of tears running down, looked at her and walked out. Juliana, who was hurt by her own words wanted to cry, but then again she thought and said to herself. "*That friendship won't take her anywhere but to the depression and failure.*" As Juliana was closing the door, she heard a voice saying, "You were too mean with her". Juliana turned and saw Caleb trying to speak. Juliana ran up to his bed, and grabbed his hand and exclaimed with joy.

"Oh my god . . . You talked!"

Caleb tried to move his head to face her, but it caused him pain.

"No, no don't do that. It's ok baby, I'm here." she said trying to help him.

"I don't know what happened."

"It doesn't matter, it's all over." she said giving him the sweetest look.

"The first thing that I worried was you . . . I, I love you." he said.

"I love you too sweetheart." She said kissing his left hand. "I love you too much to let you die."

Caleb breathed deeply. "I missed you . . ."

"What are you saying? You didn't go anywhere . . ." she smiled. "What are you talking about?" She asked again.

"I felt for a moment . . . like if I died . . . I felt like if I wasn't coming back, I felt like I wasn't going to see you again. I was scared. I was scared to think that I won't ever be able to touch you." he confessed as he started crying. "I was scared to lose you . . . Juliana I wish you could just imagine how much you mean to me . . . I wish for a moment you could wish how much I love you."

"Don't worry, don't worry love . . . you will never lose me, because there's nothing in this world that would ever separate us." Juliana responded crying. "Nothing, not even if they tell me that you have the most serious incurable disease, I will always be there with you."

Caleb smiled. "You are my little one; you are my sunshine, the sweet voice that wakes up my soul at night, in the morning. You are my little princess; you are what I wanted all my life . . . I want to be with you forever, you are the only one that I can actually be with and don't doubt of . . ."

Juliana, hearing his words felt bad from one point. As he was talking, she was remembering. Remembering all those times that she had hurt his trust, she was remembering those times when she was unfaithful to his heart. But now, that all this happened to him, she knew, she swore, she told her God, that she wasn't ever going to let temptation take over her power, her body, and her feelings. She was stronger, she was more into her own decisions, she was changed and feeling mature for the first time.

"Can I ask you something?" Caleb said.

"Of course, anything you want." she responded, holding his hand.

"Did you ever crossed the line and stopped being faithful to my heart?"

Juliana stayed quiet, looking, staring at his eyes. He was bad, about to die. It was a tragically moment should she keep on lying?

"Juliana?" he said again.

"Yeah?" she responded.

"Can you answer the question?" he seemed worried.

Juliana sighted, and deeply breathed again. "No, of course, I had never cheated on you Caleb. I have always been faithful to you."

Caleb smiled and held her hand stronger. "Thanks! I'm so happy to know that you are the one that I've always needed with me. Thanks my love, thanks for showing me what love really is. I'm here, about to die . . . and your presence will make my pain sweet, taking care of me . . . taking care of this boring man . . ."

Juliana interrupted. "Don't say that . . . you aren't a boring man, and of course I was going to be here, next to you . . . because I love you . . ."

Juliana got closer to her lover, and kissed his dry lips. She kissed them closing her eyes letting her tears fall on his face.

"What's wrong?" he asked.

"I guess I must be happy . . ."

"Why?"

"I'm happy to know that you are alive, and that nothing happened to you . . . I'm happy just seeing you here talking, moving and of course, loving me." She responded.

Caleb, wanting to hugged her tried to move his arms but it was too much effort.

"Don't move, it's not good for you." She said trying to hold him down.

Then, a nurse went in the room. She was a short, chubby lady who was wearing a white small hat, white long skirt, and white shirt, which had a small title on top of her left breast with her name on it.

The nurse looked at Caleb and said. "Oh wow, you opened your eyes . . . that was fast."

"My mom once told me, that everything bad in this world don't die soon." Caleb said being sarcastic.

"Caleb please don't say that." Responded Juliana.

"Don't worry, is normal that patients from emergency talk like that." said the nurse smiling.

"What do you mean?" Juliana asked.

"After they have fainted or they haven't been awake for any circumstance, they always wake up saying phrases, quotes with no type of meaning. Do you understand me now?" The nurse said, checking his pressure.

Juliana smiled at Caleb. "Oh well, I guess she is trying to call you crazy."

"Hmm . . . something like that . . ." the nurse said writing on her checklist after finish checking his pressure.

Caleb laughed and then softly touching his belly screamed. "ouch!"

"Does it hurt here?"

"Yes, a lot! Every time I want to move, and right now, when you just touched."

"Well, you shouldn't move too hard then, remember that you just got stabbed. And I'm not talking about a minor stab; they stabbed you on the chest. 1 cm closer and you wouldn't be here alive. Those criminals knew what they were doing."

"Please, please don't talk about it. I think he had enough for today."

The nurse looked at Juliana and asked. "Isn't your father in charge of the police department of Manhattan?"

"That's correct."

"He was here earlier, he told me he is going to take the case."

"When did he say that?" Juliana asked.

"Like a few minutes ago . . ." said the nurse who was about to leave.

Juliana worried, asked. "What do you mean by few minutes ago? I thought he left like around an hour ago, when did you speak to him?"

The nurse, who was walking to the door, stopped, giving her back at her. "Hmmm . . . before he left, I already told you." Said the nurse and rushed.

Caleb surprised, looked at Juliana and asked. "Baby, what's wrong with you?"

"Nothing. Why you said that?"

"You seem too paranoid about your dad talking to people."

Juliana breathed deeply. "It's just that . . . I don't know . . . it's so strange, this whole situation. I mean, I didn't know my dad was going to take your case, I thought I had to go to the police department and pay for it."

"I can't believe your father is taking care of my case . . . I thought he didn't like me."

"I know . . . he made the detective that was going to take your case quit."

"Quit? Why?" Caleb asked.

"The detective told me that my dad was going to fire him if he was involved in this." She said helping him to get comfortable on the bed.

"Wow, your dad is weird . . ."

"And then, the detective asked me how did I know if my dad didn't have anything to do with all this?"

"What?"

"Yeah I know, he's stupid."

"No wait, what do you mean he said that?"

"He asked me if my dad had something to do with this entire situation. Like trying to say that my dad was involved in this crime. I got so upset, and I told him to leave too, what a stupid moron!"

"And what if he is right?"

"What?!"

"Juliana, you know your father wouldn't act like this about my situation. I mean, you know he wouldn't even be this interested about my case at least if he had something to do with it."

"What are you saying? How could you talk like that about my father? What is wrong with you! My father may be a really mean person but he wouldn't kill anybody!" she raised her voice with a mad tone.

"Honey, I'm not saying that, it's just that it surprised me the way that he seemed so interested in my case."

"So what? Maybe he wants to help!"

"Yes, you are right maybe he does want to help, but I'm saying why would he fire the detective and tell him that he was going to kick him out of the investigation department and all that?"

"I don't know Caleb! Maybe my dad noticed like me that the detective was stupid! And you are getting stupid too, how the fuck are you going to say that my planned all this to kill you?"

"Baby I wouldn't say this to hurt you . . . I didn't mean it like that."

"Caleb you said it, and you thought about it. What's going to be next? How are you going to tell me that you love me when you think that my family wants to kill you?"

"Baby, please calm down, you don't have to be screaming." he asked her nicely, trying to keep her calm in the room.

Juliana crying responded. "I don't care!"

"Oh please, don't cry, baby please I'm getting a headache."

"So what! Fuck you and your headache!" Juliana walked out of the room and slammed the door as she closed it.

25 minutes after Juliana walked out of the room, detective Robin got in Caleb's room.

Caleb looked at him strange and asked, "Who are you?"

"I'm detective Robin, I was in charge of your case."

"I never asked for a detective."

"Well, sir, you don't have to ask for anybody to take your case, I was in the place where you got stabbed, and I wanted to talk to you about it. Maybe you want to investigate about these people that tried to kill you." The detective responded.

"For what?" Caleb asked. "I don't remember their faces, I'm getting well, I don't think there's going to be a point sending them to jail when they won't ever give me back all this time and pain that I'm feeling."

"Sir, I'm here to help you. I really would like to investigate what really happened to you. You are not any common citizen. You are somebody important in this city. You know in how long you appeared in the news? The newspapers today were talking about Mr. Smith getting stabbed, detailing in the front pages."

"I don't care, I just want to get well, and go back to work."

"I heard Microsoft and possibly Mac would offered you a contract . . . how long would it take you to sign it after the news increase your popularity?"

"What? How do you know about that?"

"Sir, I'm a detective"

Caleb looked at him suspicious and said. "Look, just stay out of this."

"Why? Are you scared of Mr. Russell?" the detective asked.

"Why are you saying that?"

"I apologize; I shouldn't have come in the first place." The detective said and got up from the chair where he was sitting at, and walked up to the door.

"Wait!" Caleb screamed making him stop. "Are you the one who thinks that Isaiah had something to do with me getting stabbed?"

D. Robin turned. "It was some ignorant thought that I said."

"No wait. Tell me, I swear I need to know. I just got into an argument with his daughter about all this. I don't think you'll say something like that for no reason." Begged Caleb.

D. Robin walked up to his bed and sat on the chair. "He told me to get away from this case. He knows I just got in the department of investigation. He told me he was going to kick me out if I was around. He said he was going to take charge of it."

"Why would he say that?" asked Caleb getting more into the topic.

"I don't know, I don't want to think badly."

"What are you saying?"

"I don't want to talk crap, because I'm not sure of what happened in the past . . . but as you know people talk. I've heard that he is a man that doesn't play games. He is powerful, and he does anything to get what he wants. My father used to work with him."

"And why don't you tell your father about it?" said Caleb trying to put a solution.

"My father is dead" Robin responded.

"Oh, sorry to hear that." Caleb said regretting his last sentence.

"It's ok."

"How did he die . . . if you don't mind me asking?"

"In an accident, the train ran him over."

"Wow!" Caleb said raising his eyebrows.

"He was driving with Isaiah Russell . . ."

Caleb interrupted. "My girlfriend's dad?"

D. Robin breathed deeply and said. "Yes, your girlfriend's dad. They were going to investigate who killed Officer Baron; he was in charge of the police department of Manhattan at that time. Russell and my father were really close friends. He was really there for us, especially after my mom died. My dad was worried; he really wanted to know who killed Baron. One day, Isaiah Russell called my dad really early in the morning, around 4 a.m., apparently he told him that he found where Baron's body was at. I remember my dad kissing me in the forehead and leaving. I've always been part of this crime life, ever since I was little, when my dad used to come home, and go to his office, and study the cases. I was somehow sneaking to see the pictures of the investigations. However, that day I had a bad feeling, I felt like I wasn't ever going to see my father again. I grabbed my bicycle and I tried to follow my dad, but I got lost in the way. When I got to the place where he was with Isaiah Russell, all I saw was Russell looking at the train passing as fast as it was coming, I heard a man screaming *"don't push me, don't push me!"* and when the train stopped . . . I saw a pair of shoes that I recognized, and as I got closer to the scene, I saw my dad's body pretty much destroyed on the railroad. I didn't say a word since that day I was mute for years. All I remember was Isaiah Russell standing in front of my dad's body like if it was nothing. I ran over to my dad's body to touch him, and he was destroyed, all his bones were broken."

"Your dad was killed." Said Caleb.

"No one ever found who killed Baron . . . and later on, months after, Russell became the head of the police department, and he still in it."

Caleb interrupted. "Hold up, so if your dad wouldn't have die that means that he would have been in charge of the police department?"

"Yeah . . . probably."

"Do you think that Isaiah killed your dad?"

D. Robin breathed deeply and looked at Caleb. But when he was about to answer, Isaiah came into the room.

"Detective Robin, I'm surprised you are still here, didn't I tell you I was on charged of Caleb's case?" Isaiah said and laughed hard.

"I called him, Mr. Russell." responded Caleb.

Isaiah looked at Caleb with a very deep mean look and said. "My dear Caleb, you are awake!" He smiled, and then looked at Robin.

D. Robin got up from the chair, ready to leave. "Well, I'm going to leave. I hope you'll feel better Caleb." He said putting the chair next to the table that was next to Caleb's bed.

"Alright Mr. Robin it was a pleasure talking to you." responded Caleb.

D. Robin walked out of the room, leaving Isaiah and Caleb in a conversation.

Isaiah sat on the chair and looking at Caleb said, "So . . . what was that fool doing here?"

"Not much, we were talking about the place where you guys found me."

"Are you sure Caleb?"

"Why would I lie to you?"

"You can lie to me all you want for now. Later, I'm going to need your trust and collaboration to find out who wanted to kill you."

Caleb sighted deeply. "Don't worry Mr. Russell I will collaborate with you."

"What was he telling you Caleb? Was he trying to fool you with his words?"

"What? No, not at all."

"I know Peter Robin as I knew his dad, before he died. His dad tried to kill me. But he couldn't." Isaiah responded.

"I don't know what are you trying to say with all this."

"I was guessing that he told you about his father's murder."

"Yeah, yeah he did." Caleb said getting a little nervous. He feared to put Robin out there.

"Well, let me clear the story Caleb." Said Isaiah getting up from the chair, walked closer to his bed, and stood up next to him. "I don't want you to think I'm a killer. He tried to push me to the train. He tried because he knew if I'll die he was going to take charge of the police department in Manhattan. He pushed me and I fell, I fought back and I ran; I ran away. When I turned back I saw him, and I also saw a man, a man who was wearing a black mask. They were talking, and as they were talking I heard them screaming. Then, I closed my eyes and when I opened them I saw the man pushing detective robin's dad to the train."

"Why didn't you do anything to save him?" asked Caleb looking confused.

"It was too late already. I ran to see if he was ok, but the speed of the train threw him far away. The train was coming fast, and even if I tried to stop it, I wasn't going to help it. When the ambulance and my co-workers got to the scene detective Robin's father was already dead."

"So strange, his son told me that he heard his father screaming don't push me, don't push me . . ."

Isaiah looked at him worried and scared. "That's a lie. I feel sorry for Peter sometimes. He believes that his dad was strong, but he wasn't, he tried but he wasn't. His body was destroyed. The most curious thing was that the doctors said that his brain was still working. I'm telling you all this because I need you to trust me, I don't want you to do anything against me on the low. People talk bad about me because they hate that I have everything that they couldn't have."

"Mr. Russell, I don't want you to think that I doubt of you. You are my girlfriend's dad; I know you wouldn't plan anything against me. But as I said I don't want to press charges on anybody, and I don't want any cop, or any detective to take this case. I want to leave it like this."

Isaiah sighted deeply and said. "Caleb, Caleb. If you do that, those criminals are going to see you as weak. You won't have freedom when you'll be back on the streets. They'll try to do the same, especially now that you are all over the news. They won't stop until you are dead. And tell me Caleb, what's going to happen when you are on the streets, going to dance, or to the movies with my daughter? They are going to try to kill you again, and who knows, hurt my daughter too. I don't want my daughter to get traumatized, or get killed too. I'm going to do this case for your protection and my daughter's."

Caleb remained quiet and looked at him, listened to his words, listening to his promises.

"I need you to tell me that you trust me enough to do this . . ." said Isaiah.

"Are you going to do this by yourself?" asked Caleb.

"Yes, I don't need anybody else to work with me, I'm Mr. Russell who can go against me?"

Caleb sighted. "Ok. I trust you. I'm going to let you do this Isaiah."

Isaiah got up from the chair and smiled, and looking at him, 2 tears started falling down through his cheeks.

Caleb looked at Isaiah worried and asked. "Isaiah? Isaiah, are you ok?"

"Yes, yes, I am ok. It's just that, it makes me feels good to know that you are going to help me to do better, not only to myself, but you are also going to strength the relationship with my daughter."

"Yes, but you don't need to cry please."

"Oh yeah, I had to. Caleb I want you to forgive me if in any situation I made you feel bad or uncomfortable. You are a good person, and I like you for my daughter. You are a great man. God bless you." And as Isaiah said, he walked out of the room cleaning his fake tears. Caleb, surprised, closed his eyes. It was too much of a day for him.

Isaiah, on his way to his car, made a phone call.

"What the fuck is wrong with you Jesse!" he screamed.

Jesse, was the main thieve. He was the one that got paid the most by Isaiah to stab Caleb.

"What you mean! I did what you wanted it!" Jesse responded.

"He didn't die!" Isaiah said furious.

"That's not my problem Mr. cop. I did what you wanted it and that's it."

"No, it's not!" Isaiah screamed again. "Did you at least find me the info about his brother?"

"I did. He drug deals here in Brooklyn, Manhattan, Queens, and sometimes around Soho. White boy plays the role saying he a business—man. He uses his brother address not to get caught, but this motherfucker is making money."

"What is he selling?"

"White girl, weed, mushrooms, and acid . . . them white people buy a lot of pills, but he makes money here with the coke and weed."

"Does he has any young girls under his care?"

"Yea, I think he's fucking a young bitch down the block. I always see the same cab taking her and bringing her back. We all know she messing with someone outside the projects, we all think is him."

"Follow her."

"Fuck you."

"I'm telling you to follow her."

"That has a price."

"I already paid you, and more than the rest."

"Ha! This all has a price Cop, Caleb was a different package, now his brother is another, this nigguh makes money with the drugs, so if you want me to give you the info, pay me."

"We need to meet up." Isaiah responded.

"For what? I already told you, I was going to stabbed him, paid the other 2 niggas that were with me, called 911 saying that a man was dead. That's it Mr. Cop, I'm not going to do anymore for you."

"Listen, you better meet up with me right now, or you'll get the consequences."

"Consequences? Haha" Jesse laughed. "The only person who's going to be looking bad and have the consequences is you Mr. cop. I'm a random nigga who has been in jail before. If I get arrested right now, I go to jail later nothing happens. But if you get caught on your bullshit, the whole world is going to talk about you. The whole Manhattan is going to be disappointed about your actions. Every cop in the city is going to hate you, and so your family, so don't try that bullshit with me." He said and hung up.

"Hello? HELLO!!" Isaiah closed his phone and threw it. He was furious, but he needed to bring his enemy closer, and getting his phone from the floor he dialed a number and the phone started ringing. He was calling another one of the thieves.

"James?" said Isaiah doubting.

"Isaiah?" responded James. James was the one who pointed at Caleb with the gun.

"Yeah, look, do you want some money?" Isaiah asked.

"Depending, what I have to do?" James asked.

"I can't talk about it on the phone. Let's meet up. I'm driving to Brooklyn right now. Where do I meet you?"

"Go to Bed Stuy, and when you get there go to Marcy project. When you see a green building, call me."

"Ok. I'll call you when I'll be there." Isaiah said and hanging up, he started driving over there.

Isaiah Russell had the necessity of sending people to kill for more money and power. He did not know why, but there was a big urge in his heart that used to tell him that if he didn't kill, he wasn't going to be satisfied. He had everything he wanted. He lived in one of the best cities in Manhattan such as Soho. He went to the best schools around, was well educated, and never had a "necessity" in life. But he did have a major problem, the one he was good at it. He liked to kill. He enjoyed seeing murders, and just thinking of torture he was satisfied. He didn't know why, but he had the necessity to kill Caleb, a successful business man, who was in love and pretty much living with his daughter in one of the most privileged cities in Manhattan, like Tribeca. He knew that, and he also knew that he was in love with her. But that wasn't enough for him, he didn't care if he loved her, he wasn't going to let his daughter go. Even if Caleb was everything that any man could wish for the happiness of their daughters, he wasn't going to let them be together. Perhaps, the fact that both men were powerful and wanted the same thing was what was producing this hate that was consuming Isaiah's heart and hurting Caleb. They both wanted Juliana, but in Isaiah's eyes only one could had her, and that was himself. He was her father in his eyes, and everybody else who didn't know the truth. If he was going to share his precious daughter with somebody, it was going to be with his own-self.

Isaiah on his way to one of the so called "*most dangerous cities in Brooklyn*", locked all his doors and held his gun on his left leg. While he was driving through the streets, he stared at the young guys standing in a corner shaking hands with friends, and between those hands the dirty money was exchange. The more he was driving, the deeper reality was getting. He was looking at young girls, as young as his daughter getting in luxurious cars. He knew those were those girls that were getting down for a small amount of drugs and money. He was looking at the homeless, or how do they call them? "*Crack heads*" picking up pennies from the floor, begging the drug dealers sell them some.

When he got to the project, he stopped across from the tall old blue building. He called James, and this one saying, "*wait for me.*" Isaiah waited. When James was coming out of the building, he said hi to a bunch of guys that were posted up outside the building with their bikes in the middle of the sidewalk.

James walked up to Isaiah's car, opened the door and got in.

"So, this is the famous Bed Stuy?" Isaiah asked looking around as if he was disgusted.

"It's really calm today, as you can see."

"Calm?" Isaiah responded being sarcastic. "I just saw girls giving, getting head down the street. I've seen the *wana* be *scarfaces* on the corners, young little kids, selling crack."

"Man, that ain't nothing new. That's everyday's homework . . . you should know that . . . oh ma' bad I forgot you only do top class crimes." Said James looking at him and then looked at his gun. "So, what do you want in a hood like this?"

"I need you to do me a big favor."

"Is money talking?"

"Yes, I'm going to pay you."

"Who I *gotta* kill now?"

"Nobody so far, but I need you to say that you stabbed this man." Said Isaiah seriously.

James got loudly and said "What! You crazy son?! I ain't going to jail!"

"Look, we are going to do this, listen to me!"

James loudly still. "Man! How you want me to chill the fuck out, what the *fucks* wrong with you! How you going tell me to say that I stabbed that rich white man? Son you got issues son!"

"LISTEN!" screamed Isaiah, who was getting angry.

"Hey, hey, hey man, chill ok? Don't be coming here giving your white power shit attitude."

"Can you listen?" said Isaiah.

James sighted deeply. "Ok. Ok son, talk."

"I need you to say that you stabbed Caleb Smith. I'll take you to jail like saying you are one of the men who planned this. I'll leave you there, in one of the best cells; I'll talk to the guards so nothing happens to you. Until we prove that this other man did it."

"What *chu* mean?" James asked.

"I need you to get me some of your men. I need you to tell them to kill Jesse."

"Jesse? What Jesse you talking about son? My man, my brother Jesse?! But . . . he did a good job for you! What the hell?!"

"Look, Jesse is a snitch, he told me not to talk to him about shit anymore or he was going to talk to the cops and say that I sent all of you to kill Caleb. He was going to snitch on us."

"Are you serious?"

"He got angry when I asked him to give me information about Caleb's brother, I don't know why . . . you really think I like sending to people to kill people? I don't like wasting my money like that, but I have to do it, and I'm doing you a favor as well. I'm paying you for your safety. I'm going to pay you to kill a snitch."

James stayed quiet and looking through the window exclaimed loudly, "Oh shit!"

"What?" Isaiah asked, and looked to the other side.

They were looking was how a man holding a gun pointing it a young kid.

"What the fuck is wrong with that *nigga*!" said James looking as if he wanted to hit somebody. "How the fuck is he going to shoot that little kid!" he yelled.

"Why is he doing that for?" asked Isaiah.

"Maybe drugs problems."

"Get out of the car; I'm going to call some back up. I'm not letting a kid get killed."

Isaiah started calling some police officers while he was looking at the little kid getting on his knees, with the head down.

"Yo Isaiah do something about it man! That *nigga* wants to shoot that *jit* (little kid)!"

Isaiah finished talking with some cops, looked at James. "Get out of the car and stay down. The police is coming and I don't want them to see me with you. I'm going to arrest that man right now, get out of the car."

"Ok man! Don't be telling me how to walk; I know what to do in these cases." Said James getting out of the car, bending down, being careful that no bullet was going to get him. Isaiah getting out through the same door that James got out, slowly took out his gun, walked up to the front and pointed the gun at the man from far.

Isaiah screamed. "PUT THE GUN DOWN!"

The man, who was pointing the gun at the kid, was giving him the back and said, "WHAT THE FUCK ARE YOU! A COP? BECAUSE IF YOU AIN'T NO COP MOTHER FUCKER YOU DYING TOO!"

Isaiah was bout to talk, when the sirens of the police cars were coming closer and closer. Everybody who was around the block was hidding.

The man, who was pointing the gun at the kid, grabbed the kid by the neck and screamed, "I'M KILLING HIM! I'M KILLING HIM IF YOU DON'T MAKE THE POLICE GO AWAY!"

"I'M GOING TO COUNT UNTIL 5 IF YOU DON'T PUT THE GUN DOWN I MAY HAVE TO USE FORCE AGAINST YOU!" Isaiah screamed back at him in response.

The man screaming responded. "WHAT THE FUCK! DO SOMETHING THEN! I DON'T GIVE A FLY FUCK! JAIL IS A SECOND HOME TO ME JUST TO LET YOU KNOW! FUCK THE COPS! FUCK THE GOVERNMENT FUCK Y'ALL!"

While the man was arguing with Isaiah, the police cars stopped in front. They all opened the doors and stood up behind them. There were 4 police cars, 8 officers, 6 were men and 2 females. All of them were pointing at the criminal.

"PUT THE FUCKING GUN DOWN!" Isaiah screamed again.

The man nervous screamed. "OK! OK I'M GOING TO DO IT." He pushed the kid to the floor, and this one scared ran to one of the police car, crying.

The man was getting down pretending he was going to put the gun down. Isaiah then, slowly walked up to him, keeping the gun up. When the man was about to put the gun down, he felt Isaiah's hand touching his arm, and out of nowhere he turned and punched Isaiah with the gun. Making him fell on the floor and his gun fly away.

One of the police officer then, shot at the man on the knee, and another police officer shot him on the back.

The man fell on the floor, and Isaiah got up. He got on top of the man, put the handcuffs on him, and then called the ambulance.

The police officers started closing that area with those yellow stripes that say "DO NOT ENTER".

One of the police officers ran up to Isaiah and said, "Mr. Russell, are you alright?"

"Yes, thanks for asking." Said Isaiah, who was drying the sweat coming down his forehead.

"What were you doing here by the way?" the police officer asked.

Isaiah looked at the cop not knowing what to say, and responded "Undercover . . ."

"By yourself?" The police officer asked again.

"Yeah, I got a phone call, a random phone call, and they told me that something was happening here. So I came, I didn't tell anybody because I didn't want to bother."

The police officer smiled. "Sir, how could you say that . . . You are the best person that anyone could wish they could have as a boss. I'm very proud of you, and I wish one day I'll get to work with you."

Isaiah stared at her beautiful eyes. She was new cop in the department. She was about 25 years old, 5'4 and her smile was the most beautiful that he had seen so far in the department. "Sir, are you ok?" She asked again.

"Hmm . . . yeah, yeah, sorry. I was day dreaming I guess." He said nodding.

The police officer smiled.

While, Isaiah and his team were waiting for the ambulance and were taking notes, pictures on the street, his wife, Dara, was at home nervous, eating her nails, walking around in her room. She had a bad feeling, and even if she wanted to talk to Juliana she knew she wasn't going to tell her anything.

Dara got her bag and walked downstairs. She saw Juliana coming in and crashing looks; she stopped on the last stair and turned around.

"Juliana!" she screamed making her stop.

"What?" Juliana responded while she was turning to face her mom.

"Are you ok?"

"Mom, get out of my business please."

"Baby, I just want to help."

"You are not helping! You never did and you won't!"

"Juliana, I just want to know if your boyfriend is ok. I haven't met him, so at least I want to let you know that I really wish he'll get well."

"He is good. He woke up today." She said calming down her anger.

"In what hospital is he at?" her mother asked.

"I don't want you to go and visit him mom!"

"I won't my dear, I was just wondering." Said her mom looking down.

"He is at the Belview hospital on 28 street."

"Oh ok, and what bout his family? Do they know he is at the hospital?" asked Dara looking worried.

"Her brother. He just found out that Caleb is at the hospital."

"Oh. How are you doing? Are you feeling better?" asked her mom looking at her belly.

"Yes mom. The pregnancy symptoms are not attacking me yet."

"Juliana, baby, are you sure you want to keep that baby?"

"Yes mom! I already told you I don't believe in abortions."

"My dear, I'm just saying. You are young; you just finished high school . . . I need you to think with the right head."

"Mom! You are fucking annoying me! Bye woman bye! I can't stand you." As Juliana finished talking, she walked away directing to her room. She believed that the hate for her mother was becoming stronger.

VI.

SHE IS YOUR NICE

Days passed by, and Dara, was getting already adjust to the way that her daughter was treating her. She really wanted to get closer to her like they used to be. So she thought and decided, that maybe if she goes to the hospital to visit her boyfriend, she will get a chance to be friends with her own daughter again. She also was going to meet for the first time the man who was having her little girl crazy. She was going to see for the first time the reason the why of so much tragedy in her family. And what she didn't know was that she was going to see after many years, her own brother.

When she got to the hospital, she walked to the front desk, where a nurse was arguing with an old man.

"Yes, I already told you! Now, go sit down and I'll be with you in 5 minutes! Only 5 minutes!" screamed the nurse.

"Excuse me?"

The nurse looked at her and said, "Yes?"

"I want to see a patient, but I don't remember his last name." Dara responded.

"Only family can see patients, sorry."

"No, you don't understand. He is my family, but . . . he changed his last name, and I don't know it." Dara insisted.

The nurse looked at her with a mean look and responded. "Do you at least know the name?"

"Yeah, yes of course. Caleb." Said Dara ending the sentence with a smile.

"Oh, I know who you are talking about. He is your daughter's boyfriend isn't he?" the nurse said closing the book where she was looking at. "I know your husband. He is one of the greatest officers that the city of Manhattan could have had. Yes, I was speaking to him, today earlier."

"Oh." Dara said putting her purse back on her arm.

"Room number 322. Take the elevator to the third floor and walk to your right."

"Ok, thanks." After the elevator, the doors opened and she walked out. She looked for room 322, opened the door, and when she was about to talk, she saw Caleb. She stayed standing at the door for a good minute. She felt her stomach going around, and her heart feeling fear, sadness and a bunch of crazy emotions mixed together. Her eyes were wide-opened as if she was looking at the nothing. Caleb, who was laying down on the bed, stared at her. He felt like he wanted to talk but he forgot how to. He felt as if his tongue wasn't there anymore. He felt as his heart had stopped for a good minute. The impression from both was incredible. Dara, breathed deeply sighting as she closed the door. Caleb got strength from his inside, sat up slowly, looking firmly at her. They didn't have words for each other.

Dara walked slowly up to him, not saying a word, but just looking at him in the eyes.

Caleb slowly dropped tears, his face turned red, and he deeply sighted. Slowly, he covered his face with both hands and started to cry. He cried as a child. He cried like if he was about to die, he cried as he was feeling pain. He cried and cried not saying a word.

Dara looked at him, and sat on the chair that was next to his bed. She wanted to touch him, but she put her hands back. She wanted to call him by his name, she wanted to call him "brother", but she refused, and stayed quiet. Caleb kept on crying, and crying like if he wasn't going to stop. He started grabbing his head and then his neck, making his face looked up to the roof. He smacked his head several times. He couldn't stop crying, he felt like there was something in his chest that was stocked and wasn't coming out.

Dara wanted to talk, she wanted to tell him, "*My brother what are you doing in this room? This is my daughter's boyfriend's room, please tell me they gave you the wrong room . . . my brother I want to also hug you but I don't know if I should hug you cause I miss you, or cause I feel bad about all this tragedy.*" but she stayed quiet.

Caleb softly cleaned the tears from his face, looked at her and still dropping tears, he wanted to talk. He needed to say something, but he stayed quiet as well. The words weren't still coming out of his lips.

"Caleb . . ." she said softly as if she was whispering . . .

Caleb felt like if cold water was falling on his back. He felt like if his stomach wanted to come out through his mouth. He was in shock. He felt confused.

"Caleb . . ." said Dara again.

Caleb deeply sighted. "Lily . . . why?" (Lily was the real name of Dara, which she changed before getting married, to eliminate her past from her mind. Or at least try to).

"Please don't say anything . . . I beg you, don't say anything please . . ." she said walking closer to him, slowly.

Caleb started crying. "Lily why? Why you denied me?"

Dara started crying. "Caleb, my brother please forgive me . . ." she said getting on her knees.

"Lily please tell me why have you done such a thing?"

"Caleb please . . .

Caleb with a weak voice kept on saying "Lily, oh Lily! Why did you get to that point? What did I do? You don't love me? Why did you even change your name?!"

"Caleb! Please, I beg you don't ask me anything tonight." She said dragging herself on the floor towards his bed on her knees.

"Lily, when mom . . . when mom told me that you said I was dead . . ."

Dara interrupted crying kept on saying, "Caleb please . . ."

"Lily my heart broke in pieces . . . In so many pieces that you won't even be able to find them . . . Not even a lab would be able to find the biggest one."

"Please, please my brother stop" she said getting up. "I have reasons why I said what I said."

"What reasons could you have? What can be so bad? Tell me . . . Why are you so embarrassed of your past? Nothing can change it!" Caleb screamed turning his face red, full of anger and sadness.

Dara crying. "Caleb . . . I thought you were dead for real . . ."

"Oh please, don't lie to yourself. Don't lie to your own lies. You don't know, how I've prayed to God to make me see you again." Caleb said trying to sit up on the bed. "You don't have idea of how much pain I had when I found out that my own sister was denying her family, denying her roots just to please her husband."

"Caleb, I did it because I didn't want to lose him."

"What were you going to lose? NOTHING!" he screamed until his face turned red.

"No, no, you don't know . . . Caleb . . . you don't know what have you done!" she screamed back at him, explaining him with her hands.

"Me? I tried! I worked hard to get what I have now, but I'm not going to talk about your mistakes my sister. I'm not going to tell your husband about your lies. I'm not going to tell Joey and mom that I've talked to you."

"Joey? Oh god! Have you talked to Joey?" Dara asked wiping her tears.

"I live with Joey now . . . he is back from the army. He has too much drama; I'm not going to let him get with this one." responded Caleb trying to calm down.

"I didn't deny him . . ." she said turning her back on him.

Caleb closing his eyes said, "I know . . ."

"Caleb . . . I want to see Joey . . . please . . ." she said turning back to face him again.

"I'm going to tell him about you, don't worry."

"I'm sorry. I'm sorry for making you have this bad time; this bad experience Caleb. But God had paid you back. You are a good man."

"Lily, you don't get that money comes and goes as fast as it is?"

"Caleb, you have everything in the world that once we all wished once and . . ."

"Lily, you are nothing but a materialist person . . . I wonder if your kids love you enough . . ." he responded interrupting her.

Dara closed her eyes and stayed quiet.

"Tell me something my dear Lily do your kids love you as much as I do?" he asked making Dara looked down, falling on her knees full of tears running down her face.

"What is wrong with you now?" Caleb asked worried.

But Dara kept on crying . . .

"Lily . . . how did you find out about me in the hospital, if you don't talk to Joey . . . Lily, how did you find out about me being here?" Caleb asked very scared.

But Dara kept on crying . . .

Caleb's voice changed and started dropping tears again. "Lily, who told you about me being here?"

Dara couldn't talk because her cry was stronger than her words.

"Lily, please . . . tell me, tell me who told you about me . . . Lily, oh Lily, please don't leave me with these scary feelings . . . tell me what is going on!" Caleb screamed. He was confused; he wanted to know what was going on, his doubts were all over his heart and mind. He felt his stomach in pain, but the pain of something bad; he felt that that pain was going to transform into something horrible.

"Caleb . . . Caleb my daughter told me about you here."

Caleb closed his eyes and opening them again slowly "Lily, Lily who's your daughter Lily . . . oh please don't tell me that what I'm thinking is happening, please . . ."

"Oh Caleb, oh my dear Caleb, I want to die! I want to . . . die!" she said crying hugging him strongly.

"Please answer Lily, who's your daughter? "

"Caleb . . . my daughter has your seed inside her belly . . . my daughter is Mr. Russell's daughter . . . my daughter is Juliana. And my name is not Lily, is Dara . . ."

Caleb felt like thousands of knives were stabbing his heart. He felt like he couldn't breathe. He felt like if he didn't have any more chances to live, he wanted to get out of the hospital. He wanted to get out of the city, he wanted to go somewhere, he just wanted to disappear. He had never felt so miserable as he was feeling right now. He had never felt so much disgrace in his entire existence.

"Caleb, your niece is pregnant and so in love with you . . . oh Caleb, I knew something what's going wrong . . ." She said crying trying to kiss his hands.

But Caleb couldn't talk, he let his soul crying and fainting. He closed his eyes, bite his lips until these ones started to bleed; he grabbed the sheets of the bed so hard, so strong, leaving the marks of his courage, of his angry on them.

"And the worst is that she is not Isaiah's daughter . . ." Dara said moving away from him.

Dara looked at Caleb, but this one kept on looking at the sheets, holding them.

"She is the product . . . she is the product of one of many rapes that our stepfather did to me. She is our stepfather's daughter. She is the reason why mother hates me so much."

Caleb closed his eyes and opening again and asked "No, NO! WHY!!! WHY DID YOU DO THIS?! IF YOU WOULD HAVE NEVER EVER LIED, MAYBE WE WOULDN'T BE IN THIS SITUATION! WHY!? FUCK!!! I WANT TO DIE!!" He screamed hitting himself, ripping off all the tubes that were connected to the machines.

Dara tried to stop him by hugging him saying, "I did! I did tell mom about it Caleb I swear! She knew, but she told me she was never going to talk to you about me. Oh Caleb, I want the devil to take me with him, you don't know how much I want to die and just turn to dust. Caleb, how are we going to tell Juliana that she loves her uncle . . . Tell me, how are we going to tell her that her uncle is going to be the father of her baby? . . . How are we going to tell my husband that my stepfather raped me, and that his daughter is his precious Juliana . . . How am I going to face the reality to her? To God? To the society? . . . tell me because I can't . . ."

Caleb wiped his tears, and looked at his sister "You said what to Isaiah? You told him that Juliana was somebody else's daughter?"

"Yeah . . . I told him, that one of my boyfriends left me when I was pregnant, and he still took me with him. He was 27 when we got married. Mom signed the papers for my wedding . . . She knew I was already pregnant by him . . . by that monster . . ."

"Mom had contact with you when we were in those houses?" he asked.

"Yeah, she only talked to me once . . . she told me that I was going to pay for everything that I did to her." She said I was going to cry blood for her broken heart.

Caleb looked at Dara and asked "So . . . mom hated you since always?"

"I guess . . . because I know a mother can't be jealous of her own daughter for nothing . . ."

"Oh my dear Lily, or Dara? I don't even know how to call you anymore. Why you lied so much . . . Why you created all this drama for? Don't you know that all the lies come out soon or later?"

"Caleb, don't be cruel with me, please . . . I beg you . . ."

"What are we going to do with Juliana now? That's more important than anything . . ."

"I don't know . . . she told me . . . she said that she was going to keep the baby no matter what . . ."

"Caleb . . . she is so in love with you . . . you just don't know. She disrespected her dad, our family, everything just for you."

"I didn't know about this . . ."

"I know you didn't know about this, I know her . . . she does everything she needs just to get what she wants . . . oh Caleb I know her too much."

"I love her . . ." Caleb responded.

Dara got loud and hysterically. "What are you saying?! She is your niece! Don't you understand? She has your blood!"

Caleb closed his eyes, and opened them again and loudly responded, "What was I suppose to know! I didn't fucking know Lily! All this is your fault!"

"Yes it is my fault, but I didn't know she was going to fall in love with you! How was I supposed to know that you two were going to walk on the same way once?"

"If you would have had contact with me, if you would have talked to me, she would have known who her uncle was . . . oh my god! What am I going to do! Tell me Lily, tell me what am I going to do with the love I have in my heart for her? Tell me what am I supposed to do with that seed in her belly? Tell me what am I supposed to do with myself! Because I love her . . . I love her so much . . . you just don't know . . ."

Dara hugged Caleb getting up from the chair, making it fall on the floor. "Caleb, my dear, my sweet Caleb please . . . please forgive me . . . I didn't know this was going to happen. I didn't know a small lie was going to be a big problem."

Caleb kept on crying on her arms, as he was lost.

"Caleb, please forgive me . . . please stay quiet about the situation, please . . . oh please . . ." she begged him.

"How? How can I be quiet about this? How can I just closed my eyes and don't miss her?"

"Caleb . . . I'm sorry, I hope God and you will forgive me . . . please . . ."

"Dara, I miss her now, I miss her face, her lips . . . I just want her with me . . ."

"Forget about her please, forget that she was yours, please . . . Caleb try."

"I can't . . . is not going to be easy just to run away . . ."

"There are so many beautiful women in the world, in the city that would love to be with a handsome man like you . . . oh my dear Caleb please forget about her . . ."

"I don't care . . . I don't care about the rest . . . I just want her . . . she is my sky, my good morning, my dream alive . . . don't you get it? Or is it that you never have loved before?" he said while he kept on crying.

"Yes I have. I love her, that's why I'm asking you to do this. Caleb, Caleb listen to me, we are going to do something ok? Listen to me . . ."

Dara wiping his tears said, "We are going to keep this secret with us for now. We are going to keep this as a secret Caleb . . . please just do it . . ."

Caleb interrupting. "No, no I cannot . . . I want to but I just can't, that's too much pain . . . look at her and pretend that nothing happened . . . I'm going to feel like a piece of shit, worst than shit; I don't know what am I going to do in front of her pretty face . . . I don't know . . . Why did you tell me this Lily, you should have never told me this."

"I think Juliana is coming, wait." She got up and looked through the clear glass of the window. "Yes, she is walking over here . . . Caleb, let's pretend that nothing happened please, stayed quiet . . . I trust you."

Caleb cleaned his face, and waited for Juliana to open the door of his room.

Juliana walked in. She looked at her mother, and then at Caleb, she felt something was wrong.

"What happened?" she asked.

Caleb couldn't talk, he didn't even want to look at her in the eyes; He was scared. He was worried he was sorry, it was hurting him the fact that he couldn't love her anymore.

Juliana walked up to Caleb's bed and said, "What's wrong my love?"

"Nothing, everything is perfect, don't worry about it." Dara responded instead of him.

"Mom I'm not asking you, I'm asking him . . ." and looking at Caleb asked, "What's wrong Caleb? Why have you been crying for?"

"Nothing, don't worry . . ." he said trying not to look at her.

"Why don't you want to look at me? Did my mom say something bad about me?"

"No, everything is good I already told you." He responded while he was looking at the wall.

Juliana turned to looked at her mom and screamed. "Mom, what the fuck did you say to my boyfriend? You better keep your mouth shut god damn it!"

Caleb raised his tone of voice. "Juliana! Your mother didn't tell me anything but amazing things about you, how could you talk to her in that way?!"

Silence took over.

"Sorry . . . I thought she said something bad . . . you don't know her . . . she is always talking crap." Juliana said and looked surprised to her boyfriend.

"No she doesn't . . . she is an amazing woman. Believe me, when your mother is gone, you are going to miss her the most." He said making Juliana looked at her mom, and then looked at him back, confused.

"Give her a hug. But not a random hug, give her one of those hugs that you haven't gave anyone . . . Show her through that love how much you love her." He said turning his face to look at her and Dara.

Juliana sighted, and walked up to her mom, who opened her arms and extended them waiting for her daughter's to get together with hers.

Juliana closed her eyes and hugged her mom.

Dara closed her eyes as well. She has never been as happy as she was now, after many years a hug made her day, week, her life. A lovely hug from her daughter made her smiled and cried.

Looking at Caleb, she dropped two tears and smiled, and strongly hugged her daughter.

Juliana amazed 'bout the situation asked, "Mom, what's happening? Why are you crying?"

Dara softly whispered on her ear. "I love you. You are the best thing that happened to me. You are the most amazing girl that any mother could ever ask for."

Juliana didn't want to ask anything, and finishing the big strong hug, Dara said bye to her daughter and Caleb, and walked out.

Juliana turned to face Caleb. "What happened Caleb that you don't want to tell me?"

"Nothing I swear."

Juliana smiled, and taking out from her small book bag, showed him an album.

"What is it?" he asked.

"An album . . . well my album, when I was a baby." she said sitting next to him.

Caleb opened the album, and looked through the pictures. He let her speak while they were looking at the pictures. He felt like crying again, but he had to hold it, he didn't want her to ask more questions. While she was talking and talking, pointing at the pictures. He kept on staring at her eyes, at those lips that once made him feel in heaven. He wanted to tell her how much he loved her, how bad he wanted her. But again, he held it. He needed her away from him. He knew it was bad for him having her around. But the bad was already done, the mistake was already created, the tears, the pain, everything was going to get worst he knew. But why, that was the question, why he kept on asking on his head. Why was the word that was going around his cerebellum in circles? Why God put so much drama in his life? Why he have to let her go? Why couldn't they be happy? Why, why, why?

"What's wrong with you Caleb? You are really getting me mad . . ."

"Can I, can I ask you something Juliana?" he said looking at a picture.

"Of course!"

He looked at her and asked, "Are you going to keep the baby?"

Juliana smiled and said, "Oh, that . . . yes, I am. I was thinking and I think it's the best decision. I don't believe in abortions and today when I went to church, I talked to this priest. We talked for about an hour, and he told me that what I have is a blessing. A blessing that God sent me from heaven, and . . . I want that blessing with us. Because . . . with you and I together the baby won't ever feel lonely, the baby would grow up happy in a hateful world. Our baby would be able to know what love is since today, since this moment. I know you and I can work it out. I know we will be the greatest parents in the world, and I love you, that's why I want to keep this baby."

Caleb stared at her face, and couldn't talk.

"What do you think?" she asked smiling staring at him.

Caleb still stayed quiet. He didn't want to say a word. He was scared to hurt her with his words. How did all this happen? What's going to happen later on? He wondered.

"Caleb?" she said again.

"Yeah, yeah I heard you. Honey, I think, hmmm . . . I think you should go home because I'm really trying to sleep and I don't want you to be bored here for me."

"Oh no, don't worry about it baby. I'll entertain myself with anything I'll find my way." She said sitting on the chair next to him, putting the album on top of the night table next to him.

"Juliana I'm really trying to sleep and I want you to go away." He said raising his tone of voice.

"Caleb, are you ok?" she asked.

Caleb raised his tone of voice. "Yes! Yes! Of course I'm ok, what could be wrong?"

"What's wrong with you? Why are you talking to me like this?"

"Don't you get it? I'm telling you, and I told you nicely I don't want you to be here with me. Now please Juliana get out of the room because I don't want you here!"

Juliana in shock looked at him strange got her purse, breathed deeply and walked out of the room.

Caleb felt bad, he felt like the worst person on earth. He felt worst than food directing to trash. He didn't want to say it, but he had to, he needed to be strong with her. He couldn't let his love increase or it will kill him.

Suddenly, the nurse came in. Caleb looked at her and went back to mind his own business on his mind.

"Wow, I love the way that you made that poor girl cry." The nurse said smiling in a sarcastic way about the situation.

"What?"

"You think is nice talk to females like that? I don't get men these days. They have something good in their hands, something precious and just because they know they *got it on lock*, they think they can play with it as they want." The nurse said as she finished preparing his medicine.

Caleb preferred not to say anything.

"Here, take it."

"What is it?" he asked.

"It's a pill that is going to make you feel better. How do they call it? Stress-killer."

Caleb looked at her, looked at the pill and swallowed it.

The nurse smiled at him, handled him water and said, "I hope you'll feel better."

Caleb didn't like that nurse at all. Since the first day he met her and saw her standing right there next to Juliana's dad. He didn't like her. The nurse walked out of the room, and went straight to make a phone call. She looked around making sure that nobody was around very suspicious.

"Yeah?" responded the person on the other line.

"Mr. Russell?"

"What happened? How is he doing?"

"He is good; he just finished arguing with your daughter."

"He was what?"

"He argued with your daughter. I saw her leaving the hospital, crying."

"Crying?"

"Yes sir, crying."

"You gave him the pill?"

"Yes I just gave it to him."

"Perfect, I hope that son of a bitch die slow, shocking with it."

"Another thing sir."

"What?

"Your wife was here too."

"With my daughter I guess"

"No sir, she came alone."

"What!"

"They were arguing, hugging each other. She got out of the room crying as well."

"Who the . . . ok . . . Thanks for the information. Call me when the bastard is dead."

"Ok sir. Good night." said the nurse and hung up.

Isaiah was upset; he wondered why his wife went to the hospital for. What did she have to talk about with Caleb that he didn't know of? Maybe she went to ask him to leave Juliana alone? But hugs the nurse said. Why would she be giving him a hug for?

Isaiah got up from the chair where he was sitting at. He was at his office in the police department. He walked out of the place, walked up to his car, and drove as fast as he could. He was going to solve everything with his wife.

When he got home, he threw the door when he opened it. He went upstairs as fast as he got home. He walked up to his room, hoping that his wife was there, and there she was, in bed, reading a book.

Isaiah slammed the door as he got it making her stare at him in fear. "WHAT THE FUCK WERE YOU DOING AT THE HOSPITAL WITH THAT MAN?!"

Dara, who got scared of his behavior, and dropped the book, and stood up. Her hands felt the fear and started shaking.

"ANSWER DARA, I'M NOT FOR YOUR FUCKING LIES!!"

"I don't know what are you talking about . . . What are you saying!" she answered scared walking backwards.

Isaiah grabbed her by the neck and said, "Listen bitch, you better tell me what you were talking about with that man! RIGHT NOW!" he screamed pushing her towards the bed.

"Stop Isaiah! What is wrong with you!" she said trying to talk while he kept on shocking her.

"Talk!" Isaiah dropped her on the bed again.

Dara coughing hard said, "What is wrong with you now!? You never used violence in this house!"

"Dara talk God damn it!"

"What has happened to you Isaiah?! Did the devil go inside you or what?"

"No he didn't, but he's about to if you don't fucking tell me what you went to talk to that man for? Hugging him? Crying? Tell me, tell me Dara because I'm not stupid!" Isaiah kept on screaming as he was grabbing her by the hair moving her around.

"Ok, ok I'm going to tell you . . . I don't know how, I don't know how you are going to take this Isaiah." Dara looked at him, and walked up to the window of her room, and looking through it, she started talking. "Do you remember when I was living with my adopted family do you?"

"Yeah of course, how could I forget" he replied.

"Do you remember I was 1 month pregnant already?"

"Ahuh . . . but nobody knew that."

"Isaiah, Isaiah . . . oh my Isaiah how can I tell you this . . . how?!" she said looking scared, fearing his furious and violence.

Isaiah sat down and said trying to calm down. "Just talk, I'll listen . . ."

"Isaiah, remember that I told you that one of my boyfriend's left me pregnant right?"

"Yes!"

Dara dropped tears. "It wasn't any of my boyfriends who left me pregnant . . . it was my . . . it was my stepfather . . ."

Isaiah stayed quiet, he didn't want to talk.

Dara started crying, walked towards the big window and stood next to the curtains. "My stepfather used to raped me and my brothers."

"Brothers?" Isaiah asked surprised "But . . . the only one that you told me about was Joey."

"Yes, my stepfather only used to raped me and him; he never got to raped my other brother."

"Are you talking about the one that died?" he asked looking confused.

"Yeah . . . Caleb." She said.

"What? . . . Dara what are you saying?" Isaiah said standing up from the chair.

"My brother's name was Caleb." She said turning around, facing him from far.

Isaiah breathed deeply.

"He is not dead . . ." she said looking and putting her head down.

"What? What do you mean . . . I don't understand." Isaiah asked nodding his head over and over.

"My brother, the one I told you about is not dead . . ."

"And . . . what that has to do with you going to the hospital to talk with Juliana's boyfriend? Why did you go and talk to . . ."

"Yes!" she said finishing the sentence.

Isaiah stayed quiet. "No, it's not . . . possible . . ."

"Yes it is . . ." she said crying.

"How come?" he asked looking crazy, amazingly confused and lost in words.

"It's happening, oh my dear Isaiah it is happening . . . what are you fearing right now, yes it is happening . . . Juliana's boyfriend is my brother . . ."

Dara started crying and slowly she held on to the curtains and dropped on her knees.

"Jesus!" Isaiah said in shock opening his eyes with a great impression. "Why . . . why did you lie to me all this time Dara? Why couldn't you tell me about your brother being alive?"

"I don't know . . . I don't know why I lied for . . . I'm sorry! Please . . . I beg you forgive me . . . forgive me my love . . ." said nodding her head.

"Forgive you? Dara, you know I hate lies, I hate LIERS!"

"I am sorry! I did it because I was so in love with you! I was scared that you weren't going to marry me! You just don't know." She said crying, trying to grab his hands.

"Scared?" he asked. "Scared of what Dara?! I was in love with you! Even if your past was extremely messed up I was still going to be with you because I loved you! How could you doubt me! How could do such a big mistake with me?!"

"I am sorry!" she screamed again crying on his hands.

"No Dara, I'm sorry but I can't be with you . . ." and as he said he moved her away from him, pushing her. Dara started dragging herself up to his knees, and hold them saying, "Please, forgive me my husband, please forgive me . . ."

"Oh Dara please, get off me! I can't, I can't be with you . . . at least tonight, I can't be with you . . . GET OFF ME!" he screamed.

And screaming and crying, Isaiah got the keys of his car and walked out of the room, leaving his wife on the floor crying. Juliana who was on the hallway, started running up to her parent's room, as soon as she saw her father coming out so angry.

"What's happening?" she asked his dad.

But Isaiah didn't stop and kept on walking.

Juliana worried, ran up to her mom's room, and seeing her on the floor. She hugged her, hugged her tight. "Mother, what happened? Why are you crying?"

Dara didn't speak; she just cried hugging her daughter.

Both, mother and daughter stayed there on the floor, hugging each other.

Isaiah got on his car, and drove away. He had such a heavy day, and planning go to a bar and try to refresh his mind, he received a phone call that made him park in a restaurant to answer the call.

"Hello?" he said looking forward through the big window.

"Yo Isaiah. It's James son."

Isaiah sighted deeply. "Yes, what happened?" he asked feeling uncomfortable.

"I killed him . . ." James responded making a pause in between his words.

"Killed? Killed who?" Isaiah said raising his tone of voice.

"What you mean who man!?" James said giving him attitude over the phone. "Jesse! I did as you wanted. I did it all by my own. Tomorrow come pick me up and locked me up. I'm going to say that I was the one that stabbed Caleb."

"No, it's not necessary to lock you up anymore . . . you killed before I arrested you . . ."

"What you mean?! You are not going to pay me?!" James asked screaming.

"I'm going to pay you for killing Jesse, that's it."

"What you mean!" James screamed. "Man you said if I get him killed I was going to jail and you were going to pay me for it, now do what you promised."

"Look, I'm only going to pay you on what we agreed. You killed him; I'll pay that, that's it. You never went to jail, so I won't pay you more."

"Man!" James screamed again. "How you going play me like that man! You promised me more money! If I would have known that you weren't going to pay me more I wouldn't have killed my friend!"

"You didn't do what I asked for. If you want your money then good, if not I keep it, you choose." Said Isaiah removing the seat belt off him as he started driving, getting back on the lane.

"This weekend. This weekend I'll pay you." Isaiah responded taking a deep breath.

"Man what you mean this weekend?" James asked mad. "I thought you were going to give me my money tomorrow or something!"

"Don't you get it?" said Isaiah changing his tone of voice. "The money comes from somewhere, so wait until this weekend and keep your mouth shut."

Isaiah said and hung up.

On the other hand, at the hospital, Joey, Caleb's brother was visiting Caleb. Joey opened the door of the room where Caleb was at and saw his brother on the bed, half awake, half asleep

"Caleb?" Joey said.

Caleb turned and faced him. "Hey!"

"Sorry I couldn't make it faster; I was making sure that the house was safe." Said Joey approaching to his bed.

"It's ok my brother . . ." said Caleb trying to sit up.

"So . . . how are you feeling?" Joey asked.

"Calm, but terrible."

"Where is Juliana by the way?"

"That's the problem." said Caleb sighting.

"You guys got into a fight?" asked Joey surprised.

"I wish . . ."

"What happened now?"

Caleb started crying making Joey's face turned the happy expression to a worried one. "What, what's wrong Caleb?" Joey asked getting up from the chair.

Caleb crying breathed, and tried to talk. "Joey, Joey . . ." he said having tears running down his face. "Joey . . . today I met Juliana's mom."

"And?" Joey asked worried and insisting.

"She was Lily . . ." Caleb responded crying even more intense.

"What are you saying?"

"Joey . . . Dara Russell is Lily Smith . . . our sister!" Caleb screamed while Joey turned white, he couldn't talk.

"She came and took my breathed away; I couldn't believe that my sister was standing here in front of me."

"What the . . ."

"She came because she wanted to talk, she wanted to meet Juliana's boyfriend! But she ending meeting her own brother . . ."

"Oh my! What . . . what did she tell you?" asked Joeyscared.

"She told me she denied me. She told her husband that I was dead . . ."

Joey looked down. He didn't know what to tell his brother. He was trying to put himself on his shoes and try to feel for a moment the same pain he was feeling. But as everybody knows, it is hard to put one on somebody else's situation, especially when they are going through a lot of disgraces, and awful things; Things that not only hurt the heart and mind, but also the soul.

"There's no sorry . . . she denied me. She said it was the best thing to say about her past . . . and another thing . . ." Caleb said looking down to his sheets, grabbing them strong.

"What?" Joey asked.

"Juliana is not Isaiah's daughter . . ."

"She is our stepfather's daughter . . . the last time that he raped her, Lily got pregnant."

Joey couldn't believe what he was hearing. He couldn't even talk. He breathed deeply trying not to stutter and said, "Are . . . you, are . . . you . . . serious? So . . . that means that . . . So that means that Juliana is our niece?!" He asked rising his tone of voice, feeling strange. He had that look and feeling in him as if he wanted to throw up, or as if he wanted to make something come out of him.

"Yes! Yes! YES! SHE IS OUR NIECE!!! AND I, AND I LOVE HER!!!" Caleb crying desperately screamed. "AND THAT'S NOT THE WORST! SHE IS . . . (he sighted) SHE IS PREGNANT!" Caleb said putting his hands around his mouth, as if he wanted to cover them.

Joey looked at Caleb overwhelmed, in shock and with the eyes wide opened.

"I forgot to tell you . . . she is pregnant . . . the condom broke . . ."

"Oh my god Caleb!" said Joey putting his hands on top of the table as if he was leaning on it.

"I know . . . there is not too much to say . . . I guess I wasn't meant to be happy."

Joey looked at Caleb, and when he was about to give him a hug; Caleb started coughing.

Joey got scared, tried to hold him from the back repeating his name "CALEB! CALEB! WHAT'S WRONG!?"

Caleb started to throw up. He was coughing and coughing harder and harder.

Joey going crazy opened the door and screamed on the hallway. "HELLO! HELP ME! HELP ME PLEASE!! MY BROTHER IS DYING! . . . ANYBODY!"

Two doctors who were standing in the middle of the hallway ran up to Caleb's room and held Caleb, who kept on throwing up. They put oxygen on his nose, and called two other men to transfer Caleb to emergency room.

"WAIT!" Where are you taking him?" Joey asked walking behind them as fast as he could.

"*To emergency room!*" one of the doctors responded. "If we don't take him now, he could die throwing up." All of them got out of the room and ran to the elevator. Joey, who went back to the room, picked his book bag and ran out from the room, going through the stairs.

As soon as Caleb's life was in danger, the news ran to Juliana's ears. She did the impossible, and got to the hospital as soon as she could in the company of her mother.

When Joey saw Juliana arriving didn't say a word but try to avoid her. He knew the truth, but didn't want the night to get worst. He looked at Dara, and wanted to hug her after so many years. It was his sister at the end of the lifetime. He loved her.

"Joey do you know what's wrong with him?" Juliana asked desperately.

"What do you mean?" Joey answered looking back at her.

"Today earlier, before all this happened, he treated me like straight shit. He told me to get out of his room, that he didn't want me there. I was wondering and thinking so much today . . . Why would Caleb do that? I mean I didn't do anything bad . . . I'm really worried Joey . . ."

Joey knew why Caleb was acting in that way. He knew, and he was trying to avoid her because he didn't want to love her anymore. He knew that all these news were going to hurt Juliana badly. The situation was getting worst and worst every minute that was passing by. Joey knew that the one and only guilty person of all this drama was his sister, Juliana's mom, Isaiah's wife, Dara, but he decided to deny it.

"No . . . I don't know what's up with him Juliana, when I got to the hospital to see him; he was already being transfer to emergency . . . but just wait until he gets better . . . I'll talk to him, I promise."

Juliana smiled. "Ok . . . thanks!"

And as they finished talking, a doctor came out.

"Caleb Smith' relatives?" the doctor asked.

"Yes, I am his brother . . . is everything alright?" Joey asked.

The doctor sighted, "Your brother is lucky . . . he is alive . . ."

Joey and Juliana sighted deeply at the same time, smiling looking at each other.

"What happened to him exactly doctor?" Dara asked while she was hugging Juliana.

"Apparently somebody gave him a strong pill that caused problems to the heart, and also poisoned his water." said the doctor cleaning the sweat on his forehead.

"Are you serious?" Joey asked feeling unconvinced.

"Yes, you should call the police and talk to your brother as soon as he wakes up. This is a way of murder."

"But . . . the only ones that were with him were the nurses weren't them? Juliana said as if she was asking the doctor.

"Well, that's why you guys need to talk to him to find out who gave him that pill. But for now, he needs to be in the hospital for at least 1 more month. He needs to get better from the stabs and now from the poison."

"Ok, doctor thanks a lot!" Joey, Juliana and Dara said sitting back on the sofa.

"God . . . Everybody wants to kill Caleb, why? I don't get it." Juliana said.

"*Today at 2:40 pm on a project in Brooklyn, the police found the body of a man on the door of his house. The police said that this probably was one of the many gangs that have been killing, and dealing with drugs lately. Apparently, this dead man was one of the main suspects on the stabbing of Caleb Smith. But so far, we don't have more information, we will back as soon as we'll have the results. Back to you Michel.*"

"You heard that?" Juliana said after the news changed.

"Yeah, your father never told me that he already had some suspects."

"Yeah, he never told me about it either. But you know what? He is like that, always doing his thing on secret."

"I think you should go home and rest my dear. It's not good for the baby, and so it's not for you."

"No, what are you saying, I want to stay . . . I want to be the first person that Caleb sees when he'll wake up." responded Juliana rubbing her belly.

"Juliana darling, I don't think is a good idea. I really think you should go home. Look at your mom, she is tired as well, and she is here for you only."

"Joey don't tell me to go away, is there something going on that you guys don't want to tell me?"

"Something? What else can we have? There's nothing hidden Juliana. I just think you should go home . . . I promise I swear I will call you as soon as Caleb wakes up."

"Ok . . . ok fine, I'll go home then."

"I knew you were going to understand. C'mon, wake up your mom." Said Joey getting up walking up to the big window, which gave the view to the backyard.

Juliana smiled and sighting softly, moved her mom.

"Juliana? What happened? How is Caleb?" said her mom while she was opening her eyes. Dara looked at her daughter, and then looked at Joey. She got up and walked up to him. "Are you going to stay with Caleb?" she asked.

"Yes, don't worry." He responded giving her a mean look.

"Please take care of him Joey."

"I will." He said, looking at Juliana who was picking up from the floor her book bag, walked up to her mom. "C'mon mom lets go home. Joey is going to stay here."

Dara and her daughter said bye to Joey and walked away.

Joey sat down, and just waited until the doctor be back to tell him at what time they were transferring Caleb to another room.

Everything was getting so complicated; everybody seemed to be changing or switching personalities. Everything around Caleb was going awful; everything for his world was turning black and white. Apparently, destiny didn't want him to be happy. He had no freedom, it seemed like if something, or somebody was watching every step that he was taking. Everything, just because he fell in love with somebody with who he shouldn't have, his niece, the daughter of his own sister, the product of a violent act. She was also the daughter of Isaiah Russell, a dirty cop who didn't play games and didn't do anything, but just disappear people if he doesn't like them. The money, the power that he had gave him all type of strength to destroy people. But as one knows, and many say, love is stronger than any evil force. Love is the most powerful weapon that can fight anything in this existence.

VII.

ISAIAH, THE MURDERER

That night was full of emotions that were undefined. But that night changed a lot of people's mentalities.

Do you remember detective Robin? The one that Isaiah Russell asked to get away from Caleb's case? Well, he didn't obey his words, and decided to take a risk, a risk that could ruin his career, and reputation; a risk that could also lead him to death.

The next day early in the morning detective Robin drove to Marcy project, in Bed Stuy, Brooklyn. He drove to where the murder of one of the suspects took place.

Getting out of his car, he looked around the place, looked around and with a lot of luck he found a card, and in the back it said James Johnson. As he got out of the building, he walked around and started asking if anybody knew this James Johnson.

As we know, James was the one who killed Jesse, the man who stabbed Caleb. James was the man who got paid by Isaiah to plan this murder, and now, his future was in Detective Robin's hands. Robin walked and walked for about 30 minutes. The place where he was at was dangerous and not good for a "rich looking man" in the hood. He was about 6'0 ft, light skin, blue eyes, very handsome Jewish guy, but he was just an undercover detective, who was working alone, with no back up.

When he was about to leave, he heard two young boys talking loudly about shotguns. Detective Robin walked up to the young boys, and pretending that he was looking at the magazines that were around, he stood there listening to their story.

Detective Robin looked at one of the boys and asked, "What's up kids, can you do me a favor?"

Both kids looked at the detective worried.

"Can you?" detective Robin asked again.

The taller kid looked at him and looking at his friend, and then looking back at him said. "Sure, what *'chu* want?"

"You heard about the gun shots from last night right?" Robin asked.

"Yeah . . . why?" The tall kid responded.

"Just wondering . . . my friend who lives around here told me about it. And well, I'm looking for my friend . . . but he told me to meet him up like in one hour."

"And?" the tall kid responded.

Detective Robin looked at him trying to invent something else and said, "I was wondering if you two live around here?"

The other kid getting in the conversation said, "Yeah, but what do you need *yo*?"

Detective Robin showed the card with James name printed on it. "Do you know this person?"

"I don't know his last name, but I know a James . . ." the short kid said looking at the card.

"Oh, so if I describe him would you tell me where can I find him?" Robin asked.

The short kid stayed quiet.

Detective Robin smiling at the kid, said one more time "Don't worry, I'm not a cop, I just want to talk to him about something personal."

"Then if he is your friend describe him." The tall kid asked Robin seriously.

Detective Robin thought twice, he didn't have idea of how this James looked like. So he had to think twice and hard.

"Well . . . he is tall about 5'9, 5'8 maybe . . . he is black, . . . and he is a real *'niggah'.*" The detective smiled at both kids. He felt nervous for using the n word.

"Oh I know who you talking about . . . he is Jesse's homeboy."

"Jesse?" Robin asked confused. "What Jesse are you talking about? You are talking about the Jesse that got shot yesterday?"

"Yeah . . . him." The short kid said looking at his tall friend, who was looking nervous. "They were like best friends. But then, they just stopped talking from what we know right *niggah*?"

The short kid looked at his friend expecting an answer.

The tall kid looked at detective Robin, and then at his friend. "Let's get out of here man, we don't have to be talking to strangers anyway."

"No wait!" Robin exclaimed. "At least tell me where he lives at?"

"Ok . . . but it has a price . . . and don't tell anybody . . ." the tall kid said scared.

"I swear, I won't . . ." Robin responded pulling out his wallet handling the kids $20 each.

"He lives one block away from here, in the tall blue building." The tall kid responded grabbing the money.

"Do you know the apartment number?" Robin asked again.

"Fuck outta here white boy, I ain't getting in shit. C'mon lets go." He left grabbing his short friend.

Detective Robin stayed at the store staring at the magazines, and breathing deeply, he started walking to that building. That building that by his mentality it was going to take him to make one of the worst criminals in the world be discovered, and that was Isaiah Russell. When he got to the door, he looked through that hallway which had no light. He stepped in and looked through the mail; he was looking for James's apartment. Finally, after he found it, he walked upstairs, and introduced his right hand on his coat pocket, where he had his gun. He was staring at the bluefish walls that were mixed up with graffiti and other colors were making him know that he wasn't welcomed there. *"Fuck cops"* . . . *Killer was here"* and different kinds of signs were printed on the walls. When he got to the apartment, he took a deep breath and knocked on the door. He knocked once. He knocked twice. When he was about to knock for the 3rd time, the door opened slowly, and a chain that locked the door was holding from the inside to the outside. A black man opened the door, and sizing detective Robin from head to toes asked, "Yeah?"

"Does James Johnson live here?" Robin asked seriously.

The black man, who was James Johnson, asked. "What *'chu* want?"

"Does he live here, yes or not?" Robin asked one more time.

"Yeah, it's me." The black man responded.

"Hi, how are you. I'm detective Robin, and I work in the police department of Manhattan." Said Robin showing his batch.

James looked at him worried. "So?"

"I would like to ask you some questions." said Robin putting his batch back on his pocket.

"About what? Jesse's murder? So just because I'm black and from the hood you are going to profile me as the main suspect? I don't have anything to do with Jesse's murder."

"How did you know that I'm here for that?" Robin responded.

Silence took over.

"I was guessing . . . Ya'll cops always investigating and interrogating people for nothing, so I was just saying . . ."

"I'm not here for that. I'm here to ask you for something else, ask you a couple of questions."

"I don't have time for it officer, and if you don't have a warrant for your investigation then *Ima* ask you to leave." James was closing the door, and Robin stopped him from it extending his hand and holding the door.

"What *'chu* doing man!" James screamed.

"I want to talk to you about Isaiah Russell."

"Who's that?" James asked.

"Don't play with me, I know everything . . ." Robin responded.

"About? I don't know what *'chu* talking about man!" James was about to close the door, when the detective held the door again.

James looked at Robin angry. "Hey what *'chu* doing man! Who the fuck *'chu* think *'chu* are! *Ima* call the police god damn it!" he screamed again.

"Go head call them so you can get arrested for being a suspect of Jesse's murder!"

"MAN WHAT *'CHU* TALKING ABOUT MAN! WHAT THE FUCK!" screamed James loudly.

Detective Robin took out of his pocket the white card that he found on the floor, that had James name written on it. "I can arrest you right now for this. I bet if I take it to the lab it would have your fingerprints."

James looked at it and his face turned worried and scared at the same time.

"You are fucked! If you don't want problems just open the door and answer the following questions I have." Robin said making him looked at him with anger, and taking off the locks and chains that were separating them. He opened the door and let him come in. They sat down on James's brown couch, which was covered by clothes.

"You want something to drink?" James asked Robin. He knew Robin had him on his hands. So he was being nice with him, he didn't want to go jail.

"No thanks." Robin responded.

James looked at him and sat down.

"I want you to tell me the truth." Robin said.

"About what?" James asked leaning back

"Look, money can't cover it everything or can't buy it everything. I want to know who killed Jesse Jones."

James sighted. "I already told you I have nothing to do with it."

"You don't have anything to do with it?"

"Nope."

Detective Robin looked at his hands which were sweating, rubbing each other and said, "Then why a paper with your name printed on it was there?"

"Shit . . . I don't know man, maybe I was the next one to get killed, what the fuck do I know?" James said with an attitude.

"So weird that the first person that found that crime was Isaiah Russell . . . and you say you don't know him . . ."

"I don't . . ."

"You do . . ." said Robin convinced.

"What makes you think that?" James asked.

"How much you get serving per day? 1000?" Robin asked.

"WHAT!?"

"If I give you money to kill somebody, let's say $15,000 dollars, wouldn't you do it?" Robin asked making James get up from his sofa and screamed. "Yo son, you getting me mad ass hell, what the fuck is the point of all this?! Why are *'chu* telling me this shit for? You think you going to get something? No!"

"Why are you getting loud? Are you nervous?" Robin asked.

"Nervous of what? I didn't kill him!" James screamed hysterically.

"Then who did it?" Robin asked again.

James screamed. "I DON'T KNOW!"

"Why did you kill your friend James? Why?"

James screamed. "I DIDN'T KILL HIM! IT WASN'T ME!"

Detective Robin raised his tone of voice. "WHY DID YOU GIVE YOUR FRIEND A PRICE JAMES? YOU KILLED FOR MONEY? HUH!"

James was going crazy for so many questions, and started throwing the things that were around him.

"WHY ARE YOU SO NERVOUS? ARE YOU SCARED YOU MAY GET CAUGHT? TALK! WHY DID YOU KILL YOUR FRIEND! Robin kept on screaming all over his face.

James turned to face him and screamed "I DIDN'T WANT TO!"

The silence came for a couple of seconds. James closed his eyes and detective Robin stayed quiet and sat back on the couch. James turned back facing the window.

"Who made you do it James?" asked Robin walking up to him.

James breathed deeply. "Why you care? It's not your business son! Stay away from this!"

"For what? Why? I'm not scared to die James . . . I'm not scared to die as my father, who also died by Isaiah's hands."

James turned and faced him again. He was surprised.

"Why did you kill Jesse? Why Isaiah Russell would send people to kill that man?"

"If I tell you all this bullshit, what's going to happen to me?" Asked James.

"I'm going to try to help you." Robin said staring at him. While James was sitting back on the couch.

"How? Getting locked up? Hell no! I already know this law shit. *Ima* apply the 5th amendment." James said.

"So now you are going to stay quiet?"

"I already told you what you wanted to hear . . ."

"I need to find out why Isaiah Russell sent you to kill Jesse . . ."

"Ok . . . *Ima* tell you son, but I need something that will guarantee me that I won't go to jail at least not for now . . . I have a daughter. Her b-day tomorrow, and I want to see her."

"My dad would be disappointed, but I won't say shit, I swear." said Robin begging James to tell him the story.

"Isaiah wanted to me kill Jesse so nobody could found out that he was the one who tried to kill Caleb Smith."

Detective Robin stayed quiet, in shock; he couldn't believe what he was hearing. The entire situation was getting fixed little by little, now he knew why Isaiah Russell asked him to stay away from Caleb's case. "Why did he pay you to kill him?" Robin asked.

"Jesse didn't want to do anything else for him, so Isaiah got mad and asked me to kill him . . . he's going to pay me $27,000. He wanted Jesse to go to jail as one of the suspects from Caleb's case, with the promise that

Isaiah was going to get him out and a couple of guards would take care of him too. But Jesse didn't care anymore, he stabbed Caleb and that was it. Jesse also found out that Caleb's brother is drug dealing, and messing with underage girls . . . Jesse wanted more money, but Isaiah wasn't putting up with it."

"So then, he asked you to kill him?" asked Robin.

"Yeah, he asked me to kill Jesse because Jesse told him before that if Isaiah would tried to do anything against him. He was going to tell the news, and the police department about his plans, and this *niggah* got mad, and asked me then to go to jail with his conditions. But . . ."

"But what?" Robin asked.

"But I fucked it up. I was supposed to go to jail today, and send some of my homeboys to kill Jesse tomorrow, so then Isaiah would have said that I was innocent and that the criminal was Jesse and since they were going to find him dead, nobody would have suffered . . ."

Detective Robin interrupting, "And like that everybody would ended up happy."

"Right . . ." paused James. "Isaiah with the great reputation, and me still in the hood but with money."

"When is he going to pay you?" asked Robin.

"He said this weekend . . ." James responded looking down to his shoes.

"Are you sure?"

"I trust him, he knows I have his life on my tongue. He better know what he is doing because I don't play games." James said looking at him seriously.

"What if he doesn't pay you?"

James got mad and raised his tone of voice. "Yo what the fuck? What is this son!

Detective Robin laughed, and said, "Sorry to ask you all this, but I had too . . ."

"Man you *ain't* had to ask me shit. I already told you what I know and what you wanted to know." James responded with a big strong attitude.

"You want to do business with me?"

"Business? You a dirty cop too?" James said with a fake smile

Detective Robin sighted. "Isaiah Russell killed my father . . ."

James sighted twice and breathing deeply. "Wow, sorry I wasn't expecting to hear that . . ."

Detective Robin looked down and said, "If he wouldn't have ever killed my father the city would have been one of the most safeties cities in the country. My father would have become the head of the police department, but Isaiah pushed him to the train, and won what he wanted."

"How you know he killed your father?"

"It was pretty obvious, but being part of the justice doesn't mean that bad people go to jail, it's about someone paying for a crime. Isaiah pushed my father and ran out; he let my father get ran over by the train. Now look at him. Sheriff of the police department, have the money, a beautiful daughter that everybody wants to fuck, and what else? Oh yeah, he kills people on the low too."

"How, how did you start suspecting that Isaiah had to do with all this?" James asked.

"That same day that you guys stabbed Caleb Smith I got there like around 4 pm, the only person that got after me was Isaiah Russell, and we started arguing. He told me to stay away from Caleb, the hospital and his case. He knows I'm a good investigator just like my father, so he knew I was going to find out the guys that stabbed Caleb and he knew I was going to make them confess who the main head of it was. And that was him."

James stared at him, drank water and kept on smoking the blunt that was on top of his marble table.

Detective Robin tried not to get too sensitive and tried to keep on saying the story. "I found the man that saw everything the day that Isaiah killed my father. That day that my father died the only thing that he kept on saying was that somebody pushed him. And the only person that was with him that day was Isaiah Russell. But no charges were pressed against him just because he was a cop of high rank, a very respectful officer. The same day that my father died I went back to that place, and I found a man who was walking around there. He was the member of this gang, a <u>crip</u>, a tall skinny man who had an eye green and the other blue. He was always walking with his dog. We started talking about gangs; I had to act like I was on his same crew. At the end I started crying and I asked him about the crime that happened that day. He told me then, that he saw everything. He saw when Isaiah and my father had an argument before the train got there. He told me that Isaiah Russell got out of the car running across the train rails. He ran to a small abandoned house that still is there until today. Then, he told me that my father ran behind him, and since he couldn't see him anymore, my father started walking back to the car. On his way back to the car he told me that he saw how Isaiah put on a black mask and a black shirt and ran behind my dad and hit him in the head with a bat, and then he laid him down on the railroad. When my father woke up it was too late, the train was running over him already. Then, at that moment Isaiah appeared in the picture and pretended that he didn't know anything. That's why I want to destroy his image, that fake image that he has been pretending to have since long ago. He killed my father; he killed him for money, for power, for things that didn't belong to him. All those things belong to my father and me."

James stayed quiet; he didn't want to get involve in more situations. He felt like detective Robin was being honest, but at the same time he didn't know if trusting him was the best thing.

"Sorry for wasting your time, perhaps I should come back some other time." Said Robin getting up from the sofa and walked up to the door.

James putting his drink on the table said "Hey yo! Detective Robin . . ."

Detective Robin turned and said "Yeah?"

James sighted. "What favor you want me to do for you?"

Detective Robin sighted and walking back up to him said. "Thanks!"

James looked at him and said "Favor pay another favor, you should know that."

Detective Robin sat back on the couch and observed his table, his TV, just his place around.

James looked at him and then took off the covers that were on top of his plasma TV. He took off the covers from the couch where he was sitting at. He turned on most of the lights and took off the covers that were on top of stuffs.

Detective Robin was amazed for so much expensive things in the room. He wasn't expecting James to own all that.

Then, sitting back on the couch, he looked at the table in front of him and said, "Oh wow, I didn't know you had an I-phone, and I-pod, diamonds? Wow, you must have been doing good things to pay all this."

James smiled and sitting on the chair said, "Man, I do what I *gotta* do for living. If I have to kill a cop for a Lamborghini, I'll do it. If I have to rob a bank to get a mansion I'll do it. The only thing I don't do is rape, that *ain't* me."

Detective Robin looked at him with a serious look and said "Why this life James? Why this life when you could have had another one, way better."

James sighted and putting the blunt that was on the table to his mouth said, "It's easy, and plus is the only thing that my parents left me as a gift."

Detective Robin asked, "Where are your parents?"

James, smoking tried not to cough and said. "My parents? He laughed. "My parents are dead to me. Those two *ain't* shit, and I'm happy that they *ain't* living no *moe*. I never needed them bitches, fuck them." said playing with the smoke that was coming out of his lips.

Detective Robin sighted and said, "I need you to declare that Isaiah tried to killed Caleb . . . and I need you to say that Isaiah was the one that sent you to kill Jesse."

James started shocking with the smoke and loudly said "What the fuck! That's the favor you want man? You crazy! Hell no! NO!"

Detective Robin trying to stay calm said "I'm not asking you to go to the police department . . . I'm just asking you to call and say it in an anonymous way."

James breathed deeply and said "Look man, I thought I was going to do something for you, but I can't do that . . ."

Detective Robin looked at him and getting tired of the situation said raising his tone of voice, "Ok, I'm going to leave your house, I swear I won't bother you anymore but at least tell me something . . ."

"What?" James asked.

"Tell me how Isaiah Russell planned all this. How many people he paid to cover this work, give me names, and I swear I won't say your name, I promise." Detective Robin said throwing a hopeful breathed.

James looked at him got a paper and pen started writing on it.

Detective Robin didn't say anything; he stayed quiet and waited patiently.

James looked at him and handling him the paper said, "Here."

"What is this?" detective Robin asked.

"This is the place where we took his wallet at, and then this way was the streets that we were supposed to run to get to the alley. These two points were the policemen that were working that day around the alley where we stabbed Caleb. And this is the nurse that collaborated with us too." James said pointing at the points that he drew on the paper.

"Nurse?"

James put the pen down and said, "Yes, a nurse was involved too."

"So you don't know the names of the officers that were working that day, and you don't know the name of the nurse?" Detective Robin asked.

"*Naw*, the only person that knew about it was Jesse, but as you know he dead now. So I can't tell you nothing else son."

Detective Robin got the paper and putting it on his pocket stood up and said. "Thanks! This is going to help me a lot."

James looked at him and then remembering something said, "Yeah but yo! This has a price son, I didn't tell you all this for free"

"How much you want?" Detective Robin asked.

"How much you have?" James responded.

"Just write down the price on that paper and I give it to you right now." Detective Robin said thinking that he was going to write a low number.

"Here." James said and showed him the paper.

900 just for information, it said on the paper.

"Are you serious? Just for telling me?" Detective Robin exclaimed.

"Shit, I should have charged you more son, I don't do nothing for free and fuck no I wasn't going to give you all this for less." James said showing him a smile.

"Ok." Detective Robin sighted and took money out of his pocket. He started counting his dollars bills, placed them on the table, smiled and walked up to the door.

James got the money and counting it said, "Yo!"

Detective Robin turned.

"Good Luck!" James said putting the money back on the table.

"Thanks." Detective Robin said and opening the door walked out.

VIII.

BACK OFF ROBIN

While at the hospital, Juliana was praying and praying in the church that was next to the Emergency building. She was so scared, she was feeling disgrace about everything that was happening. She couldn't believe how such a great person as Caleb could go through all this. It wasn't fair she thought, and it wasn't. Caleb was a great person even since he was little; he was scared to hurt people and hated violence at all. He always wanted to live peacefully and be with his family, and even if his sister and mother rejected him, and treated him the worst. He still had the best intentions inside his heart; feelings that we feel that don't vanish even with hate. Juliana stayed praying, whispering to God her wishes. She was talking to him as if he was in front of her in body and soul. She closed her eyes and then, she felt a hand touching her shoulder softly. She turned to see what was on top of her shoulder. It was an old white hand, and then slowly she lifted her head up and looked at the priest. He was an old man who always had a smile on his face, and talked with so much sweetness.

Juliana got up and said, "Father, oh father, why the soul that I love the most have to be suffering so much?"

The father held her two hands and smiling at her said, "My dear, as our Lord said once, everything is meant to be . . . Remember that the good souls always go through hell in order to get to heaven."

Juliana confused by his words asked, "And, what does that means?"

The father responded. "Our Lord gives a temporal suffering for an eternal good."

Juliana sighted and said. "I hope so, you just don't know. I've been crying day and night, I've been missing him and asking God every night why is he going through all this . . . Why so many people hate him when he is so amazing, so good, he is the nicest person I've ever met . . ."

The father started walking slowly to the front while Juliana was talking, and then said, "Don't worry about the devil, don't fear him . . . You shouldn't because if your faith is bigger than anything in this world, God would remember that, and he'll help you. Remember that nothing is more powerful than love, and God loves us all, he'll save you if you know how to love."

Juliana smiled and drying her tears with her hands said. "Thanks! You don't know how good you made me feel today. For the first time in years, I haven't felt so, I don't know how to explain it, but today I felt like hope came my way."

The father smiled at her and said, "God is with you my dear."

Juliana hugged the priest. She looked at him and smiling walked away from him.

She felt relief, she had the biggest and sweetest smile on her face, and she felt peaceful. She sat down on the bench that was in front of the church, and she stayed there, meditating, thinking wondering, planning what was going to happen after today. Staring at the garden that was in front of her, and looking at the birds that were floating on the lake, she stayed quiet, and started tearing again. Even if she felt better after talking with the priest she still had a small fear in her heart. She felt like something was going to happen, something very bad. She was scared that Caleb may break up with her; she was scared that something might happen to her love.

At that moment, detective Robin who got to the hospital parked his car and before getting out, he saw Juliana sitting on the bench alone. He wondered what could have been wrong, but he didn't want to get close to her. He thought that maybe a simple question was going to make such a big argument. So he kept on walking, walking on that white day, but she was beautiful, and she looked more beautiful that day. Quiet, peaceful, her innocence was attracting him, her whole self was unedifying in his eyes, and not thinking twice he walked up to her.

Detective Robin stood next to the bench and looking at the view said, "Nice day right?"

Juliana looked up to see who owned those words and said, "Oh, yeah, very nice."

"Have you been here all day?" he asked.

"Something like that."

"How's Caleb?"

"From bad to worst . . . What can I say Mr. Robin, everything has been happening to him. I don't know why or how, but I have a feeling . . . you know, I think somebody wants to kill him on purpose. Somebody just envies him a lot and don't want to see him up there."

"What happened now?" detective Robin asked.

"You didn't know?"

"Know what?"

"Apparently somebody tried to poison him . . . he is in emergency getting well. A nurse I guess gave him a pill that was going to stop his heart and he would have ended dying." Juliana said looking at the lake.

Robin stared at her face.

"I don't know why all this happens to him. He is not a bad person, he is one of the greatest men that this world could have, and people just want to see him dead."

Detective Robin was figuring out things. Now he understood better what James had told him. And looking at back again at Juliana detective Robin asked, "Can I ask you something Ms. Russell?

"Yeah . . . yes, of course."

"Who do you think this person could be?"

Juliana looked at him confused and worried and asked, "What do you mean? I don't know who could have planned all this. But a strong reason that person may have to do it."

"You don't know anyone that hate you or him, or just hate you two because you guys were together and happily in love?" Detective Robin asked.

"Not really, well, my parents didn't want me with him, but they are not the ones that did this." Juliana said expressing confusion.

Detective Robin stayed quiet for a few seconds, then got up and told Juliana. "Look, I have to go, I really didn't want to bother you with any questions. Every time I try to ask you something or talk to you we always end up fighting. You think I think your dad is a bad person, but I'm just trying to find out and solve your boyfriend's case.

"I didn't say any of that, but it's good that you quit this conversation before it turned to an argument. I wasn't going to take no type of crap today and that's for sure."

"Ok, then I guess I'll see you when I see you. Take care" Detective Robin said and walked away, trying not to look back. She was beautiful, a turn on, a goddess that he knew he couldn't let in his heart. She was Isaiah Russell's daughter and that was enough for him to know. She was happily in love with Caleb Smith, a successful man who could give her everything in the world; and the perfect man for her.

As he was walking to the emergency building, he saw Joey, sitting on the waiting room. He approached to him and started a conversation. They went from a hi to a coffee to stay awake and try to calm down. Detective Robin was asking him what really happened, how was Caleb doing, he wanted Isaiah Russell to go to jail, he wanted to take revenge for his father's dead. He wanted somebody to pay for that crime, he wanted the real killer to get his price, and that was Isaiah in his eyes.

Later on, Juliana walked inside the hospital, and found out that Caleb had already opened his eyes but he couldn't talk that much. She knew everyone else was eating, and not thinking twice she walked in the room at the time that the doctor prohibited the visitors to go in.

She checked that there was no one around and opened the door softly and saw him. She stared at him sleeping peacefully. She got closer to the bed so she could touch him while he was asleep. Those minutes, those seconds were enough for Juliana to touch his hands and remember all the times they spent together. She kept on staring at his face; she wondered why everything was going wrong. Why she had a feeling that Caleb was going to break up with her? Why was she thinking that he was trying to avoid her? She was stress thinking if she should she kiss him; she wanted to feel him one more time, but then again, she thought. He may wake up if she makes a noise, he may feel uncomfortable. So she stopped her desires, and right when she about to leave, she kissed his hand and walked away.

As soon as the door closed, Caleb opened his eyes. He tried not to cry and suffer. He wanted to call her name, he wanted to stop her but it was better if he stayed quiet. He needed her away from him, take her out of his heart, and mind. But how could he forget about somebody who he was deeply in love with? How could he run from something that he believed belonged to him? How was he going to stop his heart from beating fast whenever he sees her? How was he going to stop feeling butterflies in his stomach every time she was around? It was a hard decision. It was a hard time for him. One day he had to tell her the truth. One day she was going to find out, and that day had to be soon before the seed that she had in will begin to grow. That day had to be coming soon because if not things were going to get worst. His heart was in her hands, he was going crazy; he didn't have the courage enough to let her go, but the only solution to this problem was either him disappearing or the death of the baby.

As Juliana waited for the elevator she saw the nurse that was taking care of Caleb walking by her way. She thought the nurse was going to recognize her, but this one apparently didn't, and kept on walking. Juliana thought the nurse was going to turn to the right at the end of the hallway, but she stopped at Caleb's room and walked in.

Juliana knew that nobody was allowed to go inside Caleb's room, and upset about it she walked towards the room. In the room already, the nurse smiled at Caleb while he was pretending to be asleep. And walking closer to him the nurse started saying *"You ruined my plans idiot . . . well, at least you are going to die soon. You were lucky that they found you on time, because if not you would have been dead and I would have got my money on time."*

Then, unexpectedly, Juliana opened the door and loudly screamed. "What are you doing here?"

The nurse turned looking really angry and said, "Excuse me?"

"I said, what are you doing here?"

The nurse laughed in a sarcastic way and responded, "I'm a nurse, what else can I be doing?"

"The doctor prohibited everybody to come here for a certain time. I'm going to ask you to leave the room, you know you are not supposed to be in here."

"Look, I'm going to tell you something ok? I do not care if you are Isaiah Russell's daughter. If you mess with me I'm going to mess with you back. Don't try to get me angry young lady, because if you look for me you are going to find me." The nurse said.

"Isaiah Russell? Isaiah Russell, who the fuck is Isaiah Russell you stupid bitch! You think I care if you are friends with my dad? I don't really know why all of you people are so scared of him. But let me tell you something else, I don't care who you are, I'm not scared of you, and yes I already looked for you, what the fuck are you going to do?"

"You don't know me girl."

"What the fuck are you going to do?"

The nurse looked at her and getting the papers that she was holding when she got in the room, sized her and walked out. Juliana stayed in the room and sighted deeply. She was already getting sick of all this stress and drama. She got her phone out of her purse and made a phone called.

"Joey? Hey! Look, I think you should come already to Caleb's room and stay here."

"What? Where are you?" Joey asked.

Juliana breathed deeply and said, "I sneaked in Caleb's room . . . I wanted to see him. But then, I saw this nurse . . ."

"What nurse? He is not allowed to have anybody going to his room." Joey responded

"I know, that's why I'm telling you to come, I don't trust anyone around here anymore . . . I've seen the nurse that used to take care of him before coming in . . . we argued, and whatever. Look just come because I really want to stop with all this drama for today, I want to go home, and if I go home I have to make sure that he is going to be safe ok?" Juliana told Joey.

"Ok, I'm going to be there in a few minutes . . ." Joey responded.

"Alright, I'm going to wait for you here." Juliana said and hanging up the phone call, she looked at her lover once again, walked out of the room, and waited outside in the hallway for Joey.

On the waiting room, Joey was finishing his conversation with detective Robin.

"I'm going to call you tomorrow I guess." Joey said.

"Yeah, that would be great. I really need your cooperation Joey. If you want to find out exactly what went down in your brother's case, we need to find out every little thing." detective Robin said.

"I know, I know . . . well, take care man. I'll talk to you tomorrow." Joey said and shook hands with him.

When Joey got upstairs he saw Juliana sitting on the floor in the middle of the hallway.

"You must really love my brother." Said while he was walking up to her.

Juliana, who was on her knees, lifted up her head and smiled.

"C'mon, go home baby girl; it's not good for you to be like this." said and held her hands as she was getting up.

Juliana sighted and said. "I do love him, of course I do, and I really don't care about my appearance anymore. The make up, the extensions, getting my nails done, nothing matters to me anymore. I just want him to be good, healthy and love me again."

Joey erased his smiled and tried not to look like he knew something was going wrong.

"Joey, I know Caleb has talked to you about what's on his mind, and don't try to lie to me because I know you know something."

"I don't know what are you talking about . . ."

"Joey please, don't lie to me. I think I have had enough with all this already. I mean, everything has been going bad in my life. I feel like Caleb is avoiding me, like if he doesn't love me anymore and . . . and that is killing me . . . I can't with it anymore."

"Juliana, I think you should go home, relax and . . ."

"I don't want to go home damn it!" Juliana interrupted raising her voice. "I want things to be like before, and if he doesn't love me anymore then I want him to say IT! Joey . . . Have you ever been in love before?"

"Yeah . . . yeah I've been in love before . . ."

"Then you should understand how I'm feeling. Do you think I like seeing him on that bed?! Laying down, doing nothing? You think I like how everybody that knows about us have tried to separate us and now they almost killed him? I don't like that! I DON'T! And I feel like I'm going crazy . . . I, I just can't anymore, please understand me!" Juliana screamed as she kept on crying. Joey hugged her. He knew exactly what was going on, but he couldn't tell her that her boyfriend, the love of her life was her uncle. Joey looked at her, wiped her tears and said, "My dear, I don't want to see you crying . . . I have so much love for you Juliana, but the truth is that I don't know anything that you are going through with him. Caleb and I haven't talked; he got bad before we got to talk. I couldn't even say hi to him, as soon as I got here he was already being transferred to ER."

Joey felt bad as he was looking at her walking to the elevator. He felt bad about the whole situation. It wasn't her fault that she fell in love with her own blood. It was her mother's fault for not telling the truth and for not having enough communication with her own daughter.

Outside of the emergency building, detective Robin was sitting on the bench smoking a cigarette. It was already 7:00 pm, the night was very dark, so dark that one could see the stars moving slowly and actually see the moon in its perfect shape. Detective Robin then, saw Juliana getting out of the emergency building, walking towards her car. Detective Robin didn't miss the opportunity and throwing his cigarette on the floor and turning it off by stepping on it, ran to Juliana's direction.

Juliana who was opening the trunk turned and saw him coming.

Detective Robin stopped yelled, "Ms. Russell!"

"May I help you?"

"Are you busy tonight?" Detective Robin asked

"Why do you want to know for?"

"I was wondering, maybe you would like to come with me and eat something."

"Detective Robin, don't you hate my father?"

Detective Robin laughed. "I think that's between your father and I, I don't think that has anything to do in asking his daughter to go eat."

"You are funny Robin . . . and you try hard, very hard". She said as she walked to the front door.

Detective Robin walking behind her said, "I was just asking Ms. Russell, I don't see anything wrong with two people going to eat."

Juliana stopped and said facing him responded, "Don't you respect that I have a boyfriend? And that I'm pregnant?

"Who says I'm trying to get at you in that way?" Robin responded.

Juliana stared at him for a couple of seconds, got inside her car, and turning the car on she started driving backwards to get out of the parking. Detective Robin walked as fast as the car was moving. Then, Juliana stopped the car and putting the window down she screamed, "You son of a bitch!" and drove away.

Detective Robin amazed by her words laughed.

She was moody, very moody lately.

When Juliana got home, she looked at her mom on a white chair out in the garden. She stopped her car and let her driver take it to park it.

"Mom, what are you doing sitting here?" Asked as she was getting closer to her mother.

Her mom looked at her and smiled. "Sit down my baby."

"Dad hasn't come back right?" Juliana asked.

"No . . . Juliana, I'm not expecting a lot from your dad anymore."

"Why? Mom, I don't want to get involve in your businesses, but I really want to know why were you guys arguing that day? Does he really hate Caleb that much?"

Dara looked at Juliana making a face expression that was saying a lot, but she stayed quiet.

"Mom, what's wrong? Is there something that you and dad are hiding and don't want to tell me?"

"What are you saying . . . You don't have any reason to doubt us baby, just forget about it, believe me it wasn't big." Her mom said massaging her daughter's hands.

"If it wasn't that serious then, why my dad got so mad? Mom I'm not a little girl anymore, you can talk to me."

A fake smile came out from Dara's face; she knew she had to invent something so her daughter could stop interrogating her. However, the big question was how far was Dara going to go for her daughter's love? Was she going to keep as a secret the reality that her daughter was going to find out sooner or later? Was Dara really going to act like nothing happened and let her daughter live in a lie? Was Dara going to hide forever that the father of her daughter's baby was her own uncle, her own brother?

"Mrs. Russell, Mr. Isaiah is on the phone." Her maid said holding the phone.

"Thank you Carmen."

As the maid walked away, Dara felt relieve to know that there was nothing else to talk with her daughter.

Juliana got up and whispered on her mom's ear "I'm going inside, I'm tired, tell dad I love him." She kissed her mom on the cheek and walked away.

On the phone, the conversation got worst as soon as Juliana left.

"I heard her don't worry." Isaiah said on the phone line.

"Where are you Isaiah?" she asked.

"None of your business. You should be the last person to ask what, where and with who am I with." He responded with a terrible attitude that hurt her sensitive heart.

The silence took over the conversation.

"I'm sorry Isaiah . . ."

Isaiah interrupting said, "I want the divorce."

Dara stayed quiet and changing her tone of voice responded, "What?"

"I said I want the divorce, I don't want to be with you anymore."

"Isaiah, my love, please listen to me, we don't have to live this way . . . Please stay with me, don't leave me." She started to cry desperately. "Oh please, Isaiah don't do it!"

"I already took my decision, tomorrow I'm going to pass by the house and I'm going to tell Juliana . . . I'm going to tell her why we are separating from each other."

"No, no please, don't do that, you can't do that . . . you'll kill her with your words." Dara begged to Isaiah.

"Kill her? Why would I kill her? Kill her because I will tell her the truth? Oh please Dara what's wrong with you? What kind of mother are you?!"

"Isaiah, please, I beg you . . . she is my life, I don't want her to hate me . . . please don't tell her anything!"

"Dara, Juliana already hates you enough. If I tell her the truth nothing would change. I'm telling you, get ready because I'm going to tell her everything; I rather see her crying than being with somebody that she can't be with." Isaiah responded with cruelty.

"Isaiah . . ."

"See you tomorrow Dara." He said and hung up the phone.

Dara stayed outside in the garden, crying, crying as much as she could, she felt like her tears were the only ones that were going to help her do something. She didn't know what to do anymore it was too much. What she was going through was enough. She loved her daughter so much, that she didn't want to see her cry, and so that night she planned something to keep her daughter away from her dad.

In contrast, detective Robin who was in a bar near Isaiah's Russell hotel was drinking talking to one of the bartenders, then talking a random lady that sat next to him.

"Are you from here?" the girl asked.

"Yes I am."

"I've never seen you around . . . and I go out a lot. I go to parties, clubs, bars, always out having fun . . . how come I haven't seen you around?"

"I don't go out much."

"Wow . . . that's crazy . . . this town is ready for single people, single young people to live it up, and you are telling me that you don't go out . . . when . . ."

As the chick kept on talking, he turned and observed a black BMW parking nearby. He kept on looking carefully while his new friend was trying to touch him. But his eyes opened wider when he saw Isaiah Russell getting out of the car and with him the nurse that was taking care of Caleb

Smith. He thought once, he thought twice, why was Russell at this time, at that place with that woman? He saw how the nurse was running to the back of the car, with a big brown luggage. Where was she going? Why was she still wearing her uniform? He kept on asking himself.

Detective Robin looked at his new young and wild friend and whispering on her ear said, "I'll be right back."

The woman responded, "Where are you going?"

Robin walked out of the bar as fast as he could, and hided behind the big trash can that was by the main door of the bar. He took out his camera from his long coat's pocket, and started to take pictures. He walked and walked closer to Isaiah and the nurse trying not to be obvious, trying not to get people's attention, when he saw Isaiah giving money to the nurse. Quickly, detective Robin took one, two, three pictures. She was receiving the money, putting it in her purse as she was walking to another car. A red car that was parked not that far from Isaiah's. Robin kept on taking pictures.

When the nurse finished talking to Isaiah, she got in the car, and drove away. Detective Robin ran to another exit of the bar and got on his car. Robin waited for Isaiah to get inside the bar, and when he did, he started driving behind the nurse. He had to follow her; he had to see what was going on. Why was Isaiah giving her money for? Why would he be such a close friend with that nurse? As he kept on driving behind her, following her, turning right, and left, she finally stopped outside of a beauty supplies store. He waited on his car until she got out.

30 minutes later, she came out with different bags, and trying to look through them, the wig, make up, and other accessories fell off the plastic bag when this one broke. The nurse looked around her to see if someone was watching her. She opened the backdoor of her car, threw all the accessories in it, closed it, walked to the front, got in, and drove as fast as she could. As he was following her he was noticing that she was taking the airport's route. Why was she going there for? Certain things weren't right in Robin's head. First, Russell giving her money, then a different car, then the wig at the beauty supply store . . . why? Robin kept on wondering. Suddenly, she stopped in one motel, then, drove to another one, and to another, and the same routine repeated for couple of hours. Finally, at 4:50 am, she got out of one of the motel, and drove her car to the back; she was parking outside Room number 5. She opened the door slowly and Robin kept on taking pictures, everything was an evidence for him. Every

little thing, every step, every detail meant something for him to finish this puzzle that was driving him insane. Why did Russell pay her? Why was she staying near the airport? Where was she going? Why the wig and accessories for? Robin had no warrant, he had nothing to stop her and interrogate her. He kept on thinking and thinking, smoking cigarette after cigarette, filling his head with strange thoughts. However, he had probable cause; he knew everything was linked up to another. Caleb's assault, the thief who died after the assault, James confessing, someone poisoning Caleb, then the nurse that took care of him suddenly stopped working. What was going on? He couldn't confess to the police department about James's confession . . . He promised him he wasn't going to arrest him. How was he going to arrest the nurse when Russell was protecting her? How was he going to just jump into a big conclusion, he was just like his father. They both loved to get in cases that seemed like they didn't have an exit. They both loved getting in the deepest situations just to help the rest of the world, even if they had to put their lives in danger. Robin remembered, and missed his father, he wished he was alive so they could make justice together, and remembering the last seconds that life gave him to hug his father he started remembering how Russell killed him. Robin hated Isaiah Russell. He knew he wasn't a common individual; he knew and believed that Isaiah Russell was one of the worst human beings alive. He was the sheriff of the police department in Manhattan, he was supposed to get the criminals and lock them up, he was suppose to protect the city, and everyone in it, but in the contrary, he knew that Isaiah was the one killing, shooting, starting crimes, violating everyone's rights.

Isaiah Russell didn't care about the citizens of Manhattan. He didn't care about stopping the vandalism, drug dealers, etc. He was the boss not because he earned it with hard work, but with corruption and lies. He had a cold heart; he didn't care about anything but his own. He always wanted to rule and kill anything that was on his way. But Robin also knew that the only thing that he adored was Juliana, and that was probably the reason why all this drama started. And it was truth. He raised her way before she came out her mother's belly. He saw her growing up as he wanted, he fed her with his own beliefs, and he wanted her to have his mentality. He used to take her to the courthouse and show her around when she was little, showed her the crimes, and everything that he discovered to "protect the city", making Juliana see him as a God, and adore him. She was in his eyes the son/daughter he never had; he wanted her to be the child that his wife never gave him.

At the hospital, Joey who already changed clothes was sitting down on a chair next to Caleb's bed, reading a book. Caleb wanted to talk, but he couldn't. He wanted to talk to his brother, but he was scared that he wasn't going to be able. He knew what happened, and why he was laying there. He remembered everything, but he was scared to say a word. What has happened to his brave character? What happened to the Romeo that got everything that he wanted in life? Why was his own sweet self-going through so much tragedy for?

Caleb who was looking at his brother sleep, tried to move, tried to open his mouth to say a word, but his fear, the fear that he had thinking that he had lost his voice was coming over and over again. He tried to talk, so he started saying slowly the letter "A", then on the same way he kept on going with the letter "B" and kept on until he got to the letter "Z".

Around 12:25 pm, he sat down on the bed and tried to say loudly his brother's name.

12:36 pm, his brother was still asleep. Caleb wanting to talk to somebody, slowly got up from the bed, and walked straight to Joey's chair. But my dear Caleb wasn't walking as a 35 year old was suppose to. He was walking as an old man, shaking and trying to control his body's movements, which were failing. The stab and the poison got his body in the worst state ever. When he got to Joey's, he touched his hand and softly whispered. "Joey . . . Joey please wake up."

Joey opened his left eye first and then the right one, jumped on his seat looked at him and said loudly, "Caleb? Gosh! When did you get up? C'mon go back to bed."

Caleb walked back to his bed and laying down they started a serious conversation as Joey helped him to lay on the bed.

"Joey . . . I need you to go to the police and tell them who tried to kill me." Caleb spoke but his voice wasn't working, he had lost it, he was very sick.

"What are you saying? Who tried to kill you?" Joey screamed.

Caleb trying to talk opened his mouth and slowly moved his lips saying, "Isaiah, Isaiah Russell . . ."

"What are you saying? Isaiah Russell tried to kill you? Caleb, are you sure of what you are saying? He's Lily's husband, the sheriff of the police department . . . I don't think he'll do something like that . . . tell me, did you speak to detective Robin for something?"

Caleb nodded his head. "No, no, listen to me . . . he sent somebody to do it for me . . ."

"Who?"

"The nurse . . ."

Joey surprised opened his eyes widely and said, "What nurse?"

"The nurse that took care of me when I was in the room 320, the Dominican chubby lady . . . she is friends with Isaiah, she poisoned my water after giving me a pill . . ."

Joey stayed quiet and deeply sighted.

"Listen, detective Robin and Isaiah Russell hate each other . . . there's no way that Robin tried to brainwashed me, he is a good man . . ." Caleb said again dropping all his weight in the bed.

"Caleb, Caleb, listen, detective Robin talked to me and I don't know . . . I feel like there's something that he is hiding. I don't like Peter Robin, I think he is full of shit, and if he came and told you is because he wants you to be against Russell."

"No, no, listen to me Joey . . . Isaiah Russell asked detective Robin to stay away from my case, he prohibited to him, and I asked why and Isaiah didn't say anything . . . believe me, Isaiah tried to kill me, and he sent that nurse to do it."

Joey convinced by his words asked. "Why would Isaiah Russell hate a simple detective as Robin? Why do they hate each other so much?"

Caleb sighted and responded, "Because . . . Isaiah killed Robin's father."

Joey was shocked about it.

"Yes, it's truth, I'm serious . . . if Isaiah wouldn't have killed him, Robin's dad would have been the sheriff of the police department of Manhattan."

Joey stared at his brother and looked to the sides with his thought on mind and said, "I can't believe it, then . . . why he never paid for that crime in jail?"

"Robin told me that until this day nobody knows anything of what I just told you. They know somebody pushed his father to the train, and the only one that was there at that time was Isaiah Russell, but then he said that he saw a man pushing him . . . 2 weeks later, Robin went to the place where his father was murdered at, and he told me he talked to a man, who had stayed around the train station for years. He told Robin that he saw when Isaiah pushed him." Caleb said.

"But the cameras in the train didn't see Isaiah's face? I'm sorry this is just so confusing . . . it seems like Isaiah got into an agreement with somebody to kill Robin's father and take position."

"I don't know . . . Russell is a very powerful man . . . he probably fixed it all somehow."

"Who told you all this? Detective Robin? Maybe he is trying to put you against Isaiah Russell . . . Caleb, listen, I think Isaiah is a good man, I mean, I wouldn't doubt of his word, and I think you shouldn't ether."

"Joey, listen to me . . . Isaiah is a bad person, and I don't want him to be investigating my case, I don't need him . . . That man tried to kill me! I never said that I wanted detectives investigating who stabbed me I never said anything. Think for a moment please, Isaiah started '*investigating*' my case as soon as I got to the hospital, he was doing it without my authorization . . . that's not something weird . . . he knew everything, where was I stabbed, when, the time, he suddenly '*assumed*' that it was 3 thieves? I don't think so."

"You are right, but think also, maybe he did it because you are Juliana's boyfriend, and he wants to protect his daughter. You have to think that he could also be thinking what could happen if you two decide to walk around New York again."

Caleb looked at his brother with so much disappointed and said, "Are you so sure and confident of what you are saying Joey? Are you going to doubt of your brother's word? What . . . what is wrong with you?"

Joey stayed quiet and sat on the chair.

Caleb sighted deeply and said again, "Listen, the only way I'm going to get Isaiah away from me, is getting myself away from all this bullshit. And for that, I need Peter Robin; he is the only one that would give his life to put Isaiah in jail."

"Sorry Caleb but you are already stuck for life in this. Even if you want to escape to the end of the world you are already stuck in this drama forever. You got Juliana pregnant, who is your niece. Isaiah wants to kill you because you took his princess away, and Lily, I mean, Dara Russell, who is our sister denied you so many times . . . Tell me Caleb, what is going to happen when Juliana finds out that you are her uncle, and Isaiah finds out that you are the brother that never died? Tell me what's going to be next? I mean, he is going to hate me too, he doesn't know that we are

Dara's family; he doesn't know that we are her brothers. You know what's going to happen? I'm going to tell you what's going to happen. He is going to kill both of us to just to shut this secret and also probably make Juliana abort that seed of yours. That seed, that child that has no fault at all." Joey said raising his voice.

"You are right. It is not her fault, and so it's not mine. It's Dara's fault. I don't know what to do Joey, I don't . . . I don't know how to get Juliana away from me."

"I guess you have to just leave her alone, disappear from her life, tell her you guys are not meant to be, and . . .

Caleb looked at him angry and interrupted, "And what? Joey do you think she is not going to ask why? Anyway, Dara is going to tell her that I am her uncle; I mean she is not going to live all her life with that lie! C'mon! Let's stop playing games and let's stop being stupid! Juliana is going to find out what's the truth, but I won't tell her. Dara has to. I'm going to make her do it as soon as possible too . . . I just can't live with all this drama, I wake up every day angry, sad, depressed, and it's the same when I go back to sleep . . . I can't deal with this."

Joey looked at him and getting up from the chair, walked up to the door and said while he was opening it. "I'll be right back; I'm going to get coffee."

On his way downstairs, he walked up to the cafeteria passing by the front desk, and looking carefully, he saw Isaiah talking to the nurse that supposedly tried to kill Caleb. He stood there for a little hiding in the one of the columns that was nearby. He looked at them talking and talking. She was carrying a big brown box, but she wasn't wearing her nurse uniform anymore and that was what was surprising him. Then, they two started heading to the exit. Joey followed them and looked through the big window that was next to the exit. The nurse was taking the box and Isaiah was giving her some papers. She said bye to Isaiah and got in the car while Isaiah took off from his pocket a pack of cigarettes and turned on one of them and put it on his mouth.

Joey ran back to the waiting room and sat down on the sofa next to an old lady who was falling asleep. He was wondering why was Mr. Russell doing with that nurse, why wasn't she wearing her uniform? Everything that his brother had told him was making sense. Everything that Peter Robin was talking to him was fixing in the picture. Now he was a little surer about Isaiah Russell's bad intentions and everything that he does just to make people disappear to don't damage his image.

Suddenly, he felt somebody standing next to him. He looked to the side and lifting his head up he saw Russell staring at him and smiled.

"I'm surprised that you are still here . . . this late." Isaiah said looking at his watch.

Joey looked at him and looking down to the table smiled. "I have a brother to take care of."

"Where is your mother Joey? Don't you think that your mother would like to know how her son is doing?"

Joey stayed quiet and breathed deeply.

Isaiah smiled at him and touching his shoulder said, "Good night, I hope your brother will wake up soon." he said and started walking away.

"He is already awake." Joey replied, making Isaiah stopped

"What?" Isaiah turned and asked.

"He is already awake, he woke up today . . . but he can't talk." Joey said getting up from the sofa where he was sitting at.

Isaiah walked up to Joey and facing him said, "Wow, I'm . . . I'm happy he is awake, that's . . . that's good to know. I hope that my daughter would be happy too when she finds out."

"By the way how's your family Mr. Russell? Don't they miss you when you work this late?"

"My family is my job, is the only one that keeps it real with me, and my money is my love, my sex, my satisfaction . . . it accomplishes everything I want." Isaiah responded giving Joey a fake smile.

"That's good to know, I hope your money would keep satisfying you."

Joey looked at him leave through the exit door and not thinking twice; made a phone call.

"Hello? Robin, I need you to get over here soon. I need to talk to you about something . . . Yeah, yea he is awake already come please . . . Ok, call me when you get here." Joey was talking to Detective Robin and hanging up the phone he waited for the elevator.

On the other hand, Juliana, who was in her room, had the most devastated feeling in her stomach. She felt like dying, she was imagining, and feeling that Caleb, the love of her life was going to break up with her. She knew it, she told herself. So many paranoid thoughts ran around her head making herself think that she was the only guilty one for everything that was happening to him. First, they tried to kill him, now they tried to poison him so he could die faster. Why was everybody telling her that her dad had something to do with it? Juliana didn't believe anything that people was whispering. She knew her dad was a good person and loved her very much. As she was laying on her bed hugging her pillow, tears were falling on the white sheets, crying, asking God why Caleb wanted to leave her? She was loosing her self-esteem, she felt like if he was going to leave her it was because she wasn't enough for him. Her hormones made her go crazier in thoughts and wondered that perhaps, she wasn't enough physically, mentally, or maybe too ignorant. She wasn't going to school, she wasn't studying, she didn't have any goals because she was only living to please him, and make him happy. And from all that the only good thing she had was her baby. That seed which was growing everyday. The seed that expressed the love that she had for Caleb; a prohibited love that wasn't going to end, a love that brought so much pain but it just felt so good, so much pain that was going to get bigger as the clock was ticking.

Her phone started ringing as she was wiping her tears; she looked at the caller ID. It was Monique. She breathed deeply and picked up.

"Yes?"

"Juliana, please, I beg you, let me talk to you."

"Ok. Talk." Juliana responded with attitude.

"I know, we are not friends anymore, but . . . I miss you, and I'm sorry. I really do, I really want to be friends with you again. You just don't know how much I need you."

"You should have thought about that before Monique. Did you ever sit down and think about all the things that you did to me? Such as sleeping with my ex boyfriend, telling . . ."

Monique interrupted saying, "No, listen to me, you didn't care about him, you told me that."

"Monique, even if I didn't give three shits about him you should have told me that you wanted to mess with him. You lied to me. Those times when I was asking you how you got there to his house and stuff. Those days that I asked you to come see me and be with me. All this time Monique, all this time I was blind! I was trusting you, putting all my life in your hands and you just betrayed me . . . in the worst way ever, not only because you told Danny that I slept with his own dad, but also by you sleeping with him behind my back!"

"I'm sorry. I wasn't thinking about what I was doing. I just let myself go for that guy."

"I think before you think about what to say to a guy just to get his attention, you should think about the people that love you, the real people that really care about you. Not the people that just use you to get something."

"I know . . . Danny used me. Today I found out something, something really bad . . . He has a girlfriend now; they have been dating for about 4 weeks."

Juliana surprised said, "Wow . . . sorry to hear that. But you deserved it. That's what happens to people that backstabbed others."

"How could you tell me that?"

"What else do you want me to tell you? How are you going to be with a guy that made you sleep with him and his dad at the same time? Not only that, but also sleep around with his closest friends just for you to fit in his 'category'?! What's wrong with you? You are stupid, yes you are! You are an idiot! You don't think with your brain anymore Monique. And I'm sorry but I don't feel like talking to you now." Juliana said with a strong attitude hurting Monique's heart.

"Are you hanging up?" Monique asked trying to calm down from crying.

"I have to. Every time I think of you and try to talk to you I end up being hurt and disgusted . . . It's not good for me and for my baby."

"I love you Juliana. You are the most honest person I've ever met. You are the best friend that any girl could ask for. You have always been there for me, and even if now, we are not friends anymore, I want to tell you and remind you that I love you, and if one day you need somebody, I'm here for you."

"Ok thanks." Juliana hung up. She lay down on the bed, turned off her phone, the lights, and closed her eyes.

IX.

THE CONFESSION

At the hospital Caleb and Joey were waiting for detective Robin to go over and talk about how the case was coming along. When Robin arrived to the hospital, and was walking through the lobby, he saw Isaiah Russell sitting down on the sofa, alone.

He didn't want to stop and talk to him, and of course he didn't want Isaiah to see him either. As the elevator doors opened, Robin was getting in, pressed the button of the floor where he was going, but something stopped the doors from closing, it was Isaiah. Detective Robin didn't want to give him a bad impression, held his anger and all the questions that he had.

"It's a miracle to see you around here Robin." Isaiah Russell said smiling.

"Yeah, I know."

"I hope you are not here for Caleb Smith."

"What I'm doing here is none of your business Mr. Russell with all due respect."

Isaiah laughed in a sarcastic way and said, "Oh yes they are. Remember that I told you to stay away from his case, didn't I?"

"And I'm a free citizen in a free country doing whatever is my right to do to protect society."

"And as I said before, the one that has the last word is me."

"Let's keep on our own ways, and let's justice decide." Detective Robin said and walked out of the elevator. He knocked on Caleb's room glass window, making Joey turned and open the door.

"Sorry I'm late. I had to stopped and get something to eat." Robin said as he was taking his coat off and putting it on top of the chair.

"It's ok Robin, just take a sit." Caleb said with his weak voice.

"Wow you are talking. I thought you were going to take more days to get well." Said Robin as he sat down. "So, why did you two brothers make me come all the way over here for?"

Caleb trying to talk said, "I need to tell you something . . . Something that is going to help you to solve what you have wanted to solve for years."

Detective Robin laughed and said, "Solve? What I have wanted to do for years was to put Isaiah in prison for all the crimes he committed. But that's never going to happen; he is too powerful."

"I know who tried to kill me."

"I beg your pardon?"

"I know who tried to poison me as well. I know everything Robin. Now, I get everything you told me once. I'm sure that your father didn't die accidentally. That man that witnessed your father's murder was right. He was pushed." Said convincing Robin.

Detective Robin breathed deeply and looking at Caleb surprised asked. "What are you saying? Why are you saying this?! Where is your evidence?! And . . ."

"Isaiah Russell sent people to kill me I know it!" Interrupted Caleb.

"How do you know? Who told you this?" Robin kept on asking desperately.

"I wasn't supposed to live. The nurse . . . the nurse that was under my supervision did it. She tried to poison me. She gave me a pill that was going to stop my heart . . . I was going to overdose! That nurse was paid by Isaiah Russell to hurt me."

"Describe her."

"She is dark, chubby, around 5'4 has a tattoo near her neck . . . and"

"I know . . . I know exactly what you are saying . . . She is always at the front desk . . . It can't be . . . She is leaving." Robin said feeling stressed and looking confused."

"What do you mean she is leaving?"

"I've seen her with Isaiah Russell a couple of times. When I was at the bar I saw her coming out from Isaiah's car with a bag, like if she was going somewhere. Then I followed her. She is staying at this motel near by the airport."

"Are you serious?"

"Yeah . . . like a couple of hours ago." Robin responded.

"But I've just seen her not too long ago. She was with Isaiah talking. I saw them from far I was in the cafeteria with Joey. She was carrying boxes from her place, while Isaiah walked her to her car. She wasn't wearing her uniform."

"I saw Isaiah giving her money . . . She was buying wigs and beauty supplies around the motel where she is staying at."

Caleb interrupted. "She tried to kill me. I want to press charges against her. She is probably trying to fly out of the country. She knows that I'm not dead she knows it! She is probably scared that we may find out before she leaves . . . She probably thinks that since she is protected by Isaiah she will get out of this situation."

Detective Robin knew what to do, but his mind was so shock that couldn't demand his body to move. He knew that if he talks, he was probably either get fired from the police department, or Isaiah was going to kill him. He didn't know if he should tell them that he found out what he knew now. How was he going to tell Caleb that he spoke face to face with one of the delinquents that tried to kill him? How was he going to make the world believe that Isaiah Russell was hiring people to kill people? He knew he couldn't say any of that without proof, he knew he couldn't say that James told him every detail about this horrible case; he wasn't going to betray his own promise.

"I need to stop her. I need to stop her before she runs out of the country if not, we won't be able to find her." Robin said.

"I want to press charges on her." Caleb responded.

"Let's do it. I'm going to write everything that you just said and you are going to sign it, then I'm going to take it to the police department." Detective Robin said getting a piece of paper and a pen.

Caleb started telling detective Robin how everything happened. The time that the nurse went to the other room where he was at, the time she gave him the pill, the color of the pill. He was trying to give as many details as he could remember.

When Caleb finished, Robin made him sign the paper, got up, grabbed his coat, and walk out of the room. He headed towards the stairs. He didn't want to take the elevator this time. On his way downstairs, he made a phone call.

"Hello! Yes, this is Robin speaking Justin. I need you to do me a favor . . . yes, I'm going over there right now don't worry. Look, I need you to prepare a warrant to arrest somebody . . . yeah; do you remember the case of Caleb Smith? Yes, that one. Well, he just testified about the person who tried to kill him by poisoning him . . . no, no, he doesn't know who stabbed him yet, but he knows who gave him the pill to die when he was at the hospital. So, yeah, Justin please, prepare a warrant right now. I have a paper with his testimony and his signature. Ok . . . ok . . . Perfect, thanks man. I'll be right there in a few." Detective Robin said walking towards the main exit doors heading to his car in the parking lot. However, when he was getting in his car something stopped him from closing the door. It was Mr. Russell.

"May I help you?" Robin asked with attitude getting out from the car.

"Who do you think you are?! Didn't I tell you to stay away from this fucking case?!" Isaiah Russell screamed getting close to his face.

"You are no one to be telling me what to do Mr. Russell . . . Why are you so scared that I'll take charge of this case anyway?"

"You are a punk ass detective. Do you think because your father is dead you can take charge of everything he couldn't?"

"DON'T TALK ABOUT MY FATHER! YOU KILLED MY FATHER! DON'T TALK ABOUT HIM! DON'T FUCKING DO IT! Detective Robin screamed at Isaiah.

"Why would I kill your father for? Tell me Peter Robin, Why would have I want to kill your father for? What would have I gained?"

"YOU BASTARD! I SWEAR BEFORE MY TIME IS DONE I'M GOING TO PUT YOU IN PRISON! I'M GOING TO LET THE WHOLE CITY KNOW WHO YOU REALLY ARE!" Detective Robin said screaming as hard as he could.

Isaiah looked at him and smiling said, "Go head do what you want. I'm just going to tell you something. You are nobody in this world. Nobody, and I'm Isaiah Russell. I have the name, respect, reputation, and money. I have the power. But go head, try to act as stupid as your father once tried and that's why he got killed. But something I can tell you, the one that killed him wasn't me." he said and walked away.

Robin looked at Russell with so much hate, so much hate that he wished looks could kill people. But swallowing his anger and pride got back on his car and started driving to the police department.

Russell saw from far Robin's car driving away. He wasn't happy, he was angry; he needed to shut him too. He wasn't thinking with his head, but he was thinking with his emotions, with the hate that he had in his heart.

He had already killed Robin's father, killed Jesse, sent people to murder Caleb, and now he needed to kill James, and Robin. What could happen if he kills Robin? He thought. What was going to happen? He knew Joey and Caleb weren't going to say anything. He knew that Robin wasn't big; he knew no one was going to pay as much interest as when his father died. The minutes were passing, and only the moon was witnessing all the bad that Isaiah was planning that night, and that was kill, kill and kill. Those were the only words in his head right now. He hated the fact that Caleb was alive. He hated him ever since he first met him, and he hated him more after he found out that he was Dara's brother, and the father of her daughter's baby. What he was going to do? His wife lied to him; his daughter was in love with the wrong person. Abortion, killing, and lies everything was going through his mind like a movie. He was going crazy; he knew he had to do something to solve this. However, he knew that he was already in conflict because Caleb survived. If Caleb talks he was in trouble. If the nurse doesn't get out of the country soon, he was in trouble. If James gets caught and the police fins out he killed Jesse, he was in trouble. He had to do something quick. He was already thinking, he was planning it, writing everything on a calendar.

Tomorrow, he was getting the nurse out of the country, and then at 9 am he was going to kill James. Later on, he was going to end up with Caleb. The next day, he was going to send Juliana out of the country and the very next morning he was going to get out of America for a while. But tonight, he had to kill Robin. He had everything planned already as he was driving. The criminal mind that he had was like a calculator. He had the equation going good so far, but if he presses the wrong button he had it all wrong, he thought. That was Isaiah Russell; he was feared by many and confronted by none. He was respected by everyone and loved by none.

Finally, Isaiah found Robin's car, and started following him, always staying behind two cars so Robin won't see him. As he kept on driving, he started to get worried, why was Robin taking this way? Why was Robin driving around here? He thought.

Soon when detective Robin turned to the right, Isaiah figured out that he was taking the way to get to the police station. Why would Robin be going there for? At this time? Isaiah didn't want to ask questions and kept on following. When they were a block away from the police department Isaiah made a phone call to the nurse.

"I need you to do me a favor. Yes, I think we got caught. I don't know, don't ask me anything . . . Yeah, I'm looking at him right now, he is parking on the police station. I know god damn it! Listen to me! You need to get out of the country ASAP. I don't care if you have to pay more money, but you leave fast!" Isaiah was nervous.

"Ok, Ok . . . But what is going on? Can you at least explain me why do you think Robin is going to talk against you? He has no proof Isaiah, no evidence!" The nurse exclaimed on the other line.

"Didn't you know Caleb is awake already?! I'm pretty sure they talked. Oh god I'm going to get caught if someone finds out. If Caleb talks I'm fucked. They will find out about his case . . . you, the murder of Jesse, and fuck! What the hell went wrong?"

"Those are the guys from the projects right?"

"Yeah, but James knows better. If he confesses, he goes to jail and I'll confront him in jail. I will even dirty my hands with blood and kill his daughter . . . He knows I'll have him living worst than hell . . . and you . . . you won't run out either bitch. If I get caught you get caught with me you heard?" Isaiah said with so much anger.

"What? Don't . . . don't worry Isaiah. We won't. Tomorrow, tomorrow I'm going to call the airport and tell them I want to change my ticket for Friday. But yeah, don't worry everything is going to be all right. Look, I have to go. I'm going to talk to you tomorrow morning ok? Good night." She hung up the phone leaving Isaiah frustrated and thinking about what was going on. The nurse wasn't stupid, she knew something was going wrong tonight, and she wasn't going to stay to find out. As soon as she hung, she called the airport, and asked for a change of flights. She was leaving the country tonight. As soon as she heard that her reservation was changed, she started to pack.

On the other hand, Detective Robin was walking in the police station, and headed straight to his friend's desk.

"Hey Robin, what are you doing here so late?" one of his coworkers asked.

"I have a police report to do. How have you been by the way?" Robin asked.

"Good bro, by the way I'm going to give you the invitation for my girlfriend's baby shower tomorrow."

"Oh yeah, I forgot. How many months she is?"

"7, I can't wait! It's going to be a boy." The dude said smiling while drinking his coffee.

"Good. Well, I'm going get back at you later."

"All right man." the dude replied and sat on a desk facing the computer screen.

"By the way is Justin in his office?"

"Yeah he is. He told me he was waiting for someone I guess it was you. Just go in."

Robin knocked on the door.

"Come in!" a deep voice said.

"Justin!" Robin said going inside the room and closing the door. "Look at this." Robin said getting the folder that contained the paper in which Caleb had reported his testimony.

Justin, a detective who had more time and experience than Robin was about 56 years old. He has been working at the police department of Manhattan for over 20 years. He met Robin's father before he died, and heard about the problems that he had with Isaiah.

"He wrote all this?" Justin asked Detective Robin looking at the paper.

"I wrote it. Caleb can't even move that well. The poison affected his whole body a lot. So I wrote it and he signed it to let anybody who read this know that he agreed and he is the one who sent to do this."

"I see. Where is the nurse?"

"This is the issue. I don't know why Justin, but this is confusing. I mean I'm convinced of what I know and what I have on my mind, but I don't want to say anything if I'm going to have to involved other people."

"What are you saying? I don't understand."

"I've seen the nurse that Caleb is accusing with Isaiah Russell, not too long ago. I've seen them outside the bar where I went to tonight. They were talking for hours and he gave her money. She was carrying luggages and bags. I even took pictures of them two."

"Show me the pictures." Justin asked.

Detective Robin opened his bag and took off his digital camera and handled it to Justin. He looked at him while he was holding it; he turned it on and started looking through the pictures.

He looked at the first ones that were taken outside the bar where Isaiah Russell was giving her a bag.

"How do you know that he was giving her money in this bag?"

"Look at the next picture, that's where he opens the bag and takes money out."

Justin looked back at the camera and saw Isaiah's hand holding money that was tighten up together with a shoelace.

"You are right." He kept on looking through the pictures. Then he saw the pictures of her walking in a small supermarket. The next picture was her coming out of a beauty store with bags on her hands. The next picture was a close up of what she had on her bag. She had a wig, make up, black clothes, alcohol, etc. everything seemed so weird to him. *Why would she buy wigs for?* As he kept on looking through, he saw the pictures of her opening the door of a hotel room. The last picture was the address of the motel where she was staying at, which was nearby the airport.

Justin looked at Robin and said. "Now I understand why you are confused."

"Thanks God! I don't know what to do Justin; I have something more to tell you." Detective Robin said putting his hands on his face and breathing deeply. "What is it?" Justin answered while he was moving around his office, ready to prepare the warrant.

"I talked to this guy, and . . . he told me, he confessed me about who stabbed Caleb Smith." Detective Robin said while he lifted his head up to look at Justin.

"What did he say?"

Robin sighted deeply and said, "He told me everything. He was one of the 3 guys that tried to kill Caleb . . . and he also told me that . . . he told me that he is the one who killed Jesse."

"Jesse? Isn't he the main suspect? Jesse . . . isn't Jesse the one that stabbed Caleb and when Isaiah was about to investigate he died?"

"Yes, that one. This guy told me that Isaiah Russell planned everything. He told me that he paid them to kill Caleb by stabbing him, and it was the same Isaiah who paid him to kill Jesse, the main suspect."

"But, why would Isaiah want to kill the main suspect for?" Justin asked while he was sitting on top of the desk.

"Isaiah planned it everything. Caleb was going to die, and then he was going to 'arrest Jesse' just to say that he got Caleb's case solved. But, Jesse didn't want to cooperate with him anymore, so he asked this other guy to kill him. This guy was supposed to kill Jesse after Isaiah sends him to jail, but something went wrong, he killed him before he got arrested."

"So you are telling me that Isaiah Russell was planning to pay this guy that died to go to jail just to let people know that Caleb's case was done. But since he didn't want to cooperate he sent his own friend to kill him. And this friend killed Jesse before he went to jail?" Justin said trying to get everything.

"Yes, Jesse was supposed to go to jail and died in there, Isaiah was going to hire people in the same prison to kill him, and just say that the suspect died, and bam case solved, but this guy killed him before he got arrested."

"Do you think Isaiah is going to say something about him?" Justin asked.

"Of course. He was going to arrest him and he knew Jesse was going to speak the truth in front of the judge. So before that would have happened, he sent his own friend to kill him."

Detective Robin said and looked at Justin while he was standing up from the desk and walked to the big window that was next to drawers.

"Now I get it, I understand everything. You have to tell me the name of this guy; we need to send him to court so he could testify." Justin told detective Robin as if he was having an excitement feeling.

"I can't do that!" detective Robin replied raising his voice.

"What do you mean you can't do that?! He is the one who knows everything . . . He needs to tell us what happened!"

"You don't understand, I promised this guy I wasn't going to get him in trouble. I talked to him with all honesty. You can't do this!"

"I can't do this? Robin what is wrong with you?! Do you want to lose your job or what?! You know who the murderer is; you know where all the clues are at you just need to put them out there!" Justin said loudly.

"I can't send that guy to prison! I'm here just to make the warrant for Caleb and I'm here telling you all this because I want Isaiah Russell to burn in hell. I want him in jail!" Detective Robin said with so much attitude and anger.

"I don't know Robin . . . Isaiah is too powerful. You need to say his name, I promise Robin, and I'm going to help you as much as I can. Maybe if we talk to this guy we can make him not to stay in jail for long."

"Justin, what part don't you understand? I'm not going to send him to jail. He confessed me all this and I have to find a way to put Isaiah in jail without mixing his name here." Detective Robin said and opening the door of the office he walked out.

Justin was worried. He needed to do something before this situation gets worst. Caleb's life was in the middle of this situation. Justin had a feeling that Caleb was going to die if he didn't solve this immediately, and as he finished signing the warrant, made a phone call.

"How are you, yes this is Justin, look I need you to get me the tape of the day of this case . . . case number is 980347 . . . Yea, the Smith case. I need you to get me the tape and get in contact with 2 FBI officers right now . . . Detective Robin, Peter Robin from the Manhattan department has interviewed a suspect, and we need to get him to the station to interrogate him. Ok, ok, thanks I'm going to be in my office waiting." Justin hung up the phone and picking up the paper from the desk he walked out of his office. He walked up to two officers that were in the front desk.

"I need you to go to Belview Hospital and look for this woman. Caleb Smith has reported that she is the one that poisoned him. Here is his signature and the story. I have already prepared the warrant. If she is not there, the she may be in this motel, here is the address." Justin said to the 2 officers showing them the pictures from the camera.

One of the police officers asked. "Are you coming with us?"

"No. I have to go somewhere else. Look, this case is about to be solved, but first I need you to get this woman. Apparently by the evidence she is trying to run away or get out of the country using a different identification. She is around 5'5", chubby and tan skin. Here is another picture so you can identify her better. She was seen getting money from somebody. She looks very suspicious, I'm not sure if she works at the hospital anymore, but today she was seen in the hospital again getting her stuff out of there. I think that she is running away from us. I want her today with me, you heard me? Get some backup." Justin said leaving the paper on the desk.

"Yes sir." Responded both officers and walked away.

Justin hearing this walked back to his office, and sat on his desk, opened his drawer, got some pills, and swallowed them. Suddenly, someone knocked on the door.

"Come in." he said.

The two FBI officers he asked for were at his office.

"Gonzales asked us to be here for you tonight." Said one of them.

"Have you heard of the Smith case?" asked Justin.

"We have." responded the other one.

"Have you ever arrested a cop for hiding evidence from a case?"

"Go to the point." Said one of the officers with attitude.

"The Smith case is about to be solved . . . only and only if one of us talk, and bring that evidence to court . . ."

"Who?"

"Let's say the boss of the police department has been linked into this crime, and he is as responsible as the murderer of all this drama."

"One of the suspects of the Smith case has been murdered, Smith has been tried to be killed again after the delinquent died . . . I'm sure that 'suspect' wasn't the one that tried to kill him."

"Peter Robin knows it all."

"What?"

"Peter Robin knows it all. He has talked with one of the suspects that confessed who did all the crime . . . Robin has gone to the projects and talked face to face with the one that killed, and knows who planned all this . . . I just don't know what to do, what to say . . . we are all scared of Russell, he is dangerous . . . Russell tried to kill Smith . . . I know it, I believe it . . . and ouch oh my god!" Justin couldn't finish speaking and fell on the floor grabbing his arm hard. He was having a heart attack.

The FBI officers were helping him, while they asked for people to go inside the office to help.

"Get Robin!" screamed one of the FBI officers to the other."

"And you?"

"I'll catch you on this later; I need to interrogate Justin when he wakes up."

The officer looked at his partner, and ran out of the office looking for Robin.

"Have any of you seen detective Robin around? He just got out of Justin's office." Asked the FBI officer to one of the data entry employees.

"Yea he just walked out!"

The FBI officer ran out without saying thanks, and looked for Robin. Then, he saw him, sitting on a bench by the parking lot.

"Peter Robin?" the FBI officer asked.

Detective Robin turned around to face him, got up, and walked up to him and said, "Who are you?"

"I'm Gonzalez Sam, FBI"

"I can see that, but . . . who asked you to come?" Robin asked feeling fear coming from his head through his face.

"Justin told us everything Robin . . . we need that evidence, and I'm not asking you to bring it to court, I'm demanding you to do it."

"You don't work with me . . . look, I really don't care if you are the FBI, or CIA . . . you have nothing to do in this case . . ."

"I asked you nicely and believe me I don't have to do that . . . I just do it because I've known your father way before you were born . . . and . . ."

"Don't talk about my father . . ." Robin interrupted.

"You have to bring that man to testify in this case . . ."

"I can't." responded Robin.

"You have to . . ."

"I don't have to do shit."

"Robin . . . Robin GOD DAMN IT! THAT MAN HAS BEEN TRIED TO BE MURDERED TWICE AND YOU ARE FUCKING SAYING THAT YOU DON'T WANT TO BRING THAT DELINQUENT TO TRIAL BECAUSE YOU GAVE YOUR WORD?! HUH?!"

Robin stared at him, in silence.

"Robin your father would have been so disappointed if he would hear you right now."

"I'm going to ask you and repeat again DO NOT TALK BOUT MY FATHER! DON'T PUT HIM ON THIS!"

"THEN DO THE RIGHT THING! THINK FOR A MOMENT! THINK ABOUT THE FACT THAT THAT MAN IS GOING TO LIVE UNDER A SAFER ROOF IF WE SOLVE ALL THIS DRAMA! THINK ROBIN! HE IS GOING TO HAVE A CHILD! THINK ABOUT THAT! WE NEED THAT SUSPECT IN HERE, AND WE NEED IT NOW!" The FBI officer pulled out a piece of paper from his pocket and said, "Here is the warrant . . . either you tell me and I'll go get him with back up and make you look like a snitch . . . or you come with me and we talk to him face to face like a man of word? You decide Robin . . ."

Detective Robin looked at him furious, but at the same time he knew that he was wrong. He should have arrested that guy and never offered him or gave him his word. But it was too late; he already opened his mouth and talked about this situation. And yes, he knew that if his dad had been alive, he would have been so disappointed of his actions.

Robin breathed hard and deeply and said, "Let's go in my car."

"Thank you Robin, now I see your dad in your face, I hear him talking as you are speaking."

"Oh by the way, Justin already sent two cops to look for that nurse, and also gave them the camera to identify her better."

"The camera? Are you serious?" detective Robin asked worried and scared.

"Yes the camera, why?"

"Holy fuck! Isaiah is in those pictures . . . Smith's brother is in those pictures as well . . . this is going to get ugly!"

"Why would Smith's brother be in those pictures, what's going on?"

"Don't worry about it, I need to go back and get that camera!"

"You can't! Whatever is in that camera is good enough for us to solve this! Leave it as it is!

Robin was nervous and scared, needed to make a phone call to Caleb; he needed to talk to his brother before.

Everybody was having a bad night, but not everybody was going to keep the same enemies and the same dramatic days. Isaiah, who was at the hospital, walked up to Caleb's room, opened the door making Joey and Caleb stare at him.

"What are you doing here?!" Joey yelled.

Isaiah looked at Joey and looking at Caleb said, "My dear Caleb! You are awake! I'm happy for you!"

"Can you please get out of my room?" Caleb tried to speak as loud as he could since his voice was weak and gone.

Isaiah standing there smiled and then looked at Joey.

"You heard my brother, now please get out!"

"I'm going to tell you something Caleb Smith, many times I have tried and I did the best for my daughter, but now she is fucked because of you. Do you think I don't know the truth yet?

"What truth? What are you talking about? Look, get the fuck out of my room before I call . . ."

"Call what?" Isaiah interrupted. "Call who? The police? (He laughed) oh please my dear Caleb, I am the law! I am the police! And you can't do shit!"

"Who the fuck do you think you are? Don't fucking come over here trying to demand things . . . You are nothing but a dirty cop that thinks that by sending people to kill other people is going to clear your history!" Joey screamed.

Isaiah laughed. "Don't even try to army toy; you are a nobody here in this world. How many people raped you at war huh? Do you want me to ask you how do you get your merchandise?"

"What are you saying . . . ?"

"What am I saying? Ha! Joey, my dear Joey . . . I, I don't understand why the Smith brothers are so stupid, how come you are so slick to damage other people lives and you can't even do anything to prevent your own brother from dying?"

"What is he talking about?" Caleb interrupted.

Joey walked up to Isaiah ready to punch him in the face, when Isaiah interrupted. "Don't you dare before I arrest you right now for aggravated assault, and dealing with drugs . . . I have all the evidence Joey . . . don't play with fire because you are going to get burnt."

"I know everything Mr. Smith. I know you are my wife's brother, and I also know that the woman that you have left pregnant, my daughter, is also your own niece."

"It's truth. I know Juliana is my niece. I know your wife is my sister, the sister that denied me and said I was dead." Caleb responded sadly.

"And you must know that Juliana is my life, even if she is not my real daughter as the world and herself think it is."

Joey who walked to the other side of Caleb's bed stood up next to Caleb and stayed quiet looking at Isaiah.

"What are you saying?" Caleb asked.

"Your stepfather. Manuel Smith. He left her pregnant when you guys were separated. When I met her she was 1 month pregnant and I loved her. When we got married I loved her as well, and when she gave birth to Juliana I loved her more. But all that love disappeared when she confessed me all this, and today I hate her more than ever. The only reason why today I am who I am is because of Juliana, my daughter. That's why Caleb, I want you and need you out of her life. Don't worry if she is pregnant, don't worry about anything, I will take care of everything; she doesn't need to destroy her life with you. I want you to disappear, and I want you to do it as soon as possible, because if you don't leave her I swear Caleb you are going to regret it." Isaiah said as if he was holding his hate on his right hand.

"Are you threading me?"

"Take it as you want it, I don't care. Just tell Juliana that you hate her, tell her that you don't care about her and that's it." Isaiah said.

"I don't fear you Isaiah. I know you sent that nurse to kill me, I know it. You two thought I wasn't going to survive, but look at me. I'm here, and I already pressed charges against her. The police probably already got her, and if she talks you are going down. Probably from there I'm going to find out who stabbed me." Caleb said trying to get up from the bed, but he couldn't.

"The one that stabbed you is dead. Didn't you see it on the news?" Isaiah responded.

"I know there were 3 not only one. Mr. Russell who are you trying to fool? I'm going to find out who tried to kill me and if it was you, then you are going to pay for everything."

"I'm going to ask you please to get out of the room Isaiah." Joey said opening the door.

Isaiah stared at Caleb deeply, and walked out of the room. He decided to take the stairs instead of the elevator, and made a phone call.

"Where are you?"

"Oh my god! Mr. RUSSELL! THERE ARE TWO POLICE CARS OUTSIDE THE MOTEL!" the nurse replied afraid.

"What are you saying woman? Maybe they are looking for something else."

"Oh god! They are knocking at my door! Oh my god! Please Isaiah do something!" the nurse said while she was peeing on her pants from being so nervous.

"Check through the window."

The nurse obeyed him and screamed. "THEY ARE HERE! OH MY GOD WHAT I DO?! PLEASE MR. RUSSELL HELP ME! I FEEL LIKE I'M GOING TO DIE! OH MY GOD! I WANT TO TALK TO MY MOM, PLEASE . . . I BEG YOU HELP ME!!"

"CALM DOWN WOMAN! Nobody is going to take you to jail . . . Just open the door and ask what they want, but do not say anything! You heard me?" Isaiah said and hung up the phone while he was getting out from the stairs exit.

He was nervous, and scared that his plan was going to fail, not thinking twice he made another phone call.

"Where are you?!" Isaiah asked the person on the other line.

"Home, what's happening daw?" the guy on the other line said.

"We need to talk seriously, right now." Isaiah said nervous.

"Yo son, you know what time is it? I'm sleeping, I ain't want your drama right now."

"Look, Caleb is not dead!"

"What the fuck that has to do with me?"

"He already pressed charges on me, two cops already went to arrest the nurse that I sent to poison him." Isaiah said again going crazy.

"Yo, I don't give a fuck son. I don't care if they caught that bitch, that ain't my motherfucking problem. I'm just *gonna* tell *yuh* something man, I did what you asked me to do. I killed Jesse so he wouldn't talk, and you didn't even pay on what we agreed on. So now, you better handle that shit as you can *cuz'* I ain't going to jail and you best believe that."

"James, please. I need you to do something, I don't want to get caught and of course I don't want you to get caught."

"What *'chu* want?" James replied.

"I need you to get out of your hood; I need you to go far. I don't know California, Miami, Massachusetts I don't know another country, I don't care, but I need you out!" Isaiah asked nervous, he felt his heart coming out of his mouth.

"I ain't going nowhere motherfucker. I already told you, I did so many fucking favors for you and you still haven't paid me. Now, *Ima* tell you something son. If you don't pay me by tomorrow morning I won't help you. And the police better not know about me, because I swear if I get caught you get caught with me you heard? I don't play that shit"

"What are you trying to say? That I'm going to jail with you?" Isaiah asked

"*Niggah* listen, if I get caught you get caught with me. If I die you die with me. If I don't care about killing for money imagine what would I do for my freedom." James said and hung up the phone.

Isaiah was mad, nervous, worried, and scared. He didn't know what to do. He knew they were going to catch the nurse or probably they already had her in the police car, arrested. He needed James's help. He knew if the nurse was going to prison for poisoning Caleb, she was going to testify against him, and he needed to do something to keep her mouth shut. He was sweating, biting his tongue and the sides of his mouth as he was chewing the gum that he had very hard. He knew if James was caught, he wasn't going to stay quiet, he knew James was going to fuck him up if he loses his freedom. Not thinking twice, Isaiah ran to his car and started driving to Bed Stuy.

As he was driving to one of the most dangerous projects of New York, Detective Robin and the FBI officer that accompanied him got to James's building before he did, closed the building, and holding guns with them, they ran around the building calling backup as the they were going upstairs.

At 3:45 am Isaiah parked his car.

At 3:47 am the nurse was taken to the police station to be interrogated. She believed that Isaiah was going to get her out if the situation gets worst. As she was crying she was thinking what to invent not to mention Isaiah.

At 3:55 am, Juliana woke up in the middle of her dream having a bad feeling. She felt like something was going wrong. She got up from her bed, walked toward her mom's room and knocking once, knocking twice she went in. Her mom was sleeping deeply. She walked up to her and moved her once, moved her twice, but her mom stayed sleeping.

Feeling bad and not wanting to wake her mom up walked out of the room and went fast to hers. She got dress, got her phone, the keys of her car and got out of her room.

"Hey, it's me Juliana." She said on the phone as she was leaving her house.

"Wow, that's surprising . . . I thought you hated me." Monique answered on the other line.

"I can't be mad at you even if I want to, I need you in my life." Juliana responded.

"I'm happy to hear that." Monique said. "I can't sleep either."

"OK. Good because I need you to come with me somewhere."

"Right now? It's 4 in the morning where would you want to go right now?"

"I found an address and a phone number in Caleb's apartment and I think that's the main reason why Caleb doesn't want to be with me anymore."

"Are you, are you serious?!"

"Yes I'm serious. I want to go now, I don't care if I'm pregnant or not Monique. I want to go and find that bitch."

"What does the paper says?" Monique asked curiously.

"The address is in Queens, and the name is this one Loren S."

"Fine, I'll go with you, are you picking me up?"

"Yeah I'm heading over there right now. I'll be there like in 10 minutes, there's no traffic."

"OK, I'll be ready." Monique said and hung up.

Juliana was driving as fast as she could; she needed to get to Monique's place as soon as possible. She was dying to know who this Loren S. was. What would her name and address be doing on a piece of paper in Caleb's personal book? She was ready to go and do something crazy to that woman, a woman that she already hated and didn't even see.

When she got to Monique's house, she waited outside and Monique came out wearing jeans and long black shirt.

"Damn." Monique said looking at Juliana surprised.

"What?" Juliana asked

"You look really angry, what's wrong with you?" Monique asked getting inside the car and closing the door.

"I'm about to murder her, if she is what I think she is."

"What do you mean? What are we going to do?" Monique asked putting the seatbelt on her.

"We are going to look for her. I got her address, and we are going to see who she is. I want to see what she has that I don't, what she has that made Caleb left me. Nobody is taking my man away, he is my baby's father and she should have known it, and if she doesn't, then tonight she will."

Monique looked at her scared. She was afraid that Juliana's jealousy would get far from what she was capable of.

As the car was going and the night was the witness of all this drama and hateful feelings that these people was living. They didn't know that the only one that was going to suffer the most was the baby that Juliana had in her belly.

Juliana finally got to Queens and slowly drove around so the streets and the numbers wouldn't confuse her. She was looking carefully at everybody around. When she got to the building that the address said, she parked the car and breathing deeply she got out of the car with her friend Monique. She wasn't worried about how dangerous the neighborhood looked. She was worried and impatient to see the woman that was taking her place in Caleb's heart.

Looking at Monique she said. "I'm scared."

"Me too, this shit doesn't look nothing like home." Monique said looking around scared.

"No 'cause of that Monique. I'm scared to face her and find out things that maybe I don't know yet."

Meanwhile, at the police station the nurse who was already being interrogated kept on crying, falling or throwing herself on the floor begging for her freedom.

"You know you have the right to remain in silence and talk to an attorney, or you can waive your Miranda rights."

"I don't know anything I swear!" the nurse said crying.

"I'm guessing you didn't understand what I've just said."

"Please let me go, I want to speak with my mother, look I just peed in my pants, I want to throw up, I feel like I'm dying alive. I didn't do anything! Take my Miranda rights, take whatever you want but please let me go."

"Tell me something that can make me believe you. I have here, a couple of pictures, it's you and Isaiah Russell. He's giving you money outside of a small shopping center where you came out with wigs and other beauty accessories. Then, in this other picture you are entering a motel. Suddenly, in the motel room that we searched when we arrested you we found wigs, *extacy* pills, cash, tickets to Dominican Republic, hospital documents, an agenda that contains the information of Caleb Smith, and Juliana Russell, as well as her father. We have also found medicine, anesthesia, etc. suddenly I found out that you don't work at the hospital anymore . . . Tell me why are you leaving the hospital for? Why did you buy all these things for? Where are you going with all these drugs, and why?

"I don't know . . . I just want to see my family."

"Why are you taking these individual's information for? Wasn't Caleb Smith your patient?"

"Yes, he was, but then I stopped attending him . . ."

"Why did you stop?"

"Because he asked for a different nurse, he didn't want me to do it."

"Caleb Smith says that you were the last person who attended him, and right after you gave him a pill, which was *extacy* and not the proper medicine, not counting his poisoned water, he almost died. Could you explain that please?"

"I don't know anything!" responded the nurse crying as her eyeliner and mascara were running down her cheeks leaving black marks all over her face.

"Then what happened? How come he says that you were the one that poisoned him? Where were you at the time that this happened?

"I don't know . . . I want to speak with my lawyer, I deserve an attorney at this time . . ."

"Ok. But I can't let you out until trial. Guards take her in."

"No, No! I can't be in jail, no please don't send me inside, I beg you!"

The nurse cried, and pleaded, but the guards who had no mercy on her took her.

"Ok, I can explain . . ."

"Explain what?" the detective asked again. "Who sent you?"

"I can't say it . . . I don't want to go to jail! Please give me a chance!" The nurse begged.

"Then tell me who sent you . . . Look either way we are going to get to the bottom of this situation. Whether you did it or not there is a tape in the hospital, and if that tape shows that you were involved, you are going to prison, not even jail, but prison for attempted of murder . . . just cooperate and help this man solve his own case."

"No, I can't go to jail I didn't do it by myself!" The nurse was turning paranoid, she felt like she couldn't hide the truth anymore. "Oh please help me! Promise me that you will help me if I say the truth, please promise it!"

The detective pressed play on his recorder as she calmed down, and started to speak.

"Isaiah Russell . . . he . . . he paid me to do it. He offered me a lot of money to kill Caleb. I didn't want to do it but I ended up doing it because I needed the money." The nurse said crying, testifying the truth and putting Isaiah out there.

The detective looked down at the table, and then to the guards, he was feeling disappointment. "Why?" he asked.

"He just hates that guy because he got his daughter pregnant, and he loves his daughter very much, he doesn't want anyone to touch her. But, this time his daughter didn't obey anything and he couldn't separate them, she went crazy for him. She escaped from home for him, abandoned everything even friends for him he said . . . I don't know . . . all I know is that he was furious because his daughter is now pregnant by him, and he believes that that child shouldn't be born."

"Can you tell me if there's somebody else that is under Isaiah's management?" asked the detective.

"I don't know about that. I just want to go home." The nurse begged again.

"So you are admitting that you were going to kill Caleb Smith by poisoned him? With what?"

"Isaiah gave me cocaine, heroin, acid, the amphetamine which is the *extacy* and the sleeping pills that we usually give to patients. He asked me which of the drugs would kill him faster, and I explain to him that if we inject him the heroin as a shot he was going to have respiratory problems, since it will create effects of GABA which causes breathing slow and then stop, so he will die faster. But someone was going to find out that someone injected something in him, and it was too risky. Then, we talked about cocaine and I told him that the cocaine was going to give him a heart attack, hyperthermia, and he will eventually suffer of brain damage. So that was our first option, and in case he didn't die he wasn't going to remember much. Finally, our last option was the amphetamines, which is the *extacy*, this was going to give him a heart attack, overheating, and brain damage, pretty much similar to the cocaine, but it will only work better if we cut the air ac of his room . . . but something went wrong that day . . . I gave him the *extacy*, and then the sleeping pill . . . but somehow his brother was there when I did it, somehow the security didn't take his break that day . . . everything went wrong, and Caleb survived . . . I regret it. I regret it a lot. It's not his fault, oh god! Now that man probably will suffer of so many things after the overdose . . . I regret it so much; I hope he will forgive me."

"Ok, save the rest for your attorney. Guards please take her in."

"NO!!! YOU TOLD ME I WAS GOING TO BE SAVED! I DON'T WANT TO GO TO JAIL, PLEASEE!!! DETECTIVE!!!" The nurse kept on screaming while the detective was getting his tape and leaving the room.

Isaiah, who was already in Bed Stuy, ran up to James's building holding his gun; He was focus on what he was going to do. He was going to kill James for betraying him, he didn't play the nice game anymore and James was losing it.

When he was already in the hallway, he walked slowly not to trip, there was only 1 light on and he didn't know what he could find in his way. He was being careful, he looked around both sides, and once there, he knocked on James's apartment. He knocked once, he knocked twice, he knocked three times and James wasn't opening the door. When he was about to knock the door for a fourth time James screamed, "Who is this!" from the other side of the door.

"It's me Isaiah. I got your money." He said holding his gun up to the chest ready to shoot James as soon as he'll open the door.

"Pussy ass *niggah*, I knew you were going to come back bitch." James said taking off the locks and the chain that was keeping the door closed. As James was cursing him out, he opened the door laughing and Isaiah didn't waste a second in showing it.

James stared at him confused, and not letting another second passed Isaiah shot his gun three times. James didn't have time to breathe and looking at Isaiah in agony, fell on the floor. Isaiah quickly looked around to see if people were coming out of their humble apartments, and seeing nothing, but emptiness, he got inside the house, put gloves on and dragged James body into the living room. He was ready to plan the way that James 'supposedly died'. Juliana on the other hand, who was outside of the apartment of the so-called Caleb's new girl, didn't want to knock on the door, then looked at Monique and knocked. She knocked many times, rubbing her belly after every knock, and the door opened.

It was an old lady who asked her nicely, "Yes? What can I do for you at this time young lady?"

Juliana looked at her surprised, looked at Monique, and looking back at the old lady said. "I'm looking for Loren S., but I think I got the wrong address."

"Oh no my dear, you are right. Loren Smith lives here. She is my sister." The old lady said smiling.

Juliana was confused. Then, she saw a woman coming in the background. She was about 5'5, red hair and blue eyes, eyes just like her mom's. She looked around her 50's, that's what she thought for a second, she felt like something was wrong, why was Caleb keeping numbers and addresses of mature older women she kept on asking her inner voice.

That same woman got next to the old lady who opened the door and said "Yes?" the woman asked.

"Hi, are you Loren S.?" Juliana asked.

"Yes, it's me. Come in I was waiting for you." The red hair woman said opening the door.

Monique grabbed Juliana by the arm and stopping her said on her ear, "Juliana don't."

Juliana felt like she wanted to destroy the woman, she didn't know what to think, what if Caleb really left her for this older lady? She didn't know what to think but something inside was telling her to take it easy.

The woman asked them to take a sit and looking at Juliana said, "Come with me please, I want to talk to you in private."

Juliana got up and so Monique did.

"No, your friend can stay here. I just want to talk to you."

"She is like my sister, she goes where I go." Juliana said while she held Monique's hand.

The woman looked at them and said, "Ok, then I'm going to tell you everything right here."

"Good Night darlings!" another old lady said from far while she was going inside her room and closed the door.

The woman stared at Juliana. "It's been many years when I asked your mother to bring you here. I always wanted to meet you."

Juliana looking confused and worried said, "Wait, you know my mother?"

"Yes, I know your mother, and I can tell that she's been lying to you for years as well." The woman said looking at her and Monique.

"Wait, what do you mean you know my mom? I mean. I'm here because I think you are the reason why my boyfriend doesn't want to know anything about me anymore."

"Your boyfriend? Who's your boyfriend? Wait . . . How did you get here?" asked Loren.

"Caleb is my boyfriend, I thought you knew that."

Loren stood up putting her hands on her face. She couldn't believe what she just heard. It couldn't be possible; the worst have happened, her thoughts kept on saying.

"Are you ok?" Juliana asked.

"It can't be . . . why did your mother let this happen?!" Loren said as she started to cried while she was sitting on the chair feeling the shock.

"What? What are you talking about! Can you please tell me what's going on?! I came here to find out if my boyfriend is cheating on me or not, and . . . and you are making all this worst!" Juliana was getting aggravated.

"Juliana . . . Juliana don't you know it yet? Caleb is not your boyfriend; he can't be your boyfriend!" Loren said loudly.

"WHAT THE FUCK! CAN YOU JUST TELL ME WHY?!" Juliana screamed.

"BECAUSE HE IS YOUR UNCLE! HE IS YOUR MOTHER'S BROTHER! MY SON!" Loren said screaming holding Juliana by the arms.

Monique had her mouth open full of shock and Juliana, who wasn't talking was quiet wanting to cry and scream, but her silence said it all. She felt like if she was trapped in an alley where the walls were closing in, and her mind was full of doubts with thoughts that were scared to grow. Juliana had tears running down her face stared at Loren and sitting on the sofa she stared at the floor. Loren, who felt guilty and felt her pain got on her knees and said, "Your mother has been lying and keeping this secret for years. She has two brothers; those are Joey and Caleb, which are my sons. I can show you pictures of them and even the copy of their birth certificates. I have their newborn baby clothes from the hospital still . . ." She said with her eyes full of tears holding on Juliana's knees, looking at both Monique and Juliana.

Monique couldn't believe what was going on. She couldn't believe that such a tragedy was happening to her best friend. Why would such a big mistake happen to her friend? Why something so big would get bigger with the presence of that baby that she had in her belly?

"You are not Isaiah's daughter my dear Juliana." Loren said crying trying to look at her eyes since Juliana had them closed.

"What are you saying? . . . That's not truth! Stop talking shit!"

"Oh yes it is! I am speaking the truth! Why would I lie about something so delicate? She is my granddaughter; she is what I am saying! You weren't supposed to born my dear, but God wanted you to come to this hell. You are not Isaiah's daughter that's truth, and Caleb and Joey are your uncles those are truths as well . . . You are the product of a rape, you are the seed of my ex husband. My ex husband raped your mom when she was about 13 and he got her pregnant with you. Then, later on, Isaiah, who is your father by name, picked your mom and you. You were a baby that nobody wanted but since you were on the way, we all started loving you." Loren said trying to make her feel "better", which it wasn't working.

"Why . . . Why are you telling me this for? Why you had to tell me this, why my mother couldn't say it . . . why?" Juliana asked while she was crying hard.

"I don't know. I don't know why your mother lied so much about her past and her real life. The only thing that I can say is that you can't keep that seed that is in your belly. That would be the curse of the whole family, it will come out deformed and it will suffer as long as it's alive. You can't keep that baby, you can't! You need to forget about Caleb, you need to forget about everything that once you lived with him. You need to start over because if you don't get away from him you will never forget him. You are young, beautiful and you are the seed that I wished I had with my ex husband. But him, he wanted your mom, he wanted to fuck her and make her his! That's why I hate your mother so much; I can't see her in pictures or in person. You don't know how bad I envied her beauty and youth. But since I love you I'm giving you this advice. Kill that seed, drink something, do something but kill it or you won't live happy, your life would be nothing but pain and suffering . . . that seed will be the shadow of your life, a shadow that will bring all these sad memories to you back and forth. Don't make that seed a not wanted baby!" Loren said with so much hate.

Juliana standing up, crying and screamed as much as her lungs allowed her. "STOP! I DON'T NEED TO HEAR YOUR SHIT! I DON'T BELIEVE YOU! I DON'T!" She ran through the door of the apartment. She ran, and ran as fast as she could, tripping over the hallway, which had no light. When she got to the stairs, she fell Monique holding her, and hugging her saying "Don't worry Juliana, everything is going to okay I promise it . . . I love you."

X.

THE UNEXPECTED ENDING

While Juliana and Monique were crying thinking how to solve this situation; Isaiah Russell was just finished with James's murder not imagining that Detective Robin along with other FBI officers were inside the building almost at James's apartment.

"Isaiah Russell is like an army, and now that we just found that the nurse confessed, he is not going to be easy to get."

Both officers started walking slow and softly. They were being careful that Isaiah or James would hear them, specially see them with the guns. When they were outside of James's apartment, one of the officers, Officer Gonzales told Robin to get on the other side of the door so they can cover up from both ways. Gonzales counted softly *one . . . two . . . three . . .* And unrepentantly, they threw the door down, and pointing with their guns they saw James's body on the floor. Detective Robin and Officer Gonzales looked at each other. They were communicating in a telepathically way. Robin stayed around the door calling the rest of the officers for back up but kept his eyes on every inch of the room. Gonzales looked around the kitchen and saw something moving. Robin was examining James's body from far holding his light on his left hand and gun on the right one, "Gonzales did you find anything?" He asked.

"Nothing."

"Hold up, back up is here . . . hello?" Gonzales answered his radio. "Yes, it's the green building . . . We are on the 3rd floor. I need 5 cars outside and 5 officers here with me now!"

Detective Robin had to walk around the apartment. He walked through the kitchen, the bathroom and when he tried to turn on the lights they weren't working. He walked to room next door and for his surprise the lights weren't working either. Then, he saw something that called his infinite attention. He put one glove on his left hand and grabbed a bag that was on the floor. He opened it and found a bunch of $100 dollar bills, as well as checks with different names. He kept on looking around the bed but didn't find anything. Finally, when he was ready to leave the room he felt the door closing. He turned as quick as speed light and saw a man standing a couple steps away from him.

"You are stupid as your father Robin. That's why he got killed, just like you are about to right now." It was Isaiah Russell.

"You can't kill me . . . they will find you." Detective Robin said without showing fear.

"Tell me when anybody has said something against Mr. Russell? Never, and that's how is it going to be. I am the man, I am the fear you feel when you are scared." Isaiah said getting closer to Robin.

"Kill me then. Kill me just like you killed my father, I'm ready to meet up with him anyway." Robin said dropping his gun and taking off the glove that he had on his left hand.

"I am going to kill you, take that money and run out through that window . . . or perhaps shoot myself to let them know that everything was in self-defense . . . You really think I'm that stupid Robin?" Isaiah laughed, and got ready to shoot at Robin's head.

Robin stayed quiet and closed his eyes ready to take that bullet. However, Officer Gonzales was hearing the conversation behind the door got ready to kick that door and shoot Isaiah before he killed Robin. But Isaiah wanted to torture Robin first, and shot him in the side of this stomach near the ribs. Gonzales kicked the door, and shot Isaiah in the arm making him drop the gun. He looked at Robin who was on the floor bleeding, while Isaiah was trying to get the gun that flew out of his hands but Gonzales stopped him and grabbing Isaiah by both arms he turned him around and put the handcuffs on him.

"You son of a bitch! You can't arrest me! Do you know who I am?!" Isaiah screamed.

"I know who you are and who you were. You shot a cop, you killed James Johnson, and you paid a nurse to poison Caleb Smith to die. You are a criminal that deserves nothing but a good execution." Gonzales said while he was calling the backups.

"Yes, I need you here, it's apartment 322, it has no lights. I have two men shot bleeding." Said Justin in shock. He couldn't believe what his eyes were seeing.

"I, I feel like I'm going to be lucky . . ." Robin said in pain.

"What are you saying man, what's wrong with you?" Gonzales responded.

"I'm lucky because I know I'm going to get to see my dad tonight." Robin said trying to hold from Justin arm.

"Don't say that, you are going to live and you are going to be a great chief, just like your dad wanted to." Justin said trying to cheer him up. 5 policemen came in the room, 2 of them took Isaiah while the paramedics put Robin on the stretcher. However, Gonzales wasn't done. He stayed in the crime scene with the other detectives searching the place and taking pictures of James's body.

Meanwhile Juliana, who was at home crying, devastated holding from Monique's shoulder who was feeling her friend's pain as well, felt like she was going to die for so many surprises.

"Juliana what are you doing!" Monique screamed as she ran behind her friend who was running in the middle of the hallway.

Juliana opened the door of her mom's room, walked up to her mom's bed and shook her.

"MOM! MOM! WAKE UP!" Juliana screamed.

Dara, woke up by jumping on the bed saying "Baby, what's wrong?"

Juliana stared at her, waited for her to sit down, got closer, looked at her mom with hate and slapped her hard.

Monique couldn't believe it.

"Why did you do that for my baby? Why do you hate me so much?" Dara asked while she was touching her red cheek.

"I want you to tell me the truth mother!"

"What?" Dara asked looking confused.

"You know exactly what I'm talking about! Why . . . Why didn't you tell me that Caleb was your brother?! Why didn't you tell me that I was the product of a rape?! Why did you keep all these secrets and never told me anything!" Juliana asked screaming and crying.

"Who told you about this?"

"IT DOESN'T MATTER WHO TOLD ME THIS! I WANT TO KNOW IF IT'S THE TRUTH!"

Dara getting out from her bed tried to hug her daughter but didn't get anything but rejection from her.

"DON'T TOUCH ME! I HATE YOU! YOU DESTROYED MY LIFE MOTHER! YOU JUST DON'T KNOW HOW YOU KILLED ME!"

"I'M SORRY!!! I DID IT TO GIVE YOU A BETTER LIFE, A BETTER EDUCATION, SO YOU COULD HAVE EVERYTHING I DIDN'T! "Dara said crying getting on her knees.

"NO! I HATE YOU, I HATE YOU MOM! I WON'T EVER FORGIVE YOU! NEVER!!! TELL ME WHAT THE FUCK AM I SUPPOSED TO DO?! I'M PREGNANT BY MY UNCLE AND YOU, YOU ARE TELLING ME TO FORGET IT? TO FORGIVE YOU? I CAN'T! I WON'T EVER FORGIVE YOU! AND I'M LEAVING! I'M LEAVING YOU FOREVER YOU WON'T EVER SEE ME AGAIN!" Juliana screamed at her mom making her shock in her own tears and walk on her knees asking for forgiveness from her daughter.

Monique who couldn't stand the situation walked up to Dara and helped her to get up from the floor.

"STOP IT JULIANA! DON'T YOU SEE THAT YOUR MOTHER DID ALL THIS JUST TO GIVE YOU A BETTER LIFE? SHE DIDN'T ABORT YOU BECAUSE SHE WANTED YOU TO LIVE BECAUSE SHE LOVED YOU AND SHE STILL DOES." Monique said screaming at her friend.

"Everybody is against me. Ok, FUCK ALL OF YOU! I DON'T NEED YOU!" Juliana screamed and left the room.

"No wait, wait! Where is she going Monique?" asked Dara hopeless.

"Probably to the hospital, she probably wants to hear it from Caleb."

"Monique, please come with me I don't want her to go crazy." Dara said as she walked to her closet. "Let me get my coat, and let's run over there before Juliana does something crazy."

Meanwhile, Caleb, who was sleeping at the hospital's room heard Joey's phone ringing.

"Joey!" Caleb tried to wake up his brother and since he didn't get any answer he threw a pillow at him waking him up.

"Ah what?" Joey said waking up.

"Your phone dickhead!" Caleb said.

"Hello?" Joey answered. "Yes . . . What? How come? Are you serious? Wow! Ok, ok thank you so much, all-right thanks man, ok . . . What's your name by the way? Gonzales? And you are with Robin right? . . . Ok thank you."

Caleb worried and confused asked his brother "What's wrong?"

"Isaiah shot Robin." Joey said surprised.

"Are you serious? So . . . that means that he is going to jail?" Caleb asked.

"Yes, and this detective or whatever he is just told me that they already caught the nurse, she is in jail she declared everything. Also, Isaiah killed the guy that killed the one that stabbed you . . ." Joey said putting his phone on top of the table.

"Wow, so much drama, this is worst than a movie. I can't believe Robin got hurt. He is such a good man. I wonder what Juliana is going to say, how she is going to react when she finds out that her dad is the biggest criminal ever." Caleb said leaning back on his pillow.

15 minutes later Juliana appeared at the hospital. She was ready to confront Caleb and ask him to either believe or forget what she already knew. As she was running through the hallways holding her tears she opened the door, and stared at Caleb.

She walked up to Caleb's bed and trying not to cry and said "Can I ask you something?"

"What are you doing here?" he responded.

Joey interrupted. "Juliana, please, this is not the time or the place . . ."

"Today I did something crazy for love . . ." she responded.

Caleb looked at her and worried asked, "What did you do?"

"Today I went to your apartment to get my clothes and I found in your personal book an address and . . ."

Caleb interrupted and said, "No you didn't. Juliana what did you do?!"

Juliana started crying and said, "Why . . . why you didn't tell me that I was your niece?! Why didn't you tell me that our love was prohibited!"

"Juliana . . . Juliana my dear I swear I didn't know."

"No, No! You knew it Caleb! You knew it and you didn't tell me anything! You and my mom knew everything and even my dad knew it and nobody thought about telling me! What was everyone thinking?! That I was going to live with that lie all my life? You thought I was going to be ignored my whole life? What's wrong with you?!" Juliana said crying pulling her hair, getting insanely bad; She didn't know how to express her feelings, she was just hurt.

"Juliana please let's go outside." Joey said.

"DON'T TOUCH ME! YOU BETRAYED ME TOO! YOU KNEW IT ALL!"

"Juliana I swear, I didn't tell you I didn't love you for nothing. I didn't want to ignore you for nothing . . ." Caleb responded crying as she was.

"You don't love me, you never did . . . you lied to me!"

"No, no, my love . . . You are the love of my life, you are the one that I've always asked for . . . please, please don't do this to me, I love you . . . I just wanted the best for you." Caleb said trying to get up from the bed.

"Caleb, everybody is telling me to forget you, but how could I forget you? Tell me how can I do it and I swear I'll do it! . . . I can't leave you! I can't let you go! You have my heart in your hands! Why can't we be together!? You don't know how crazy I'm going with this situation! You don't know how bad I want to die!" Juliana said falling on the floor crying while Joey was trying to help her get up.

At that very moment Dara walked in the room with Monique. Dara, looked at her daughter and felt her pain inside her heart. She hugged her strong and kissed her on the forehead.

"Mom! Tell me why my life had to be this way? Why did I fall in love with the wrong person?! Why can't I just close my eyes and never wake up?!" Juliana kept on saying to her mom while she was crying on her arms.

"Don't say that my dear, don't. I swear I promise my baby . . . We are going to help you through this."

"I think you should go home Juliana, if you want I can stay with you." Monique said.

"I think is the best too, she's been having too many strong emotions tonight and Caleb needs to rest too." Joey interrupted looking at Dara and Juliana on the floor.

At that moment 2 officers arrived Caleb's room with the company of a nurse.

"Caleb Smith?" A Japanese looking man said showing his plaque.

"That's me." Caleb said raising his hand.

"Mr. Smith, they just sent me from the police department to let you know that Martha Pinedo and Isaiah Russell were arrested and charged with attempted of murder for your case." The detective said looking at

Dara. He knew that was Isaiah's wife, and knew what was going on. The news suddenly started spreading in everybody's mouths as soon as they saw Isaiah Russell walking in the police station with his hands handcuffed.

"What did you just say?" Juliana said getting up from the floor.

"Are you Juliana Russell right?" Detective Lo asked gently.

"Yes. I'm Isaiah Russell's daughter and this is my mother Dara. His wife."

"I'm sorry that you had to find out this way about your father's situation.

"What are you guys charging my father of?" Juliana asked.

What could have been worse? Caleb, who was the love of her life leaving her? Her dad convicted as a murderer? Or have an abortion at this moment and end up with that seed that never asked to come?

"Monique, take me home please."

"I'm sorry for everything that I'm occasioning my dear brother. I regret all the lies I've said and all the things I did. I know that . . . if, maybe if I never lie to my husband, myself and my daughter, nobody would be suffering today." Said Dara.

Caleb looked at her feeling disgusted. "Are you serious? Are you really serious about everything that you are saying? Can you actually be that disgusting Lily?! Because your name is not Dara, it's Lily. You are a fuck up person! You are . . . You are the worst human being that is on the earth. You have no type of love for anyone around you. You are nothing but a crap in this society, a waste of space! And you want to know why? . . . Because you destroyed all of us! Yes! You destroyed me, your daughter, maybe not your husband or maybe yes, who knows why he tried to kill me! But you are the main source of why all of us today are crying and suffering! I'm going to thank you. Thank you my dear Dara for denying me, because I could never have a sister that has the same blood as me with all those hateful feelings inside!" Caleb said tearing looking strongly at her.

Dara, who was crying looked at Joey, but this one turned his back on her. She looked back at Caleb, and started walking away.

"I'm going to ask you please don't ever come back to see me. I don't want to see your face again. Deny me if you want, pretend that I'm dead as you always have . . . and I will do the same." Caleb said.

"And Juliana? You are not going to respond for that baby that is in her belly?" Dara said not turning back to look at him.

"Juliana is 18 already; I think I can talk about it with her." Caleb responded to her question in a cold way.

"She is my daughter, I have the right to know too Caleb . . . gosh! Don't hurt her too!"

"Now you remember that she is your daughter? Now you remember that speaking the truth is the best way to solve things? Dara please get out of my room! I don't want to see your face again!" Caleb screamed as much as he could.

Dara looked at him, and looking down she got out of the room. Joey couldn't, he didn't want to say anything. He knew it was better to let her go. He knew that everything that was happening was her fault. It was true. *Words are more powerful than weapons and violence.* He kept on saying on his thoughts.

When Juliana was about to get inside the car, she stopped Monique and said, "Wait, I want to tell something to my mom . . . wait, wait for me Monique." and leaving her friend with words in her mouth ran back to the hospital to look for her mom.

On the waiting room, where he mother was sitting at, Juliana stopped and stared at her. She didn't make noise at all. Slowly she walked up to her and touching her left shoulder she said softly, "Mom, everything is over already."

Dara lifted her head up, and looked at her daughter who was giving her the most beautiful smile that she ever seen in her life.

"No, not everything is over. I need to do something first." Dara said getting up from the leather brown sofa.

"What are you going to do mom?" Juliana asked worried and confused.

"Go home, I will tell you when I'll get there." Dara said and started walking to the exit.

"No, wait! I need you to go and see dad mom please!" Juliana said running behind her, grabbing her by the arm.

Her mom stopped and said "He can wait. But yes, I'll go and see him."

"I need you to tell him something."

"What my baby?" Dara asked in a lovely way.

"I need you to tell him that . . . I'll keep the baby. I won't have an abortion or give up on adoption as we both thought about doing." Juliana said looking down holding the rosary that was hanging on her chest.

Dara, who was surprised about it, took a deep breath and said, "I'm not even going to ask about it. I know, and I'm concerned that you two have a very strong relationship and you two are always taking decisions without thinking about asking me . . ."

Juliana interrupted saying, "No, no mom. The thing is that we thought that it was the best if you wouldn't find out because . . ."

"The best thing? Juliana do you know what an abortion is? Do you know you can die and do you know about the trauma that you get after it? Look, I got pregnant at a young age and I kept you, I wanted you to survive and breath, know what is life like. So why wouldn't you let this seed survive? Tell me! Who are you to kill that poor innocent baby that never asked to come to this world?!"

"Mom! Mom please stop!"

"What?" Dara said.

"You are right. But that's why I'm going to keep this baby! Because I think, and I know that he or she has the right to live and grow up! I'm sorry, I know I should have told you, or at least talked to you about it."

"Juliana, my dear, being a mom could be hard and stressful, but is the best thing that a woman can get as a gift in this world. And I'm happy that you are thinking like this at this moment. You've showed me that even if you are in bad times you can think right and not just let yourself let go by any bad feeling." Dara said and hugged her daughter.

"Let's go home, and raise the baby . . . he or she will only need love in this hateful world."

They both held each other's hands and walked away.

Months after . . . Isaiah Russell's trial day arrived.

The judge was ready to say his verdict. "Isaiah Russell, this jury has enough and clear evidence that supports that you should be charged with the following:

The murder of Peter Robin in 1984.

The murder of Jesse Johnson, an ex gang member who participated in the intent of murder of Caleb Smith in 2006.

The murder of James Moving, an ex gang member who also participated in the intent of murder of Caleb Smith, who also killed Jesse Johnson under your directions.

The intent of murder of Caleb Smith which was committed by Martha Pinedo, a nurse that worked at the Belview Hospital for over 5 years, who poisoned Mr. Smith.

You are also being charged with battery, and assault to another police officer, Detective Robin.

Therefore, this jury has found you guilty of all charges, and I condemn you to life in prison with no possibility of parole in 15 years . . . I'm sorry Isaiah." Said the judge making everyone in the room stare at him. The judge tried to save Isaiah, he felt so bad, and felt worst looking at him in the courtroom with his lawyer by his side, wearing the orange prison uniform.

While on the other side of the room was Caleb looking how Isaiah destroyed himself.

"For Mrs. Martha Pinedo, this jury has found you guilty of attempted of murder and since you are a resident of this nation only, this court will be sending a letter to the immigration services and ask for a voluntary deportation where you will be serving your sentence in your original nation for a period of 10 years. Case closed." The judge got up, and walked out of the room.

When the trial was over, the guards opened the door for Caleb to get out. Outside there was nothing but news, photographers, journalists here, more flash over there. Caleb wasn't surprised of what was going on, the "*God*" of Manhattan was discovered.

"Mr. Smith how do you feel discovering the real identity of Isaiah Russell?" asked one of the reporters who then translated the question to Spanish.

"Mr. Smith how is your niece feeling about this situation? Is she keeping your baby? Is that why Isaiah Russell wanted to kill you?" asked another reporter.

Caleb didn't do anything but kept on walking in the middle of so much traffic, and let his lawyer speak for him. *"All that my client has to say is that justice was touched and proved, and what justice wanted was done. Thank you."*

Juliana on the other hand was on the phone with her father's lawyer.

"When can I go visit him?" she asked.

"As soon as they finish preparing all these documents, just give it a week. How are you feeling?"

"Horrible. No matter what . . . Isaiah Russell will always be my father, and always in my eyes will be a good man. I wish he was out so he could see his grandson when he is born. But I guess that's not God's will anymore."

"I think we can fight for parole for next year, I'm sure. Let's stay positive Ms. Russell. Remember that your father was a loved man outside and . . ."

"I don't know and I don't want to imagine his life inside. Every prisoner hates cops . . . I guess, he is going to go have to do a lot to be in peace in that hell. Anyway, I'm going to my doctor's appointment Mr. Campbell just call me when you get a chance."

"Have a good day Ms. Russell." Said the lawyer and hung up.

As the time was passing by not everyone forgot easily about the case that touched the whole Manhattan's heart. After Russell's court day and sentence, everyone wondered about Juliana, and her situation, the baby, the love for her uncle, and the relationship with her mother.

One day, at the prison Juliana was visiting her dad leaving him pictures of the sonograms that she had.

"That belly gets bigger every time I see you my dear." said Isaiah who seemed older, full of stress, with deep eye bags.

"You see me every week dad, you shouldn't see much difference." Juliana responded.

"How is your relationship with Caleb? Do you talk to him?"

"Isaiah I don't think is the place or the time to ask those things." interrupted Dara, who was accompanying her daughter.

"It's okay mom, don't worry. Well, we don't talk much; the only way we talk is through text messages or e-mails. I try to avoid him as much as possible, but we agreed that when the baby is born he is going to take him out alone, and so I will. It's going to be very difficult to deal like this every day of my life, but I have to do it, and hopefully one day, not soon I will find a guy who will accept me with all this heavy drama that I will always have . . . like a shadow."

Isaiah stared at his daughter with sadness. "How was Italy by the way?" he asked.

"It was great! We had a lot of fun. But we haven't developed the pictures yet; as soon as I get them I will bring you some, or send them through mail ok?"

Isaiah Russell unbelievable felt incredible happy to know that his "daughter" was going to have a baby. But he also felt sad to know that she was paying all the mistakes that her mother did. While Juliana was showing him the pictures of her baby shower, she started complaining about some pain that she was feeling on her back. Then, she looked in between her legs and felt water coming down. Isaiah, nervous and worried started screaming all over the visiting room "MY DAUGHTER IS ABOUT O GIVE BIRTH! SOMEBODY GET A DOCTOR!!"

Hours after Juliana's water broke . . . Later on, after almost half of the day Isaiah was taken by a guard to the director's office.

"I'm going to let you receive this phone call for the great appreciation that I have for you Mr. Russell. Your wife is on the phone, and she needs to speak with you." Said the director of the prison.

After all, besides the fact that Isaiah Russell was one of the most intimidating persons alive, and corrupted as he could be, everyone even Supreme justices respected him.

"Hello Dara?" Isaiah said on the phone.

"It's a boy! And he's healthy!" Dara said on the other line.

Isaiah's eyes got full of tears, tears that started to fall down his cheeks, and then on top of the director's desk. That day Isaiah was the happiest man on earth. He felt an enormous joy in his heart; he was so happy that he didn't care about being in jail anymore. He was so thankful to God, that he asked the director to tell his lawyer to send him a priest to visit him so he could pray for his new grandson.

While on the other line, he heard Juliana telling her mom to give her the phone so she could talk to him.

"Hello dad? Dad I'm crying! It's a boy and he is healthy. Everything is in great condition I love him so much. You have no idea how much I want to scream, and express my love for this little being that I have in between my breasts. I wish you could be here, but don't worry I will visit you soon, and hopefully take the baby with me to jail so you could meet him."

Isaiah couldn't talk. He was in glory, he knew that he wasn't going to be able to enjoy the moment with his loved ones; he knew that after he hangs up that phone life was going to be the same again. None of the prisoners were going to care, he knew they all just wanted to fight, rape, and bully others.

"Dad are you there?" Juliana asked.

"I'm here my dear . . . I'm sorry my time is up . . . God bless that child, and please kiss him in the forehead for me."

"I love you dad . . . I love you very much, I'll be there soon."

"Bye my dear, I love you too." Said Isaiah and hung up.

While at the hospital, Caleb, Joey, Monique, Dara, and, Lucas who was Caleb's closest friend, were congratulating Juliana for the new baby.

Suddenly, Robin walks in the room, and looks at Juliana so in love with her new born.

"Robin . . ." she says.

"How are you?" he asked.

"Look, he is perfectly fine." She responded with a big smile on her face.

"I'm glad to hear that . . . very happy for you."

Caleb, who was staring at this attraction from Robin's eyes towards Juliana, interrupted and said, "Did you come from court or the police station?"

"No I actually came just to check on Juliana."

"Thanks Robin, thank you so much for everything . . . I want to let you know that I don't hate you for sending my dad to prison . . . I think there, perhaps my father would realize all the bad he has done . . . but thanks again for stopping by." Juliana said smiling.

"I got this for you, and the baby, I hope you will like it."

"You shouldn't have, thanks again." Juliana responded receiving the present.

Caleb was jealous of the situation, even if he was dying inside; he knew he couldn't do anything against this. He couldn't be with his own niece he knew it, but he also couldn't see her with another man but him.

"Robin how come you don't have a girlfriend?" asked Dara.

"Mom please leave him alone." Juliana responded as she was breast-feeding her new born.

"No, don't worry is okay . . . well Dara simply because I haven't met a woman that is willing to sacrifice nights without me, or simply because I haven't met a woman that will be able to deal with all that deals around me."

"If you would have only met Juliana before . . . maybe she would have been that one . . . you had no idea how wild this girl was."

"Mom, stop it . . . please?"

"I'm sorry."

"Well don't. I'm so happy and grateful to God that my son is here with me, and he has definitely changed my life . . . forever. Look at him, he is like an image of hope. Hope that I need every day to forgive and forget. He is to me like a second chance that God is giving me to keep on going with my life. I believe I can start all over, and just walk holding hands with him . . . I don't know being a mother just gives you a different feeling of life, like a different perspective. I just can't help but look at him, and cry of happiness and joy. He was the cause of so much drama, and pain, but still I feel like I have always loved him, since day 1, and even before he was inside me. I know that by looking at him sometimes it will remind me of all these horrible things that happened, but him, with his presence and innocence will make me forget them, and be stronger. I love him, I love him more than I have ever loved any human being in this world . . . and I just hope all of you will help me keep on going, and support me in any decision I will make."

Dara cried, but she cried because she never in her life heard her daughter speaking so lovely, so intense, so in love. Monique was amazed by how her friend changed, and how her cold heart turned into a soft piece of glass. Caleb was surprised how her rebellious ex girlfriend was so changed by the smallest thing in this huge situation. How this baby had the power to melt Juliana's heart, and the power to make someone fall in love again such as the coldest heart in the history of mankind, Mr. Isaiah Russell.

Detective Robin, became one of the best detectives and undercover cops in Manhattan. He was happy to know that Juliana and her baby were good, but felt disappointed knowing that Juliana wasn't ever going to see him with the same eyes that he was looking at her. He tried to make up a lot of things in his mind even after hearing Juliana's words he thought that by giving her time, she was going maybe give him a chance, or reject him again. So he decided to let time flow, and let destiny decide for him.

Caleb already a father felt that he was going to change and do so much for his newborn. He couldn't be with Juliana, but that didn't become an obstacle for them two to not be friends, and before he walked out of that room he kissed her in front of everybody who was inside the room. He had to let her know that he was thankful and full of love. He had to let her know that she gave him the best gift in life, and that was his son. That day, he couldn't hold the emotions inside him, and after the powerful kiss that he gave her he ran to the bathroom to cry his anger, sadness, happiness, and all these cruel emotions that were hugging his soul from the inside. That's why his seed was the shadow of his life, because no matter how many years pass by, how far he would run, he was always going to remember everything by looking at his son. All the drama that once happened was going to come back as memories, by just looking at his baby, that baby, who never asked to come, but for some reason destiny wanted here.

Justin, the detective who helped Robin solve this case, became the new chief of the police department in Manhattan, and participated in designing a park for kids, a small park that was going to be named "HOPE".

Monique, Juliana's wild best friend, got into college where she was majoring in psychology, and got engaged to Joey.

Joey on the other hand, quit drugs, and thanked his God for not letting him fall into a heaven of bad decisions, and opened his own boxing academy, which he named "THE SIN".

Dara, stayed with Juliana and her grandson until her last day. She learned so much after all this time, and figured out that family comes first over any social circumstance. She figured out that being a mother wasn't easy but it wasn't hard either. She stayed by Juliana's side and helped her raised her grandson, who they named "Israel". Later, as soon as he turned 3 months, they moved to California where they rented an apartment that was near the beach.

And Isaiah Russell . . . well, he stayed in prison until his time was done. He regretted any bad he did in the past. He couldn't believe the hate that consumed his heart. He didn't know how, or what made him that way, but it was already disappearing every night after praying and looking at the pictures of Juliana and her grandson posted on his wall. He became the most respected man in jail, everybody showed him love, even the cops that were working in the prison where he was at tried to treat him as nice as possible. They couldn't believe that a man of his "class" was behind bars. He became humble, and became a man of good, who dedicated his hours to teach the youngest prisoners to make a change in their lives and value the life that God gave them.

The end.

"LOVE CONQUERS ALL."

Printed in the United States
by Baker & Taylor Publisher Services